The explosion of need.

For one endless, aching moment Walker and Kalli stared at each other.

Lord, they had needed. They had loved.

But that was ten years ago. Ten damn years ago, Walker told himself.

His silent cautioning did him no good. His body recognized no divorce, no decade apart. It recognized only what it had known. And what it wanted to know again.

Kalli.

His Kalli.

His wife.

Dear Reader,

Welcome to Silhouette **Special Edition**...welcome to romance.

The lazy, hazy days and nights of August are perfect for romantic summer stories. These wonderful books are sure to take your mind off the heat but still warm your heart.

This month's THAT SPECIAL WOMAN! selection is by Rita Award-winner Cheryl Reavis. *One of Our Own* takes us to the hot plains of Northern Arizona for a tale of destiny and love, as a family comes together in the land of the Navajo.

And this month also features two exciting spin-offs from favorite authors. Erica Spindler returns with *Baby, Come Back,* her follow-up to *Baby Mine,* and Pamela Toth tells Daniel Sixkiller's story in *The Wedding Knot*—you first met Daniel in Pamela's last Silhouette **Special Edition** novel, *Walk Away, Joe.* And not to be missed are terrific books by Lucy Gordon, Patricia McLinn and Trisha Alexander.

I hope you enjoy this book, and the rest of the summer!

Sincerely,

Tara Gavin
Senior Editor

Please address questions and book requests to:
Silhouette Reader Service
U.S.: 3010 Walden Ave., P.O. Box 1325, Buffalo, NY 14269
Canadian: P.O. Box 609, Fort Erie, Ont. L2A 5X3

PATRICIA McLINN

RODEO NIGHTS

SPECIAL EDITION®

Published by Silhouette Books
America's Publisher of Contemporary Romance

Thanks to the staff of the Cody Nite Rodeo for their generous cooperation, especially Ray Owen and Roberta Sankey, and thanks to two genuine rodeo cowboys, John and Mark, who provided information and inspiration.

Also thanks to all those whose patient listening helped this one come to life (you know who you are) and especially to Peggy Cleaves and Angela Devine for saying the right thing at the right time.

 SILHOUETTE BOOKS

ISBN 0-373-09904-5

RODEO NIGHTS

Copyright © 1994 by Patricia McLaughlin

PATRICIA McLINN

says she has been spinning stories in her head since childhood, when her mother insisted she stop reading at the dinner table. As the time came for her to earn a living, Patricia shifted her stories from fiction to fact—she became a sportswriter and editor for newspapers in Illinois, North Carolina and the District of Columbia. Now living outside Washington, D.C., she enjoys traveling, history and sports, but is happiest indulging her passion for storytelling.

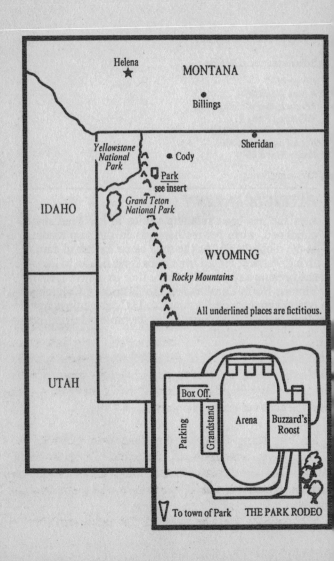

Helena ★

MONTANA

• Billings

Yellowstone
National
Park

• Cody

Sheridan •

Park
see insert

IDAHO

Grand Teton
National Park

WYOMING

Rocky Mountains

UTAH

All underlined places are fictitious.

Box Off.

Parking

Grandstand

Arena

Buzzard's
Roost

To town of Park   THE PARK RODEO

Chapter One

Stroke.

The word echoed in Kalli Evans's head as she hung up the phone with a hand that she willed into steadiness.

The word was there when she placed her own call to inform her boss she needed to take time off. Jerry Salk didn't argue, preferring the pinch of her temporary absence to the possibility of losing her altogether. She also knew it didn't hurt that her departure coincided with New York's slide into the summer business doldrums.

Stroke.

Her eyes stung. She ignored it. Tears wouldn't help.

Hanging up a second time, she pulled out her suitcase, pushed back the closet's louvered doors and surveyed her choices. Not much would translate to where she was going.

"Wyoming!" Jerry had bleated. "What on earth for?"

She hadn't bothered with details, just "family obliga-
tions." He wouldn't understand the loyalty that meant
dropping everything because Baldwin Jeffries needed her.
"He's not even a blood relation?" she could hear Jerry
asking in perplexed disbelief if she'd given him the chance.

What Jerry had said was, "I thought all your family's in
Connecticut."

"Not all," she'd said, though she had no blood ties to the
Jeffrieses.

More than blood, she was related to them by ties of the
heart.

And now Baldwin Jeffries had had a stroke that left him
unable to continue the tradition that meant as much to him
as life itself.

Five days into his twenty-first season running the Park,
Wyoming, rodeo—running it every night, rain or shine,
from the first Saturday of June through the last Saturday
of August—"Jeff" had shocked everyone who'd ever
known the indefatigable fixture of the region and sport by
crumpling to the rodeo-office floor.

Stroke.

The mirror reflected her tight face, and she acknowledged the grim word was not echoing alone.

Walker Riley.

Whatever had happened between her and Walker, she
never questioned that his loyalty to Baldwin and Mary Jeffries was every bit as strong as hers. So there could be no
doubt she would see him in Park.

She lifted her chin at her reflection. It didn't matter.
Walker Riley and the feelings she'd once had for him be-
longed to the distant past, when she had been young and
foolish. Very foolish. Foolish enough to marry him.

He could have stayed on the interstate nearly to Billings
before dropping south. Probably would have been faster.

The left side of Walker Riley's mouth twisted up, more with hard-earned self-knowledge than humor.

He'd known damn right well it would be slower-going on two-lane 291. And as for passing through Yellowstone Park . . . well, between the tourists and the way even his lionhearted camper-loaded pickup labored with the mountain roads, his rate of speed hadn't been much more than a crawl. Couldn't even fool himself he'd enjoyed the scenery. He'd hardly looked out the window beyond checking traffic now and then.

Spent too much time looking into himself. And the past.

He made a noise that caused the gray-muzzled dog to look up from its cedar-stuffed pad on the seat next to him. He laid his right hand on the dog's flank, and with that reassurance, the animal dropped its head down.

Looking into himself and the past . . .

More worthless pursuits were hard to think of.

A flash of color slid past on his left. The roof barely came level with where his elbow stuck out the open pickup window. Low and sleek, the car hurtled toward the future like a bat out of hell. Which was how fast it needed to go if the idiot hoped to pass him on the tight curves snaking through high-walled Shoshone Canyon. Why, to pass his truck like that, that jerk must have been going—Walker glanced at his speedometer and his righteous indignation fizzled—not all that fast.

He and his pickup definitely weren't hurtling toward the future. More like turtling.

He fed the pickup more gas.

Up to a few years ago, he'd been one to live in the present, taking each season as it came, not pining for the one behind or the one to come. These days he'd found himself more in accord with looking to the future. Maybe that was maturity.

The left side of his mouth rose again, though he was careful to make no sound that would wake Coat. 'Bout time he acquired some maturity, wasn't it? His birth certificate said he was thirty-three and some days his body said he was a hundred and four.

So it was a good thing he was growing up enough to give the future a nod now and then. But the past . . . ?

The past was what he was driving toward, no matter how slowly he went.

Kalli had forgotten how the wind could blow in Park, Wyoming. Even in early June. She pushed a long strand of hair off her forehead. She should have taken time to put it up, the way she'd worn it flying from New York yesterday.

Holding her hair with one hand, she squinted against the brightness, trying to read the expression of the man making his way toward her from the buff-colored brick dignity of the Shoshone County courthouse.

Tom Nathan had told her to meet him here at ten, after he'd attended a breakfast meeting of the rodeo committee.

She'd arrived at 9:40. She would have gone directly to the meeting of the independent committee that contracted with Jeff each year to produce the rodeo—if Tom had told her where it was being held. Which likely was why he hadn't told her.

Tom Nathan's leathered face gave nothing away. Neither did his habitual easy gait.

"Well?" she demanded.

He took the final three steps, stopped in front of her and sighed. He said nothing.

"Did they accept? What happened?"

"Just what I expected."

"What does that mean?"

"They're highly impressed with all that gaudy success you've been having. Had some things to say that'd turn your head right around."

"But?"

"Yeah, 'but.'"

"Damn." She turned into the wind, letting it stream her hair away from her face and burn tiny bits of dust into her eyes until they watered. "Damn, damn, damn. You'd think they'd cut some slack—for Jeff. After all the years, after all the success Baldwin Jeffries has brought them . . ."

"They haven't forgotten."

"Then why won't they give me a chance to run it for him? I know what makes a business go. Before I can advise someone to buy into a firm, I have to know if it's a good investment, and to do that I have to know if the company's working, if it can work—I have to know how to *make* it work."

"Don't have to convince me."

"All businesses follow certain similar concepts. Even rodeo."

Did they still think of her as the child who'd been Jeff and Mary's summer visitor? Or the girl who'd followed in Walker Riley's wake? That was a lifetime ago. She was thirty-one now, another person.

"They're willing to give you a chance."

"What?" Then why did Tom look as if he had something to say he knew she wouldn't want to hear?

"They just want to be sure things'll go on the way they have under Jeff and Mary. Can't blame them. Rodeo means a lot to this town. It's a draw. Folks don't just pass through Park, they stay for the rodeo, they have a meal, they buy souvenirs, they spend the night in a motel. If something happens to the rodeo, you could say it happens to the whole town."

From the first Saturday in June through the last Saturday in August, the rodeo's the daily pulse of this town. Jeff had first described it that way when she was eleven years old. That first year her father had sent her west for a summer on his college roommate's ranch. Each of the other three Evans children had followed, sometimes for one summer, sometimes two. But Kalli had returned every summer. And she knew what the rodeo meant.

No, she didn't blame the committee for wanting to ensure the rodeo's success. She did, too. It was the one way she could help repay Jeff and Mary for years of love.

"You're mostly an unknown quantity, far as they're concerned, Kalli. You know business, but you don't know *rodeo.*"

She shook her head, sensing what was coming the way an animal senses a thunderstorm.

It didn't stop him.

"They insist on having somebody involved who knows rodeo. Knows it inside out."

The storm was closing in.

"You could do it, Tom. After Jeff, there's nobody better at producing a rodeo. You'd be a consultant, someone for me to call on."

"I would if I could, you know that. But I can't be two places at once. Not even for Jeff. I've got a full plate this season and they want someone who'll be here all summer. Someone who's been around rodeo 'most all his life. Someone who knows the town and the circuit..."

They both knew the someone.

She'd decided last night, after seeing Jeff, still and frail in the hospital bed, and Mary, shaken but calm by his side, that she would stay for as long as it took to get them through this. But she hadn't bargained for what Tom was asking.

A meeting with Walker, yes, but a summer? Reaction swelled in her. Not panic— Why should she panic? No, not panic, but *wariness* about a summer of working side by side.

"It's the only way, Kalli. The only way to keep it for Jeff. And you know what it means to him...."

Rodeo was the blood that ran through Baldwin Jeffries's veins. It was, after his wife, Mary, his love. It was the children he'd never had, and it was as well loved, cared for and fretted over as herself... and Walker.

"So I guaranteed the committee you'd be having someone with plenty of rodeo knowledge working with you. And the two of you would work together for Jeff's sake."

"He might not come."

"He'll come. I called him same as I called you. He had a, uh, an obligation to fill over in Washington state, and then he was going to start driving." Something twisted in her at the certainty that the "obligation" had been to ride a bull. "Heard from him before the meeting and he agreed to whatever's necessary to keep the rodeo as his Uncle Jeff's. He's on his way. Ought to be here by tonight."

"Phew! If I'd known I'd be working harder with your help than when I was doing it all on my own, I might just have said no thank you when you offered." Roberta Chester swept salt-and-pepper curls from her forehead, swallowed long and deep from a can of soda and tried to glare at her new boss.

"I never offered to help," Kalli amended mildly. "I said I wanted you to show me how things run."

As always in moments of crisis or uncertainty, Kalli had tackled work as if it would keep the demons at bay.

"Yeah, that lasted about ten minutes," Roberta said. "Then you started showing me how to run things better."

Kalli looked at the older woman, who'd been rodeo secretary for four years. In the chaotic three days since Jeff's stroke, Roberta Chester had kept the rodeo running. She might resent a stranger coming in and taking over.

Kalli should have known better. She did know better.

"No sense looking at me like that, Kalli. I haven't gotten my nose out of joint, so there's no need for you to be thinking of ways to get it back in line."

No sense pretending Roberta hadn't hit the nail on the head, either. "I just didn't want you to think I was ungrateful. I barged in here and—"

"And came up with some good ideas. You're right, I should wring your neck for that."

Kalli grinned a little sheepishly and the other woman burst out laughing.

"New York can't be half as tough a nut to crack as we hear, if you're any sample, Kalli. Way Jeff and Mary tell it, you've got that town by the tail, holding your own with the hardest of hardheaded businessmen. But here you are worrying about hurting the hired help's feelings. Doesn't look like you're so tough, after all."

"Don't let appearances fool you, Roberta." Others had, and it had cost them. Sometimes to seven figures. "I can be as tough as I need to be."

"Good. You're going to need to be if you're really thinkin' I'll use that computer."

Kalli laughed at Roberta's dour look at the laptop she'd brought. It should serve the rodeo's needs, for now. She wasn't as sure about the endurance of the small printer.

"You'll be amazed how much easier it is to track results," she assured Roberta.

Or it would be as soon as she set up a format for them. It would take some adjusting, since times determined winners in calf roping, team roping, steer wrestling and barrel racing, but points decided bareback bronc, saddlebronc and bull riding. Keeping track of those individual results, then mixing the two types to determine overall top performers didn't fall into any of Kalli's usual systems for assessing businesses.

Kalli looked around the rectangular, one-room rodeo office. So different from her recent life, yet so familiar. Familiar from that lifetime ago when she had adored Walker Riley.

A counter the length of the room left three and a half feet open on one side and six feet on the other. The wider section held two desks, three tall filing cabinets and a cart with a telephone, answering machine and fax machine. The only object on the other side was a strip of wood under two windows. Protruding nails held clipboards with entries, standings, results, rules and notices. On the narrow south end, one door led to a closet, another to a toilet and sink. The north wall held a window and the outside door.

An incongruous setting for her high-tech computer, although the fax machine indicated the electronic age had made inroads here.

"We need that contraption to keep up with the national rodeo association in Colorado," Roberta said, as if reading Kalli's mind. "I've just now mastered it, and you're wanting me to try a computer?" She sighed. "Well, if you're willing to try teaching an old dog new tricks..."

One smart old dog, Kalli thought after little more than an hour.

"In a couple days, this will all be second nature," she assured the secretary.

"So you say."

That skeptical grumble didn't fool Kalli. She leaned back in the hard chair next to Roberta's, stretching.

"And then we should tackle getting the complete books on the computer. It can simplify billing and end-of-year statements and tax information like you wouldn't believe.''

Roberta shook her head. "Jeff takes care of that himself, just asks for a little typing and envelope-licking now and then. So it couldn't get much simpler for me.''

"Well, then it will be easier on Jeff when he comes back." She'd need to find those books, make sure everything was in order.

The automatic reminder fled nearly as soon as it formed. Unwillingly, her eyes went to the clock again. Almost six. Despite the lingering sunlight, it was nearly the hour that officially divided day from night.

He ought to be here by tonight.

She pushed the thought aside. The office would reopen in about an hour for the business of the night's rodeo, and to take future entries. Neither she nor Roberta would have much time to spare until ten-thirty or so.

"You better take a break, get some supper, Roberta.'' She pushed back the chair and stood, stretching again.

"How about you? You must be starving, since you missed lunch.''

Kalli had spent her lunch break at the hospital. She wasn't even sure if Jeff was fully aware of her presence, though she'd thought the expression in his eyes had changed when she came in. Surely that was an improvement from the night before....

"I don't feel much like eating. Maybe later.''

"Nervous?''

Kalli shot her a sharp look, but Roberta had bent over to retrieve her handbag from the bottom desk drawer.

"Because this is my first rodeo in charge? I don't—''

"I don't mean about the rodeo." Straightening, Roberta looked her in the eyes. Something about the dark brown gaze wouldn't allow Kalli to look away. Something direct, commanding and maybe a little compassionate.

"I mean about seeing Walker."

"How did you know...?"

Roberta laughed. "C'mon, Kalli, you didn't stick around the rodeo long from what I hear, but you're smart enough to know what it's like. Folks might cover a hundred thousand miles or more a year, but the circuit's like a small town. Complete with concern for your neighbors and a thriving grapevine. It's just a very mobile small town."

Kalli sat on the edge of the desk. Roberta was right, she should have known.

"I met Walker in the first few weeks I was working for Jeff and Mary," Roberta said. "Took a shine to him right away, too." Her eyes narrowed. "Don't go looking like that, girl. He never said a bad word about you. You should know him better than that. 'Fact, he never said a word about you at all. But there was talk. Even though it'd been a while since you'd left."

Kalli just bet there'd been talk. Even years later. And it wouldn't have been in her favor. Like any small world, rodeo fiercely defended its own.

"Got to admit," Roberta went on, "I was prepared to not like you, considering. Even with Jeff and Mary singing your praises. But..."

In that trailed-off word, Kalli felt an approval that warmed her.

"Thanks, Roberta. But it was a long time ago. We were kids. It's long-forgotten. And there's no cause to be nervous. This is something that needs to be done for Jeff's sake. That's what's important."

"Sure." Roberta didn't bother to make it sound convincing. "I'll run to the Sandwich Shack and pick up a burger and salad to bring back. What do you want?"

"Nothing, really, I—"

"I didn't ask *if* you want something. I asked *what* you want. But if you're not choosy, I'll pick it myself."

The door clicked shut behind her before Kalli could think of a response to such high-handed thoughtfulness.

The sound of a car engine brought Kalli's head up. The car stopped immediately outside the office; only then did she realize it had been shadowed by another. The second engine also turned off and she heard doors slam and greetings exchanged. Roberta and Tom Nathan.

She breathed again.

They didn't come in right away, and in a few seconds she knew why. A third engine sounded, deeper, more powerful than either of the first two. She could imagine it following the rock-strewn, dust-thick drive as it curved past the arena, widened into an informal, weed-dotted parking lot and eventually led to the office.

The third engine shut off, followed immediately by the opening of the office door. Roberta came in alone, leaving the door open behind her.

"Here's your supper." She swung up the gate of the counter, set a bag on the desk in front of Kalli and added in the same tone, "Walker just drove up."

Kalli recognized the generosity in the woman's warning, but didn't answer, not taking her eyes off the desk calendar provided by a local feed store. This first meeting was bound to be awkward, she wouldn't pretend otherwise. But it had all been so long ago, and she'd been over him so long. Still, her mind refused to make sense of the familiar grid of days and dates for the month of June.

Outside, Tom greeted Walker. She heard in his voice a blend of pleasure at seeing him and sadness at the circumstances. Then Tom took the two steps up to the office door. Behind him, she heard booted feet on dried earth and thought she could smell the sun-warmed dust they stirred.

Just outside the door, Walker said he'd gotten into town a while ago, then answered another question. His voice was low and slow, the cadence as basic as her own heartbeat.

"Yeah, went direct to the hospital. Jeff was sleeping, but I saw Mary. Thought I'd make a circuit of the grounds here before checking in with the office, but cut it short when I saw you folks pulling in."

The calendar snapped into orderly focus before Kalli's eyes. Of course he'd check the rodeo grounds first.

Walker was in the room. She couldn't say she'd heard him come in and she hadn't looked up from the desk, but she knew.

"Hey, Kalli."

Ten years.

Ten years since she'd seen the face she'd first seen when he was eleven years old, and had loved nearly as long. The face she'd watched change from a boy's to a man's. The face of the man she'd married...

The last time she'd seen him, as she'd given him his choice, his face had been unreadable except for the indomitable will that always was a part of him. Maybe she'd known right then what his choice would be. But she'd hoped.

Instead, he'd gone to compete and she had packed and left before he came home.

Slowly, she stood. For an instant, he was merely a dark outline against the bright rectangle of the open door, a silhouette from the past. But she knew him. That surprised her.

And now her eyes adjusted to take in the details within the outline. The jolt of recognition and familiarity shook her a little.

But as she'd told Roberta, she'd long ago learned to be as tough as she needed to be. She stood straight, her voice cool and steady.

"Hello, Walker."

Walker Riley stood there, not six feet from her, so fa‑
miliar and so unknown. None of it seemed real.

"You look good, Kalli. Different, but good."

Her chin rose at that, and she let the memories drain
away.

"You look just the same, Walker."

One side of his mouth lifted in a half grin. That was dif‑
ferent; he'd always grinned full-out before.

"Not hardly."

He crossed the wooden threshold that decades of booted
feet had worn into a smooth dip.

He did look older. But rather than softening his edges,
the years seemed to have sharpened them, so his cheek‑
bones and jaw stood out, looking more angular, casting
deeper shadows. His skin was taut and tanned.

Stepping up to the opening in the counter, he pushed the
straw cowboy hat back from where it had ridden low on his
forehead, then apparently thought better of it and re‑
moved the hat. Caught between his big, powerful hands, it
seemed to shrink. His hair, as thick and dark as ever, car‑
ried a ridge where the hat had rested.

His eyes hadn't changed, the color as vibrant as a blue
jay's back, though the creases had deepened through years
of squinting into the sun. The way he used his eyes hadn't
changed, either. His slow, open regard surveyed her from
her hair down to her toes.

Years in New York, years of confidence and accom‑
plishment, allowed her to stand steady under his look,
though she felt the tightening in her shoulders that was her
personal tension register. It jumped a notch higher at
something that flickered across his eyes as he took in her
silk blouse, matching silk slacks, sleek belt and deceptively
simple pumps. She didn't need him to tell her the outfit was
inappropriate for a night at the rodeo, she thought.

"Different, but good," he repeated in a murmur.

"I am different." She deliberately schooled her voice, leaving her words a statement, not a defense. "And I'm very good at what I do. I'll do a good job."

He met her eyes a moment longer, a slight frown tugging his brows, then nodded once. "I'm sure you are good at what you do."

He broke the look then—she hated the sense of being released—and turned to Roberta with that same, new half smile. "How's my favorite rodeo secretary?"

"Probably smarter than the last woman you used that line on." But there was warmth and affection in the hug she gave him, and in the gruff words that followed. "Glad you're here, boy. And I know Jeff and Mary are."

Walker patted her on the back before they disengaged from the hug. For a flash, his eyes came to Kalli and for that instant she had an image of being enfolded in his arms. Then he turned away, and her breath came out fast, as if she'd been holding it.

"Yeah, well, I figure even an old rodeo hand who's had his brains scrambled a few times should be able to ride herd on the setup you and Jeff and Mary have going."

Kalli felt the way she had once as a kid when she'd swallowed too much spicy, steamy chili. She could feel the burn all the way down her throat and into the pit of her stomach. A glance at Tom confirmed what Walker's tone had just told her: Walker didn't know about the committee's stipulation. And, since both Tom and Roberta were looking at her, it was clear who they expected to break the news.

"You aren't going to be riding herd alone, Walker," she said.

Chapter Two

He stilled for a heartbeat and a half, then pivoted on on[e]
low boot heel to meet her face-to-face.

"How's that?"

"The committee has agreed to let us step in for Jeff an[d]
Mary with the understanding that you can provide the r[o]
deo experience and I can provide the business expertise[.]
That's the condition they set."

"There's no need for you to stay. I'll tell them. You g[o]
on back to New York and I'll—"

"I'm staying. Until the rodeo closes for the summer [or]
until Jeff can take over again, whichever happens first[.]"
The heat in her stomach flared. "Don't you think I woul[d]
rather have handled this on my own? Don't you think [I]
would have—" She bit her lip, clamping down the word[s,]
fighting for calm. "But the committee has legitimate co[n]
cerns, and as Jeff's representatives we have to do our be[st]
to satisfy them."

She hadn't realized she'd cloaked a question in that last statement until she found herself looking at Walker, waiting for an answer. Even frowning, his face gave away none of his thoughts. But she thought she saw in his eyes . . . She drew herself taller, her shoulders tightening. Well, she wasn't looking forward to a summer with him, either.

"We'll do our best."

Walker's voice had no particular emphasis, but as Tom and Roberta each let out a pent-up breath, Kalli thought the words might have had an added message for her. A hope that the two of them would do their best to get through the summer without inflicting any more scars on each other.

"Well, great." Tom clapped a hand to Walker's denim-jacketed shoulder, raising dust. "I know you two'll do a great job and Roberta here will keep things on track, all right. Everything's going to work out fine."

"Yeah. It'll work out fine," Walker said without inflection. "How about you and me making the rounds, Tom? I got an overview, but you can reintroduce me to the details of the operation."

"Walker."

Kalli had kept her voice low, but it stopped both men before they reached the threshold.

"Walker, I think we should talk right away about changes we want to implement in the running of the rodeo."

"Changes?"

"Yes. Improvements." Impatience stirred as he continued to look at her without answering. "You know, making it better. Making it run more smoothly. More profitably."

"I always heard, 'If it ain't broke don't fix it.' And I haven't been hearing any complaints about this rodeo."

"Anything can be improved. Anything can benefit from being viewed from a fresh perspective. This rodeo's no exception."

"It's fine today. Tomorrow'll be—"

"Today! You have to look beyond today, or there won't
be any tomorrows. You haven't chan—" She bit off her
words, drawing away from the danger. Widening her stance
fractionally, she met his look and spoke levelly. "I will not
be satisfied spending a summer simply 'riding herd' on this
rodeo when I know that with a little effort I could leave it
better off than when I found it."

In the quiet, she heard the doorknob rattle under Tom's
uneasy hand. She was aware of Roberta leaning against the
counter, watching. But Kalli kept her eyes on Walker.

He'd dipped his head as if in contemplation of the worn
floor by the toe of his boot. The thick, dark hair hid most
of his face, but in the shaft of evening sunlight that fought
through the dusty window, she saw with something like
shock that a few silver strands mixed in at the crown.

Then he raised his head.

She tried to keep her heartbeat steady. No use. It was like
some reflex action. One deep look from those blue jay eyes
and her blood hammered. But that's all it was, a reflex. It
didn't mean anything.

"How 'bout if you spend a couple days getting adjusted, seeing exactly what the situation is here before you
go looking at changes?" he suggested. "Take time to get
settled."

It was so damned reasonable.

Answering evenly ranked with her top feats of mind over
lungs. "Very well. We can each assess the situation, then get
back to each other."

He looked at her from under lowered eyebrows and said
a little quizzically, "Yeah, we'll get back to each other,"
before heading out with Tom.

What was the matter with her? Under normal circumstances, she would never rush into a business and start
talking about making changes before she'd studied the op-

eration. Oh, a few stopgap, easily implemented measures like introducing the computer, but nothing beyond that. Why had she been so quick to jump in here?

Because these weren't normal circumstances. Because she hated the sense of helplessness she'd experienced when she stood by Jeff's bedside. Because—

"Let's get to work," she said to Roberta, but that didn't quiet the final possibility sounding in her head.

Because she'd needed to feel in charge, in control. Because she had been so strongly reminded of the fear and helplessness of being in love with Walker Riley.

She'd been a girl when they were married.

He'd never fully realized that. Not until he'd walked out of the dazzling sunlight into the dim, dusty office only to be dazzled all over again by the woman she'd become.

She still made him think of the mountains bathed in sunset. Brown hair tinged with russet, fair skin edged with peach, generous mouth fired with orange. Strength and quiet beauty brightened by fiery light. Her eyes were the color she'd derisively called khaki. He thought the color— silvered, pale brown, flecked with red near the pupils— matched a kind of sage he often spotted along the roadside as he drove from rodeo to rodeo. Every time he saw the sage, he thought of her.

Standing there in the office, she'd been wearing clothes draped in loose folds. Though not so loose he hadn't been reminded of curves he'd once known well. Not so loose he hadn't seen the long line of her slender thighs and remembered that though she stood some five inches shorter than his six feet, her legs were so long that when he and Kalli rode out together, they fixed their stirrups only two holes apart.

"Jeff's got a good crew up in the press box," Tom said, breaking into Walker's thoughts as they circled the arena.

"Announcer, scorekeepers 'n' all. Veteran group. You shouldn't have trouble there."

They'd passed the web of metal-tubed fences that formed chutes for timed events and moved around the stadium until they stood by the grandstand, looking across the arena to the staging area for roughstock events. This was topped by a small set of bleachers dubbed the Buzzards' Roost for the spectators who liked to watch the cowboys' preparations, with the press box above that.

A few people were already in the stands. Out-of-towners, Walker figured. People not accustomed to driving five minutes to events with easy parking.

"How about the rest of the crew?" he asked Tom. "Pickup men, judges, timers, stock sorters, chute tenders..."

"Should be fine. You know how Jeff organizes. 'Course, there's likely to be some turnover. 'Most always is. Especially with Jeff out of the picture right now. You're going to need to set some folks' minds at ease about the newcomers running the rodeo. Not just the committee, but the merchants and your crew, too. Even the cowboys. There's enough uncertainty in rodeo— They like to know who they're dealing with. Hell, you know that. But that's something Kalli might not be taking into account with her talk of changes."

Walker felt the force of Tom's look, but didn't take his eyes off the pens that held the stock for tonight's show. Horses, steers, calves and bulls. Rounded up from the Jeffries ranch west of town and trailered here, they were rotated out each night before new stock was brought in for the next day's performance. The animals looked fit; Jeff wouldn't stand for anything less. The cowboys would soon learn *that* wouldn't change.

"Could be people'll be worrying this might be less of a show without Jeff running it," Tom said. "The people in

town have felt safe recommending the rodeo to visitors because they know folks'll get their money's worth. They'll
be more cautious for a spell with you and Kalli running it.
Changes could make it worse.''

Behind them someone shouted that Tom had a phone call
in the office. "Keep going. I'll catch up with you," he instructed.

Changes... Walker had opened his eyes one summer to
find his tagalong buddy of the past six years transformed.
And the way she'd looked at him... No man could ever
want more. At nineteen, he'd been just old enough to know
seventeen was too young, and young enough to suffer hell's
torments as each kiss and touch brought them closer. He
could still sweat in memory of that summer's frustration.

Then he'd made her his. He'd thought forever.

A girl. Twenty when they'd married, just past twenty-one
when she left. Maybe if they'd waited longer the way her
family wanted, instead of getting married one week after
she finished college. Or maybe no amount of waiting would
have helped.

"Walker, you old sonuva—"

The slap on his back was nearly as jolting as the disrup-
tion of his thoughts. A seamed face beamed at him from
under a cowboy hat that barely reached Walker's shoulder. Without consciously moving, he'd nearly completed a
circuit and now leaned against the fence by the Buzzards'
Roost.

"Hey, Gulch. How're you doing?"

"I'm doing just fine for an old man, which you took
every opportunity of telling me I was when you were a
smart-mouthed kid. And you?"

Walker grinned. When he'd started rodeoing in earnest,
Gulch had been wrapping up his competitive career and
Walker had thought him ancient. Since Gulch had then
been about a year younger than Walker was right now, he

appreciated the irony. From this spot in Walker's life, Gulch Miller didn't seem such an old guy.

"Can't complain."

"You never did even when you could," Gulch said with a clicking noise that resembled disapproval, but wasn't that at all. "Wish you were back under better circumstances."

"Yeah." Walker let out a breath.

"Jeff...?"

"Doctors say it's hard to tell at first with a stroke. Takes a while to know what's what. But he's doing better, coming along a bit every day. They're talking about sending him to Billings for rehabilitation eventually. Might wait some because they're short-staffed up there, but that's not all bad since there's more folks to spell Mary here than in Billings."

"But?"

Walker felt a frown deepening. No wonder Gulch had figured there was a "but."

"He isn't talking yet. When Tom first called, I got ahold of a doctor on the rodeo committee where I was at and started asking questions. Almost every answer started with 'it depends,' but one thing he did say was that if somebody who's had a stroke isn't talking some, least making sounds the first week or so, chances are they'll never talk."

"You worrying about it won't change what's going to happen, Walker. Any more than drinking ever changed what already happened. I sure know that."

Without answering, Walker looked at the sky, still blue and cloudless even as the sun withdrew its warmth.

When he'd first met Gulch, the nickname was so long-established most people had forgotten it originated only when Miller went off the bottle—because he'd gone dry. But one morning in Pendleton, Oregon, some eighteen months after Kalli left, Walker had woken to a thundering hangover and a dim memory of a spectacularly careless ride on a bull named Killjoy, and he'd found Gulch Miller sitting in his camper.

Gulch hadn't done any more than talk and pour coffee, but Walker knew what it had cost the little man to tell about the auto accident years before that had killed his wife and baby daughter and left him, at twenty-two, healthy enough to rodeo and sick enough at heart to nearly drink himself to death.

"And that's what you're in danger of doing, Walker," he'd said that rainy morning. "But you're the impatient sort. You wouldn't wait for the booze to do it from the inside. You're trying to get stomped to death first. I'll give you this— You're getting some hellacious rides out of it, good enough to put you in the Finals come December. But chances are, you won't live to ride in them. Is that what you want?"

No, that wasn't what he wanted. And in time, he'd accepted that no matter how much he drank, it wouldn't blot out the fact that he couldn't have what he did want—Kalli.

"She looks good, doesn't she?" Gulch's matter-of-fact tone didn't hide the underlying empathy. Clearly, his thoughts had followed a similar path to Walker's.

"Yeah, she does."

"'Course, I saw her year before last when she was visiting Jeff and Mary...."

Like all her visits, it had been arranged for when Walker had let his aunt and uncle know he'd be rodeoing in some other part of the country. Not that anyone had acknowledged that. Nobody ever mentioned Kalli to him, except that once, when his mother had died two years after Kalli left, and Mary had given him the carefully written note. He'd recognized the handwriting, but not the words. He'd burned it that night.

"So I'd seen her since she became a big New York City executive. Even discounting that Jeff and Mary were bragging on her, she's doing mighty well for herself. 'Course, she was always smart as a whip.''

As he had with Tom, Walker sensed an underlying concern: *We know how you fell apart last time— We were there to pick up the pieces. Don't leave yourself open for a second time. The pieces might be too small.*

And they were right.

Gulch went on recounting Kalli's accomplishments, but Walker only half took it in. More spectators filed in, some pausing on the catwalk to the Buzzards' Roost to ooh and aah over the livestock penned below. To his right, gruff chatter and occasional raucous laughter punctuated the arrival of cowboys, preparing their rigging and their psyches for the competition ahead. Cooling breezes mingled the smells of animal and human with coffee and popcorn from the concession stand behind him.

No wonder Kalli looked different. She had cause to. While this had remained his world, she'd left it to make another—and most would consider it a better—life for herself. A life he'd had no part of.

It didn't bother him she looked different. What bothered him was she still looked so damned good to him.

"Now that the events have started, there'll be a lull," Roberta announced. Kalli felt her mouth quirk as she suppressed a smile. Woe to anyone who put the lie to that proclamation! An emergency wouldn't dare occur. "So why don't you take those feet of yours outside and let 'em take you someplace instead of no place?"

Kalli halted in midpace, the habit so automatic she hadn't realized she'd been doing it.

"Sorry. The pacing can be annoying, I know."

"As far as bad habits go, it's better than chewing tobacco," Roberta decided judiciously.

Kalli laughed. Even to her own ears, it sounded a bit ragged, but Roberta looked approving.

"I promise you, Roberta, no matter how tough things get, I won't put a pinch between my cheek and gum."

That earned a nod. "Good. How 'bout promising you'll go out and walk around awhile, too?" Before Kalli could protest, she added, "Might as well get reacquainted with the layout. Some things might've changed since last time you were here. Fresh air'll do you good, too. Besides, never hurts to let folks see you on the scene."

Kalli might have disputed the other points, but the last one was inarguable.

"You're right. I'll take a look around."

She snagged her blazer from the back of a chair, pulling it on as she headed out. Decisiveness carried her around the corner and four strides down the side of the office before impressions and memories flooded in.

An amplified voice announced a cowboy's score, slipping in the information for the uninitiated that this was a very good performance, indeed. Thus exhorted, the crowd cheered approval. Ahead of her, floodlights pasted stars against the darkening sky. The aroma of grilling hot dogs overlaid the scents of horses, cattle, sweat and hay. In a pocket of silence, she heard a muted call, then the *thunk* of a chute opening, quickly swallowed by the crowd's roar.

Twisting away, she leaned against the wall and looked out on the parking area. But the haphazard array of horse trailers, campers, pickups and every vehicular hybrid imaginable brought other memories—memories of hot, loving nights spent in just such a temporary home.

A new sound slipped in. Low, a little pitiful, yet somehow excited and almost . . . familiar. Her eyelids lifted.

A dog was framed in the open window of the passenger seat of a camper-topped pickup, dusty red and well traveled, with the right front fender primed to an equally dusty black.

"Coat?" The dog yipped excitedly, and Kalli found herself jerking open the door of the pickup and throwing her arms around the dog, tears flowing and her face being thoroughly licked between ecstatic barks. "Coat, is that really you, boy? Oh, Coat . . . Coat."

The slightly wiry texture of the dog's multicolored coat was so familiar, but the puppy of memory was now gray-muzzled and moving with the gingerliness of age. That didn't dim the unconditional joy of his greeting.

"Kalli? Kalli, you okay?"

She spun around to face Walker, standing just behind her, one hand half raised as if he'd considered touching her, then changed his mind.

"It's Coat," she said, and knew instantly how stupid that sounded. Of course it was, and of course Walker knew it. This was the puppy they'd adopted not a week after their wedding, the one she'd named after the Dolly Parton song "Coat of Many Colors," in honor of his varied tints and because she'd loved the sentiment of the song. This was the dog she'd left behind, with some muddled idea that Coat would look after Walker even if he wouldn't let her.

"You kept him."

Walker dropped his hand, and in the artificial light, the lines of his face seemed harsher. "Of course I kept him. You didn't think I'd just dump him because it wasn't convenient anymore, did you?"

Kalli straightened and brushed away her tears with the back of one hand, though the other remained in Coat's fur.

"Sorry I barged into your truck—this is your truck?" Pride steadied her voice. She caught the movement of his nod, but didn't face him. "Coat recognized me, and in the excitement, I didn't think about how inappropriate it was to get in someone else's truck."

"I don't give a damn about the truck. I heard Coat bark and thought . . . I thought I better check on him."

Something about his tone made her turn. "Is he all right? I know he's getting old, but is he sick?"

"No. He's all right. Vet says he's pretty healthy for his age, matter of fact. But he has arthritis and he can't get around like he used to. And sometimes other dogs don't respect his age, or horses get touchy, so . . ."

So he kept an eye out for Coat, Kalli supplied silently. He kept a cushioned dog bed on the passenger seat of his truck and when he heard the dog's bark, he wasted no time checking it out.

She smiled a little as she looked at the dog and thought she saw agreement in Coat's eyes: Walker Riley was still a soft touch for any creature weaker than himself.

"He recognized me," she said, hoping to share her pleasure with the man standing so close she could feel the heat of his body.

"Dogs remember who lands a boot in their ribs, but they're not wise enough to forget somebody who walks away from them."

A slap would have been less painful, but no more bracing. His quiet demeanor in the office had lulled her, had her thinking maybe they could work together without the bitter past welling up. She'd been a fool.

"I'm going to take a look around." Her words dismissed Walker and the conversation. But she couldn't resist a last hug of the old dog. "I'll see you later, Coat," she whispered, then walked away without looking back.

She ran into Gulch Miller sooner than she would have wished. His eyes were too darn sharp for her comfort. Within a network of wrinkles that had widened despite the shading of an ever-present cowboy hat, those eyes flicked from her face to over her shoulder, to the vicinity of Walker's truck.

To her relief, Gulch made no comment, instead introducing her to crew members in the snatches between their duties. Before long, Gulch, too, was called away, and Kalli simply watched the activity.

"Hi, you're not from 'round here, are you?"

Kalli blinked, bringing her focus to the young cowboy to her right. Old enough to vote, but yet to see his first presidential election, she thought to herself. Attractive, and he knew it, but still enough of a boy not to be sure that other people knew it. Something about him tugged at her.

"No, I'm not. And you?"

"Just over the border," he said with a nod north. Montana, she thought, not Canada. "Where's your home?" he asked.

Good question. "I live in New York City."

His eyebrows rose, but to her amusement he seemed less impressed than surprised at her lack of good sense.

"You visiting here?"

"Mmm. Sort of. Looks like I'll be here all summer."

"Then you'll have a chance to come to the rodeo a few more times."

"Very likely," she murmured.

To prevent his seeing the amusement in her eyes, she looked beyond his left shoulder and met Walker's assessing stare. He stood ten yards away with a group of competitors, including a blond barrel racer with her hand tucked into Walker's elbow and her side plastered to his.

No chance now the young cowboy would think Kalli was amused.

"Then you'll see me," he said, "because I'm going to be rodeoing here 'most every night. This is my summer to make the big push, make a name for myself...."

And the resemblance hit her square in the heart—he was Walker, the summer her feelings had deepened and widened from hero worship to love. She'd been seventeen.

"I've already made a start," he was saying proudly. "I won tonight, plus I got two seconds earlier in the week."

"What event?" At least the question kept him talking and prevented her from looking back to Walker—either the flesh-and-blood one across the way or the one in her memory.

"Bareback bronc. I got a real rank one. Why, she—"

"Matt Halderman. Good ride tonight."

Walker's low voice stiffened the backs of both his listeners, but Kalli suspected the cowboy's reaction was pride.

Walker extended his right hand for a shake and put his left hand on Matt's shoulder for a congratulatory squeeze.

"Thanks. Thanks, Walker." A two-time national champion praising a youngster just trying to make a name for himself was cause for a severe lump in the throat. Kalli admired Matt Halderman's poise.

She also admired Walker's adroit maneuver, even while it infuriated her. A slight pressure on Matt's shoulder with his left hand, a subtle tug with his right hand, still in a handshake, and he had the younger man turned. Without a ripple, Walker stood between Kalli and Matt.

"I see you've already met the brains of the operation while Baldwin Jeffries is laid up."

Matt's startled brown eyes came to Kalli. "Uh, yeah."

"It's nice to meet you, Matt," she said with a warm smile meant to ease any awkwardness, and extended her hand across the gap Walker had opened between them. "We haven't made it official. I'm Kalli Evans—"

"Riley." Walker's single word stepped on the heels of hers.

"It's Evans," she said more harshly than she'd intended, shaking Matt's hand, but glaring at Walker. The shadow of his hat brim hid his eyes; the bottom of his face was unreadable. "Kalli *Evans*," she emphasized. "Call me Kalli."

"Sorry. Old habits die hard." Walker's tone was as neutral as what she could see of his face. "Say, Matt, how about we talk about that ride?"

"That's great, Walker. Thanks!" Matt touched the brim of his cowboy hat. "Nice meeting you, uh, Kalli."

"Nice meeting you, Matt. I'm sure we'll see you in the office if you're going to be entering all those rodeos."

Walker stood beside the bed and looked at the man who'd taught him to ride—horses, bulls and the rough spots in life.

The outside of Baldwin Jeffries had changed, dwindled since he'd first started taking in his widowed sister's only son every summer. But Walker knew the inside would always be the same. He held one inert hand between the roughened warmth of both of his.

In his uncle's eyes he saw frustration and bewilderment, but those feelings were relegated to a minor role. Concern dominated Jeff's eyes, and Walker tried to answer that.

"It'll be all right, Jeff. I'll keep the rodeo going. Hell, the way you organize, it'd probably run itself another century, but I'll be here. Along for the ride."

And you? the faded blue eyes asked.

"I'm fine. No need to worry."

Walker? He knew what his uncle's eyes demanded.

"I saw her.... It'll be all right, Jeff. It's been years."

The blue eyes regarded him steadily a moment longer, and in those eyes Walker saw the memory of his own disbelief giving way to dazed pain. He guessed Jeff was remembering the bouts when Walker had flirted too long and too seriously with the bottle and danger, the years of careful, unacknowledged scheduling so two people who loved Baldwin and Mary Jeffries wouldn't cross paths.

He wondered if Jeff could see as clearly into him. Could he see the longing Walker had felt to touch Kalli when he'd seen her with Coat? Could he see that Walker had fought that longing by digging at the scars between them, scars better left untouched if they were going to work together this summer? Could he see that when it came right down to it, instinct had pushed Walker into staking a claim to her that he knew damn well he had no right to? And over a kid barely weaned, for God's sake.

"It'll be all right," he repeated.

His uncle blinked, turning to where Mary sat. But Walker had seen the sheen of tears.

"So, you thinking about putting your own stamp on the Park Rodeo, Walker?" Jasper Lodge asked.

That sounded innocuous, especially as spoken around a hunk of roast beef sandwich. But, since he was committee chairman, all Lodge's comments had significance. His approval or disapproval could be pivotal to the rodeo's future.

So when he'd called yesterday asking if he could come by "just to get reacquainted" with Walker and Kalli, there'd been no question that they'd say yes.

Roberta told them to make the meeting for lunch today, "because there's no surer way to soften up Jasper Lodge than through his stomach." This morning, she'd arrived with the makings for hefty sandwiches, homemade potato salad, green salad, fresh lemonade and, for dessert, double-chocolate brownies and watermelon.

They'd set up some distance from the office, at a picnic table under four cottonwoods by a stream feeding into the Shoshone River. It was a pleasant spot. Only Coat, banished to the shade of a distant tree to prevent his soulful looks from interfering with the diners' pleasure, didn't seem to approve.

"I'm looking at the operation of the rodeo, Mr. Lodge," Kalli said before Walker could answer. "We've divided the responsibilities. Walker will focus on running the competition aspects."

She'd be better off calling him Jasper, Walker thought. "Mister" reinforced her position as an outsider. Walker considered joining the conversation. Then he flicked a look at her. What was that saying about discretion and valor? He opted for discretion, and potato salad.

"That so?" Jasper Lodge aimed his question at Walker, but he couldn't answer around a mouthful of potato, onions and celery.

"Let me tell you what we have in mind, Jasper," said Kalli.

Against the red-and-white checks of the cloth Roberta had spread on the table, Kalli's blue slacks and shirt topped by a tan blazer and a brightly patterned scarf created an image of cool competence that matched her tone of voice.

Used to be a scratch would let loose her emotions from just beneath the surface—the fire, the love, the passions, Walker thought. Had they gone deeper underground or had they been smothered?

Roberta replaced their empty dishes with a platter piled with brownies and wedges of watermelon so succulent they glistened with moisture.

Watermelon. The memory hit him, low and deep in his gut. Sitting on the steps of their old trailer, the open doorway behind them airing out a day's accumulated heat. What rodeo had taken them to that spot? There'd been too many places too fast; he couldn't remember. But he remembered late-summer softness, the warmth soon to be a memory with fall clearing its throat. The last watermelon of summer—the only summer she'd carried the name Kalli Riley.

She picked up a wedge of watermelon now, in the bright midday sun. He knew it was now, but he could also see a younger Kalli holding a slice of watermelon in the private darkness of night.

He watched her bite into the sweet, unseeded tip.

Smiling at something Roberta said, she glanced at the watermelon before putting it to her mouth a second time.

God, please, let her just bite into the damn thing and be done with it. Don't let her still have that old habit. Don't let her...

Her tongue flicked out, deft, as accurate as a sharpshooter, and slid away one black oval seed from where she would bite next, then another. And a third.

Memory stirred his body, brought sweat to his upper lip, under his arms, down his back.

With the greed of youth, they'd each eaten a slice of watermelon that long-ago night, then set about sharing a third. Fascinated, he'd watched her delicate removal of the seeds with her tongue before she bit into the fruit. When his turn came, he'd taken a huge bite and a seed had caught at the corner of his mouth.

The seed, slick and smooth against his skin. The sweet taste of watermelon, the juice a cool veneer on his lips. The chuckle she gave as she stopped his hand from dislodging the seed. The soft, heated rub of her tongue as she slid the seed against his skin with excruciating slowness. The endless, aching moment as they stared at each other. The explosion of need.

They hadn't even made it all the way into the trailer, barely across the raised threshold onto the thin carpet. They hadn't gotten all their clothes off. But, Lord, they had needed. They had loved.

It was ten years ago. Ten damn years ago. The mentally gritted-out words did no good. His body recognized no divorce, no decade apart. It recognized only what it had known, and wanted to know again—Kalli.

As she swallowed a bite of watermelon, her gaze brushed over him, halted and returned. He had an uneasy feeling that despite the curtaining of the tablecloth, she knew his jeans felt bindingly tight. With a slight frown, she glanced at the uneaten fruit still before him, then back to his face. He saw the exact moment the memory hit her, and didn't try to stem his fierce satisfaction at the stunned look in her eyes and the sweep of color in her cheeks.

She looked away, dropped the watermelon rind as if it had burned her and wiped her hands hastily on her napkin.

"Jasper, now that you're done eating, would you like to come in and see our office setup?"

"Sure would."

Walker stayed perfectly still, hoping his failure to join them would go unnoticed. Kalli didn't so much as glance his way. But Lodge turned back.

"You coming, Walker?"

"No. I need to pick up stock for tonight soon as I finish this coffee."

The older man gave an acknowledging wave.

"Now, where's this portable computer I've been hearing about, Kalli?" Lodge's question carried back to Walker. "I've been thinking I might get one for home and link up to the store. Which reminds me, when're you going to come to the store and let my Esther pick out some clothes that'll make you look less like New York and more like Wyoming?"

With that less than subtle hint, the committee chairman took Kalli's elbow and started into the office.

Roberta cleared the table, removing Walker's untouched watermelon without a word. But he felt her piercing look.

"Guess you want to finish your coffee before you go out to pick up stock, huh, Walker?"

"Yeah."

"In that case, you can fold up the cloth and put it in the back of my car along with the mug when you're done."

"Sure, I'll do that." He swallowed the tepid liquid.

She picked up a box of lunch paraphernalia, letting loose her parting shot as she walked away. "Tablecloths can come in mighty handy, can't they, Walker? Hide a multitude of sins. Sins and other conditions."

Chapter Three

Damn Walker Riley. Damn him, damn him, damn him.

It wasn't fair to be sitting at a picnic table minding your own business, and be hit by a lightning bolt of memory. Damn Walker Riley.

Their paths hadn't crossed much these past two days, though Kalli heard "Walker says" a hundred times a day—at the rodeo and at the hospital, where he, too, received permission to visit outside regular hours. Of course he never showed up at the same time she was there.

She'd seen him only twice—when a cowboy stopped to look over the operation and when a curious citizen made a get-acquainted call. Both times Walker had appeared as suddenly as a storm cloud, maneuvered distance between her and the newcomer and introduced her as "Ms. Evans" in a tone that declared "hands off." Then he'd disappeared. Just as she prepared to inform him that the Riley

Personal Bodyguard Service was most definitely un-
wanted.

But she had him now. She'd ordered Gulch to inform
Walker that his attendance was required first thing this
morning at the meeting she'd called with Gulch, Roberta,
Tina, the head of the ticket office and Tom Nathan, who
was leaving today to return to the circuit where he produced a series of rodeos. She wouldn't set Walker straight
about his interference, not with an audience, but she would
make him sit in the same spot with her for more than two
and a half minutes.

From Walker's expression as he entered the back room
of the box office building for the meeting—the last to arrive, naturally—that would constitute punishment.

Barely sparing Walker a glance, she couldn't help iden-
tifying his scent, a mix of morning-cool sunshine, dewed
sage, warmed animal and well-worn leather; he'd already
put in time in the saddle.

She was staying at the Jeffries ranch just west of town;
he hadn't been there this morning. So where did he ride? It
didn't matter. She didn't care. He could ride where he
wanted. He could sleep where he wanted. If he spent every
night in his Spartan camper, it wasn't any concern of hers;
he'd probably done it often enough these past years.

And if he'd found somewhere—or someone—more ac-
commodating, that wasn't any concern of hers, either.
That, too, had surely happened often enough in ten years.
Blond barrel racers were not an endangered species, last
time she'd heard.

Coat, following at Walker's heels, split off to greet her
with a wildly waving tail and an insistent nose requesting a
good petting. She complied.

"Walker, if you'll take a seat." She pointed to the only
one unoccupied. She'd sat at the head of the table from
habit. Then, as the others left the facing chair at the end of

the table empty, as if in silent testimony to a connection between her and Walker, she'd contemplated the danger of habits.

"We were about to hear from Tina with the season attendance figures." Kalli leaned forward, balancing a pencil in a deceptively loose grip. "Go ahead, Tina."

As Walker dropped into his customary half sprawl in the chair, she gave the head of the ticket office an encouraging nod. In a soft voice Kalli had already learned belied absolute reliability, Tina recited the numbers.

Declining numbers.

"The pattern's clear," Kalli said into the silence that followed Tina's summary.

"It's natural." Walker didn't actually contradict her, but that's how it felt. "Folks aren't sure how it'll go without Jeff running the show. When they see we're running it just like Jeff, business will pick up."

"That'll be too late." She thumped the pencil eraser on the table. "This rodeo has an eighty-two-performance season. Eighty-two. It's held eleven. That leaves seventy-one. Even with a solid base, we can't afford to ride out a lull. There's not enough time to make up lost ground."

Walker didn't answer, didn't shift position, didn't look up. For all the response her words got from him, she might as well be keeping a pledge of silence.

Intent on Walker, she started at Tom Nathan's voice. "Kalli's right. If you lose the town's confidence, you won't have time this season to get it back. And next season, they'll be looking for someone they do have confidence in."

"But Baldwin Jeffries—"

Tom cut across Gulch's protest. "Jeff would be the first to understand. He knows what the rodeo means to this town, and he knows how much of the rodeo's success relies on giving people what they expect year after year."

"Or better than they expect," said Kalli. "That's what we have to aim for. To make this season so good that the rodeo committee would be fools not to recontract with Jeff."

She thought—hoped—she saw an answering spark in the eyes of the others around the table. With one exception.

"And the first step is to get ticket sales up," she added. "Any ideas?"

She listened to suggestions batted around the table, jotting down additional ticket outlets, ways to promote in surrounding towns and an open house for area residents.

"These ideas are good. And I think you're right, Roberta, about not waiting for the open house to make contact with the merchants and rodeo committee members. Take a look at the possibility of holding some lunches, then let me know.

"I hope you'll all keep thinking of ways to raise attendance, and pass them on. Now..." She paused to pull in a breath, looking at the pad, then up and right into Walker's gaze. "We have one asset we haven't exploited yet."

Everyone else around the table stilled. Only Walker moved. He tilted an eyebrow at her.

She met that blue stare directly. "You."

While the others asked what she meant, she heard Walker's quiet repetition of one word: "Exploited." Heard it and refused to back down, despite a rush of heat up her back that might have been confused with guilt. This was necessary for the rodeo—for Jeff.

"I mean the reputation of Walker Riley, national champion bull rider. From a PR standpoint, it's a natural."

"You mean, like interviews?" Gulch sounded appalled. "He's always hated that, Kalli. Remember how—"

His words shut off like a spigot. Out of the corner of her eye, Kalli saw the misery on his weathered face at having brought up the forbidden past. She did know how Walker had hated it. With his pride and sense of privacy, he'd never opened his life or his emotions for anybody.

She licked her dry lips.

"One of the best-known bull riders comes back to where he started, a knight in shining armor rescuing the rodeo for his uncle, the man who gave him his start."

When Walker's gaze dropped, she nearly faltered. She made herself go on.

"Reporters worth their salt will jump on it. The coverage should help by itself. Plus we'll copy the clips and distribute them to the motels. That should catch the tourists' eyes. And we'll send clips and videos of TV tapes to key tours and travel agents."

She went on with the possibilities, although one by one the others shifted their attention to Walker, silent and still at the end of the table. He raised his chin an inch. That's all it took to slam his gaze into hers.

"You're rushing, Kalli. Sales'll pick up. But if you go doing a lot of changing, you'll make folks nervous. They're already wondering if it'll be the same with Jeff not in charge."

Yes, she'd anticipated that answer, acknowledged it had merit. Though overcaution had its own dangers.

"That's why it's so important for you to do the publicity. Everyone around here knows Walker Riley, and trusts what you say. You can ease that nervousness, let them know the rodeo will go on as before—or better. You have the name. You have the championship buckle."

She met his look, the length of the table offering little protection from the burn of blue eyes.

"Hold off on those other moves and I'll do your interviews with the locals, but not beyond."

Her interviews. Damn him. But personal feelings had no place in a business negotiation. She let it go, and compromised. "We also do lunches with the rodeo committee and top businesspeople in town. And we send a news release to the others built around your name and title.''

He stood up slowly. From his spot next to Kalli's chair, Coat did the same.

''Right. Might as well get some use out of it. It cost enough.''

When Kalli arrived at the hospital that evening, closer to eleven than ten, to find Jeff sleeping, she tried to persuade Mary to go to the cafeteria. But Mary didn't want to leave, saying the murmur of familiar voices soothed her husband.

So Kalli updated her on the rodeo. Mary gave her a searching look, but spoke only words of encouragement and praise. Then she told Kalli of the messages of support and love that had poured in from their wide circle of friends.

No sound betrayed him, but Kalli was aware of someone at the door. She was not surprised to turn and face Walker.

''They didn't tell me Jeff had a visitor. I'll wait.''

His retreat halted immediately when Mary held out a hand.

''Walker, no. You stay here with Jeff. Kalli was just going to take me to the cafeteria for a late supper, and I'll feel so much better if you're here.''

Kalli blinked at Mary's abrupt change of attitude. After a moment's hesitation, Walker came in, bending to brush a kiss on Mary's cheek.

''How is he?''

''Better,'' Mary said with a slight smile. ''He likes to have you two come by, though he frets about the rodeo.''

Walker nodded in acceptance that Mary knew her husband's thoughts. As Mary and Kalli left, he lifted the chair

Kalli had been using, turned it and straddled it, his attention focused on the man in the bed.

As she walked with Mary to the cafeteria, restlessness seized Kalli—an urgency to do something, to tackle some project, to solve some problem. She thought of the paperwork waiting for her at the rodeo office with something like longing as she gently bullied Mary into taking more than coffee.

At a corner table, they ate wilting fruit salad and tired sandwiches, with frequent halts while one or the other stared, unseeing, at nothing. Mary finally pecked at enough food that when she sighed deeply and pushed away the tray, Kalli didn't feel the need to badger her into eating more.

"I wish he'd talk."

Mary's unexpected words made Kalli's fragmented thoughts stumble onto the realization that she'd harbored a similar wish—that *Walker* would talk to her, really talk to her. How stupid. She and Walker had nothing to say to each other. But Mary's need to have Jeff talk was very real.

"He will. Give him time. It's—"

"No." Mary cut off Kalli's assurances. "Time's against him. If a stroke patient doesn't talk early, often he never does. The nurses and the doctor hem it around with a lot of 'ifs' and 'sometimes,' but that's what it boils down to."

Kalli was silent. Mary wasn't bemoaning the facts, she was stating them. In the face of such courage, Kalli wouldn't offer empty words of reassurance.

"His body not doing what he wants, that would be hard for anybody, especially a man like Jeff. He'd get by, though. But not talking . . . I see the frustration in him and it's so fierce. Sometimes I worry that he'll just let go because the frustration's so bad, that he'll quit fighting."

"No!" Kalli's shocked denial drew no looks. The few other customers must have been accustomed to intense conversations. "Mary, don't think that. Jeff would never give up, never. He's too strong."

Mary turned to face her, examining her. "Even the strong give up sometimes," she said slowly. "Walker did. You did. Jeff could."

"He won't. Jeff won't give up." She said it with every ounce of conviction in her, but Mary's unwavering look demanded more. That was harder.

"Walker... Walker didn't give up. He might have been down for a while, but he kept going with what he wanted from life. He never gave up the rodeo." *Don't slow down. Don't linger on the thought of how he went on without you.* "And I...well, there you're right. I gave up. On the life out here. On the marriage. But the difference is I'm not strong like Jeff and Walker—"

"You are strong. If you'd given yourself some time—"

Kalli covered Mary's hand with hers. "What I'm saying is, Jeff won't give up. Not ever. You can't let yourself worry he might."

Tears welled in Mary's eyes, but didn't fall. "I must be getting old to go saying a fool thing like that about the man I've known fifty-two years."

"You just needed someone else to say the words."

Turning her hand, Mary returned the grip. "You've gotten to be very wise, child. You're right. I'd said the words so much, they didn't make sense anymore. I needed to hear a new voice. Now, c'mon, let's get up to the room."

Fueled by food or renewed hope, Mary walked smartly down quiet corridors. As they neared Jeff's room, Kalli tried to ease away, planning to leave before Walker performed another disappearing act. But Mary's firm grip on Kalli's hand never slackened, and escape would have involved an undignified tug-of-war, which Kalli would probably lose.

Two steps inside the door, they both froze.

Walker stood at the far side of the bed, one hand splayed on the wall above Jeff's head as he leaned down. With his back to them was a short, white-coated doctor, also leaning over the figure in the bed.

"Oh, my God," Mary whispered. "Jeff!"

Walker straightened. But his face held none of what Kalli feared.

"It's all right, Mary. Everything's all right. Jeff's talking."

"Talking?" Mary repeated.

She moved to her husband's side, the young doctor backing up to give her room.

"Not much volume yet," said Walker with that half grin, "but the vocabulary's 'bout the same. First thing he said was 'Mary.' I called in the doc. And Jeff got right down to business with 'rodeo.' And somethin' about somebody's parentage not being quite on the up-and-up."

The doctor's discreet throat-clearing managed to convey humor. "I believe Mr. Jeffries was addressing me."

"I wouldn't be at all surprised," Mary said with great fondness as she held Jeff's hand between both of hers.

"But now Mr. Jeffries needs his rest," the doctor added in a different tone.

"I'm not going—"

"You may stay awhile, Mrs. Jeffries," he allowed. Which, Kalli thought, was rather like someone telling the Mississippi River it could flow. "But everyone else, out."

In a surprisingly short time, Kalli was walking with Walker across a concrete plain interrupted only by a pair of pickups and three cars. After the hospital's bright stillness, the parking lot seemed dark and mysteriously alive with the currents of the night.

Walker turned with her as she headed to her car. He didn't so much as brush against her jacket. He tucked his fingers into his jeans pockets, hunching slightly into the wind that tugged at his cotton shirt. Leaving a pool of light, they dipped into darkness.

"Must have some cutting horse in him."

"What?" How could his slow voice throw her when she'd been so aware of his physical presence?

"The little doc. The way he rounded us up and chuted us right out the door."

"He was efficient."

A smile drew up the one side of his mouth. Irritation pulled at her. This lopsided stuff was getting old. Who would have thought he'd adopt such an affectation? Maybe someone who hadn't known what his smile was *supposed* to look like would accept it as genuine. Not her.

"Did Jeff really talk?"

He didn't bristle at her demand, but a shifting of shadows indicated a lift of his eyebrows.

"Yes."

She'd known him too long and had once known him too well not to decipher the conflicts in that syllable. That was natural. So was the softened quality of her next word.

"But...?"

Reaching her car, they faced each other under the spotlight from a nearby pole. Walker propped his right hip against the back door, adjusting his hat to shade his face.

"He made noises. Calling them words came more from knowing what he'd want to say. If I got Mary's hopes up... Maybe I shouldn't have made it sound so good."

"Anybody would have done that under the circumstances." Her words didn't ease his concern; she saw that in his stance. Needing to persuade him, she cupped a hand around his arm just above the elbow. "Besides, Mary told me the doctors said the important thing is the ability to vocalize. The words will come, and they'll get clearer."

A warm movement of air that might have been his sigh touched her cheek. He dipped his head, then straightened, pushed his hat back with a forefinger and grinned.

"Thanks, Kalli."

The stark light illuminated the lines and planes his face had acquired. And under that artificial glare, Kalli recognized what she hadn't before—a shallow indentation of scar tissue above the right side of his mouth. The corner that no longer lifted when he grinned.

Sharp tears scraped at her throat as she swallowed. His grin faded and his face stilled into watchfulness. She became aware of her hold tightening on his arm. The breeze-cooled cotton of his shirt provided her hand no protection from the solid fire of his skin.

How could she have forgotten that about him?

Even as a boy, his skin had run hotter than anybody else's. As a child, she'd found it odd, and saw it as raw material for teasing. As a young woman, she'd found it fascinating, and recognized it reflected a fire that ran deep within him. Now she found it frightening.

She snatched her hand away. Digging her keys out, she turned away under the excuse of unlocking the car.

She felt his look. If she had once been able to read him with a look, he'd had the same ability with her. She couldn't risk that his skill had survived in better shape than hers. She needed something more to put distance between them. To obscure from his eyes any traces of the tears that threatened and the heat that burned. Something to remind him how things had changed. Something—

"You have an interview first thing in the morning," she blurted out.

As a reminder of the canyon the years had carved out between them, nothing could have been better. Walker's expression shifted, hardening. He said nothing.

"Roberta's cousin's brother-in-law is editor of the paper over in Whiton. She asked if she should call and I said yes. He's sending someone tomorrow. The focus will be on you. So please don't disappear all afternoon the way you and Gulch have done the past couple days."

He turned away, looking over the top of the car. "You don't waste any time, do you, Kalli Evans? Not when you want something badly enough. Like publicity for the rodeo." He faced her again. "Or to get away from me."

She made no response.

He slapped his palm softly on the car roof. "Good night, Kalli."

He didn't wait for an answer before walking away.

The sweeping was adequate, but they should hose down the stands more often. Kalli made a note on the clipboard she carried for her morning inspection as she started up the back steps to the Buzzards' Roost.

Voices above her stopped her in midstep. The light, quick tones of the young reporter, Jenny Belkin, who'd shown up this morning. And Walker's distinctive deep, slow notes.

"Have you had many injuries, Walker?"

"Nothing that's kept me from going back." He said it so easily. As if the specter of his pain hadn't torn Kalli apart. As if it hadn't contributed to the end of their marriage. "When you've broken your nose in a few places, you try not to go back to those places," he added dryly. "That's what you learn in your old age."

"You don't seem old."

The young woman's words might merely represent an interviewer trying to make her subject comfortable. Only Walker hadn't sounded uncomfortable. In her mind's eye, Kalli saw the sun-streaked hair, the deep tan, the petite build of the someone Roberta's cousin's brother-in-law had sent to do this story.

"In rodeo, I'm Methuselah. Lots of cowboys my age have been retired four, five years."

"So when do you think you might retire?"

Either Walker's neutral response or her journalistic instincts had shifted Jenny Belkin's focus; reporting Walker Riley's retirement would be a coup. Or else Kalli had imagined the earlier intonation of more-than-professional interest. She didn't much like the implications of that.

"Can't say."

"But if you're not competing while you're running the rodeo here in Park, isn't that a de facto retirement?"

"I'm working too hard to be retired. This isn't what I had in mind for when I quit rodeoing."

Kalli knew what the next question would be before it was spoken. She knew because she'd heard it before.

"What did you have in mind for when you quit rodeo?"

And she knew the answer because she'd heard that, too.

Memory rose. Acrid hospital smells stinging her nostrils. Shock opening to grief, heavy and fresh. Walker, sick at heart, but when some Texas reporter asked if he'd be retiring after this tragedy, his answer coming swift and sure.

Retire? I'm not retiring. Hell, no. My career'll end when they carry me out in a pine box. Just like Cory.

God, she couldn't listen to him say those words again. She'd already relived them too often in her mind.

But she couldn't move.

Disembodied, his voice came from above her.

"I thought I'd find myself a porch and a rockin' chair with a view of the mountains and tell everybody who'll listen 'bout my great career riding the bulls."

Jenny Belkin's laugh barely reached Kalli over the buzzing in her ears. Her muscles loosened abruptly and she sat on the bottom step, staring at a drift of dust obscuring the toe of her Italian leather flat. *I need boots. When will I find the time?* She almost giggled at the inconsequence of that thought. She faced a much more complex issue.

Had Walker Riley truly changed so much?

"C'mon."

Wrenching her attention from last night's figures, Kalli looked at Walker. He'd rarely been around this time of afternoon the past two weeks, much less looming over her desk, demanding she go somewhere. "C'mon where?" she asked.

"With me. Roberta said you left the ranch station wagon for servicing this morning. We'll take my truck."

"But—"

"I've cleaned out Coat's bed, so don't worry 'bout getting your fancy clothes messed up on the way."

"On the way where?" she asked in exasperation.

"Lodge's store."

"Whatever for?"

"Clothes. That's what they sell."

"I *know* what they sell. But I don't need—"

"Yes, you do. Look at you," he ordered.

She didn't need to look at her two-piece dress with matching blazer—"fancy clothes" indeed! She'd even worn sandals. "I look all right. My clothes are perfectly—"

"You look more than all right."

At his uninflected interruption, her heart lurched. She hadn't thought he'd given her more than a glance through the four lunches, two joint newspaper interviews and staff meeting since that night in the hospital parking lot.

"Acceptable," she finished weakly, then crossed her arms on the desk, leaned forward and strengthened her voice to add, "And I'm not going anywhere."

Instead of responding to the challenge, he unhurriedly pushed a pile of papers from the corner of the desk to its center and propped himself there with his bent leg resting along the edge so his knee nearly brushed her elbow.

"Jasper Lodge is chairman of the rodeo committee."

That didn't warrant an answer.

"Could be the most important vote in whether Jeff keeps the rodeo next year."

"I know that." She kept her voice as even as his.

"And he asked you two weeks ago when you were coming by his store."

Her shoulders tightened. She said nothing.

"Asked you two weeks ago when you were going to start looking more like Wyoming and less like New York." No one else might have caught the flick of disdain in the last two words. But she felt its sting. "Have you gone?"

"You know I haven't. I haven't had ti—"

"Doesn't make good sense to me. Alienating somebody influential. Maybe things are done different in New York."

She stood, snagged her purse and reached the door. "Well, c'mon, Riley. You wanted to go, let's go. If you're going to be a chauffeur, don't keep the customer waiting."

Staring out the pickup window as neat frame buildings gave way to the taller, squarer buildings of Park's downtown, she acknowledged Walker's point. Jasper Lodge hadn't been drumming up business—at least not entirely—he'd been commenting on image and perception.

"You didn't have to be snide about New York, Walker," she said. "You could have persuaded me to get casual clothes without resorting to those tactics."

He passed Lodge's plain wooden sign and turned at the side street. A car was angle-parked, but the next spot was empty. Sometimes she forgot how far she was from New York.

"Maybe," he acknowledged as he pulled in and turned off the ignition. "But it wasn't just the clothes."

She shot him a glance and got his profile.

"I want you to get boots, too. For boots I figured I better play it safe and get snide."

Despite herself, she was laughing as Walker held open the door of Lodge's for her.

"We'll start with boots," declared Esther Lodge, Jasper's wife and the heart and soul of Lodge's store.

After a report on Jeff, an update on Mary, a blunt assessment that folks were playing wait-and-see with the rodeo and an account of her youngest's progress in college, she listened to Kalli's modest list, then set the attack.

"You looking for basic ropers? Tube shaft or scallop? Leather? Suede? Fringe? Fancy stitch? Walking heel or dress?"

Kalli sorted out her preferences and Esther quickly had her seated in the back corner of the narrow store. As she tried on boots, Kalli was aware of Walker picking up and putting down samples with uncharacteristic restlessness.

"Boots first so I can help you, because I'm leaving to go by the Carmodys' pretty soon here," Esther said. "Lolly's laid up with a bad back and she called to say those boys of hers have grown right out of their clothes, so I'm taking things by their place."

"Going by" the Carmodys' ranch involved a thirty-mile trip one way—the last seventeen miles on dirt. Oh, yes, she was a long, long way from New York.

"Don't like those?" Esther whisked away a pair of lizard boots with six-row stitching of a stylized flame. "With Lolly laid up and the doctor bills, I don't know what they'd have done if you hadn't sent those cowboys, Walker."

Kalli's gaze jerked to Walker, who frowned quellingly. "What—"

But Esther had caught the signal, and talked over Kalli. "So I'll be leaving soon. And that old rascal Jasper's not back from the bank. Left an hour ago, but I don't doubt for a second he's sittin' in the barbershop with his cronies, talkin' away. So I'll finish with your boots, then roust Jasper on my way out to Lolly's. You and Walker can look after the store while you pick out your other things."

Kalli shot Walker a look. He used to hate shopping. Eventually she'd realized that one reason was he couldn't afford much. She'd assumed he would drop her at Lodge's, then disappear. Looking after the store, he'd be stuck.

"I can trust you, Kalli," Esther added.

Trust her to choose clothes, Esther meant. Her highest compliment. When people talked about going to Lodge's to see what they could find, they meant they'd see what Esther would decide was right for them. Tom Nathan, who was on the road most of the year and divorced nearly two decades, had gotten in the habit of calling Esther from time to time to tell her he was running low on shirts, or needed a belt or jeans. She'd make a choice and send it off. Sometimes, when he got busy, packages arrived without a prompting phone call.

He wasn't the only one.

"Thank you, Esther," Kalli said, suitably modest.

"Nothing to thank me for. You got taste. Simple as that." She set aside the black high-shafted boots with a dress heel they'd concurred on. "Now, this pair with the slouch shaft is nice."

"Yes, I'll try those on."

"'Course, you don't want to use these for kickin' 'round the pens or chutes, not like a pair of ropers."

"Kalli's clear of the pens and chutes, so that's no worry," said Walker. "Long as they'll do for the office."

Kalli might have dismissed the raw note buried under his usual slow delivery as her imagination if Esther hadn't cleared her throat and muttered, "Well, well."

Kalli yanked the boots on and stood to check the fit. The man made no sense. They'd divided the rodeo—her with the business operations from the office, him with the competition from the pens and chutes. An arrangement that included a tacit agreement to limit contact that could only be uncomfortable for both. Did he want her nosing around?

Kalli went to the only mirror. Walker stood next to it, holding a man's dress boot worth several hundred dollars. From the corner of her eye, she watched his strong, battered hand caress the leather.

Fighting an urge to swallow, she hitched her skirt for a better look at the boots and concentrated on the mirror.

Walker put down the boot with enough force to rap the heel against the wooden shelf.

"I'll take these, too," she said, then added defiantly, "And let me look at the ropers."

She quickly agreed with Esther on a workmanlike pair in saddle-leather brown. Then, while Esther instructed Walker on tending the store—"Answer the phone, check the tags for prices if anyone wants to buy and write them down, but don't take their money because I don't want you messin' with my register"—Kalli selected a pair of basic jeans.

"Shirts are back in that corner," Esther told her. "We got in a new one with a pleated cape-type yoke. It's a nice cotton. The green would look real good on you."

Kalli spotted the jade shirt and knew Esther was right. But she opted for a plain white oxford cloth shirt and a soft ⸺use with minimal same-colored piping, both neu-⸺ough to blend with her casual clothes back in New

"You take those things on back, Kalli," Esther instructed as she gathered her purse and the parcel for the Carmodys. "Trying-on room's around to the left."

"Thanks, Esther. I'll leave a check with Jasper for the boots and whatever else."

"That's just fine as long as you don't let this cowboy here try to work my register."

With a laugh, Kalli slipped behind the curtain to the dressing room. But she could hear the voices out front.

"You could use some shirts, too, Walker. How long's it been since you bought decent ones? You'll look like one of those clowns dressed in rags instead of a champion bull-rider if you keep puttin' off spending some money on your appearance, boy. A champion ought to look like one."

"Esther Lodge, if you had the outfitting of me, I'd have spent all my time and money on looking like your idea of a champion and none of it being a champion."

"False economy to wear your clothes to rags. You need shirts, boy." The sound of a door closing told Kalli that Walker had been allowed no time for a rejoinder.

Slipping off her jacket and unhooking the side closure on her skirt, Kalli mulled over the exchange.

Had Walker put off Esther because he didn't feel like buying shirts? Or for another reason? Avoiding wrinkles, she laid the blazer, then the skirt across a bench.

Granted, rodeo champions weren't in the same income bracket as million-dollar baseball players or football stars, but the national title was worth a good bit. Certainly enough to not be short of money for shirts. If he'd held on to it.

She took off her sandals.

Could Walker have blown his winnings? Others had.

He'd been careful with money when they were married. But he'd had no choice. She'd never known him w̄ had money. How had he reacted?

Unsteady fingers slowed with the task of pulling on the new clothes. Images of Walker struggling financially stirred too many emotions, too many possibilities. Had he let the money trickle through his fingers? Or had it gushed away in generosity and wild times? If she'd been there . . .

She let out a settling breath as she tucked the rose blouse into the jeans and turned to the mirror.

A younger woman looked back at her. A woman with less armor against the outside world. A woman with tangled hair and cheeks blushed by sun and wind instead of cosmetics.

The woman she used to be.

A woman who didn't have the strengths she had now. Who hadn't learned the things she'd learned. Who hadn't lived the life she'd lived.

A woman who loved Walker Riley.

The eyes of the woman in the mirror widened and glistened with gathering tears. She shook her head, shattering the illusion and banishing the past.

With clear eyes, she looked at her reflection, and saw the woman she'd become. Not perfect by any means, but not a naive girl, either. Not even the clothes of yesterday could keep it from being today.

She sighed, gave herself a little shake and started unbuttoning the blouse.

"Kalli?" An elbow hooked the curtain, shoving it aside.

"Hey!" Kalli's hand closed the throat of the blouse.

"Ain't nothing I haven't seen before." But he didn't look at her. "Brought you some things."

"*Some* things? Looks like half of Esther's stock."

"Only in your size." Walker dumped an armload of blouses on the bench, spilling jeweled colors, bandanna-print yokes, Aztec embroidery and color-blocked shoulders.

"Hey, my clothes are under there." Kalli started toward the haphazard stack that threatened to iron creases into her two-piece dress and blazer.

"Won't need 'em." Walker snagged her arm.

For an instant, as she faced him in the constricted dressing room, close enough to smell the sun and dust on him, near enough to see the groove from nose to mouth that lifted so distinctively when he smiled, the possibilities of not needing clothes around Walker sizzled through her blood.

"Here, try this on. You won't go back to city clothes. Not as long as you're here."

"What makes you so sure?" Her tone was defiant, but she accepted the jade pleated-yoke shirt.

"'Cause you're more comfortable in these." He started out, then paused in the doorway to toss her another instruction. "Better get started because I'm coming back soon as I pick out some more jeans. And I'm not knocking."

She frowned, but didn't waste any time shrugging out of the rose shirt and trading it for the jade. It did look good. The slight extension at the shoulders made her waist look very small where the shirt tucked into the jeans. And Walker was right— She wouldn't get back into her New York clothes until she had to. She'd forgotten how comfortable these clothes were. Designed for a day in the saddle, they clearly ranked comfort over fashion.

She turned her back to the single mirror, then twisted to try to see that view.

"Nice."

Walker's single, drawled word had her flushing the way flowery compliments hadn't in years.

Beyond her image, the mirror showed a long, lean cowboy propping a shoulder against the doorjamb, holding a pair of jeans. She untwisted herself slowly. "Thanks."

They looked at each other, and she could almost feel the years peeling away.

No. No. Nothing could take away the years.

"For the jeans. Thanks for the jeans."

At her tug, he released his hold on the jeans but didn't budge otherwise.

"Now get out of here so I can start trying on all this."
She raised a hand, prepared to give him a slight push on his
way, then thought better of it.

He raised an eyebrow at her aborted gesture, but oblig-
ingly pivoted a quarter turn so his shoulder still rested
against the wooden frame but was now outside the dressing room. She pulled the curtain across behind him.

She started unbuttoning the shirt.

"It's going to take most of the afternoon to try on all
these clothes," she said, willing to say almost anything to
break a silence that screamed of awareness.

"Buy it all and you'll still be behind Belle Grissom."

"Belle! How is she?" She hadn't thought of the dimin-
utive barrel racer for years. Two years younger than Kalli,
Belle had already been a veteran of the circuit and had
shown the newcomer the ropes. Since Belle's solution to any
crisis was to buy clothes—preferably with rhinestones, se-
quins or both—her wardrobe was legendary.

"She's doing fine. Got divorced couple years back and
went on such a shopping spree, she had to get a bigger
place. I knew that marriage was doomed when he gave a
bunch of her things to the mission. Belle didn't miss them.
But then she saw this mite outside the mission wearing a
shirt decorated with a big glittery horse's head. Seems it was
one of a kind. Boy, did it ever hit the fan then."

Kalli laughed, Walker's words and her memories of the
people making the scene as vivid as if she'd been there. As
she tried on clothes, she prompted his stories of people
she'd known with questions and comments. Ten years,
covered in the time it took to put on a dozen outfits.

"And Sailor—remember Sailor Anderson?"

"Sure." She remembered. A charmer, the Lothario of
the rodeo circuit, who'd earned his nickname with a girl in
every "port." And she remembered Pammy, the unglam-
orous daughter of a stock contractor who adored Sailor

with every fiber of her being, yet accepted her role as his
sole unmarried female "buddy." "How is Sailor?"

Finished trying on the clothes, she pushed open the curtain as she stacked her selections and folded or hung the
rejects. She'd decided to wear the jeans and rose shirt.

"He's fine. He finally got smart." Walker resumed his
position against the frame. "Opened his eyes and saw what
he had in Pammy and married her seven years back. Two
kids and a third on the way. Sailor's settled down. His
winnings bought a couple radio stations in Texas, so he's
using his gift of gab for something more'n charming la-
dies."

Two children and a third on the way... That could have
been her and Walker. Kalli put on a smile. "Sailor settled
down? How in the world did that happen?"

He straightened away from the door. "You 'bout ready?
Jasper oughtta be here any time."

"Yes. I sure hope Jasper will take a check for all this."
Her gesture encompassed five shirts, three pairs of jeans
and a denim skirt.

"And this one."

He added the jade pleated-yoke shirt.

"No. It's not practical, Walker. You were right, I need
clothes that can stand up to the rodeo. But this is dressy.
And I have plenty of dressy clothes."

"Then I'm getting it for you."

"Walker, no—"

"I'm getting it for you."

"If I want it, I can afford it. You don't have—"

"I may not have a high-power job, but I can afford a
damn shirt."

She put a hand to his chest, instinctively trying to soothe
his harshness. The gesture seemed to shift his mood. He put
his hands on her shoulders, not gripping, just smoothing

over the fabric of her shirt. His voice dropped and slowed to his usual deliberateness.

"Dammit, Kalli. I couldn't get you things before. Not even what you needed. I'm buying you this."

"Walker." It wasn't a protest this time.

He ran his hands down her arms to her elbows, then up again. Through the fabric that covered it, the heat of his chest seeped into her palm.

"Let me give you this, Kalli."

She looked at him, and the shirt was forgotten. There was only Walker. The boy she'd worshiped. The young man she'd loved. She moved her hand higher, so cloth no longer separated her palm and his skin. The heat seemed to leap from him, firing her blood.

He stepped in, one hand moving to cup the back of her head.

In the first instant, his lips on hers felt strange. But it was only a flash, immediately lost in the heat, in sensation's explosion as his mouth pressed against hers.

"Walker." She managed the word of caution; he made it something else. Sliding his tongue inside her mouth, he opened her to deeper expressions of need. Mutual need.

She stepped back under the onslaught of emotion, but held on to his shoulders, as if she feared he wouldn't follow. But he did, that first step and then a second, pressing her against the smooth cool surface of the mirror. He slipped his arm behind her, drawing her tighter and tighter against his body.

Her hands wandered, reacquainting themselves with the curve of his skull under the thick hair, the harsh bones of his jaw, the width of his shoulders, the line of his collarbone, the power of his back.

They kissed and kissed again. Moving, adjusting. Exploring faces and throats, only to return, hungry mouth to hungry mouth.

Not as if the ten years had never existed, but as if they were being relived through these kisses. Kisses of discovery. Kisses in the pouring rain. Kisses lit by the sun. Kisses of apology. Kisses in celebration. Kisses in consolation. Kisses to shut out the cold. Kisses heated from the fire that flared from one to the other. Kisses started in anger and pain. Kisses ended in joy.

Kisses almost desperate with loss.

She felt the growing tension in him. She knew what was coming. She knew.... Yet, when Walker pulled away from her, she couldn't stop a whimpered gasp at the coldness that whipped around her. Only where his hands gripped her shoulders, holding her at arm's length, did she feel anything less than frozen.

He stilled his face, as if, without movement, his emotions couldn't be read. But the emotions concentrated into eyes that burned and crackled with intensity.

A bell announced the opening of the front door. Walker eased his hold on her until they stood separate, no contact between them. But his look didn't change, even when he finally turned and strode out of the dressing room.

She'd first seen that look before she'd understood the strange, insistent urgings of her own body.

But now she understood. Now she understood what it could do to her.

Chapter Four

"Walker? Kalli?"

Jasper Lodge's voice grated across Walker's nerves. God, he hadn't wanted to let her go. What he'd wanted to do was take her right then and there. To drive into her softness until they melted into each other. To claim her and possess her and never again let Kalli Evans out of his sight or his hold.

Which was exactly why he'd had to let her go. Thank God and a lifetime of discipline, he'd still had the crumb of sense that told him he couldn't afford—physically or emotionally—to let that situation go any further, because the only possible ending was frustration on both levels. Any moment Kalli would have realized the extent of his emotions and would have run due east, not stopping until she hit the Atlantic Ocean. Just like she did last time.

"Walker, you in here?"

"Yeah, Jasper, we're here."

Walker was aware of Kalli smoothing down her clothes, pushing her hair back, but he didn't risk looking at her.

He took another breath before walking out into the main part of the store, sparing a moment to thank Providence that Esther made the most of floor space by building displays good and high— They came in as handy as a tablecloth. He took his time joining Jasper at the register.

No sense advertising to Jasper Lodge—and thus to all of Park and a good percentage of Wyoming—that Walker Riley still desired the woman who'd once been his wife with every atom of his body. Especially certain atoms.

He wasn't sure if it was any consolation that her body hadn't been exactly neutral, either.

Physical desire for each other had most definitely survived the past decade. He wasn't particularly surprised.

But what did it mean if the body survived and the heart didn't?

"There you are, Walker. Where you been? Where's Kalli? Esther said you two were here when she stopped by the barbershop. But when I came in and nobody stirred, I thought I mighta caught the woman being wrong for the first time in thirty-six years of marriage."

"Thought you'd be back long before this, Jasper."

"Uh, well. Uh, lots of discussing going on down at the barbershop. Couldn't, er, didn't want to walk out in the middle."

Walker had diverted attention to Jasper's whereabouts because he'd felt no inclination to explain where he and Kalli had been . . . or what they'd been doing. But Jasper's obvious discomfort raised his eyebrows, and his instinct for something out of kilter.

"What's everybody discussing down at the barbershop?"

"Oh, all sorts of things. You know, that saying about ships and sealing wax and something else and kings."

"Cabbages. It's of cabbages and kings." Walker reviewed a mental picture of vehicles parked near the barbershop as he and Kalli had driven past. Around here, vehicles were as recognizable as their owners. "Must have been mighty interesting cabbages to draw most of the rodeo committee. Far as I can tell, only one missing was Dawson Fletcher."

Jasper shot him a hunted look. "We got to look to the future. It's our duty. It's what folks expect of us. You've been 'round. You know how it is, Walker."

"How what is?"

Kalli's voice, forcibly bright, broke the moment. Jasper came around the counter to take the stack of clothes from her and talked nonstop about her selections, her good taste and Esther's approval. He didn't answer her question.

But Walker hadn't expected him to, any more than he'd expected Jasper to tell him what they'd been talking about at the barbershop. He knew, anyhow. The future of the Park Rodeo. The question wasn't what they'd discussed. It was if they'd decided.

He was still puzzling that as he and Kalli got into his pickup, her packages stowed behind the seat. But the quality of her silence soon penetrated the air that swirled around them from the open windows. And another puzzle took precedence.

Kalli.

She stared out the passenger window, leaving him only a slice of her face to consider. It was enough.

Reaching across the gulf of seat she'd left between them, he laid a hand on her forearm where it rested across her lap. She jolted. Not that he needed that reaction to know her regrets.

"It's all right, Kalli."

"Of course it is. I know that." Squaring shoulders that already looked tight, she turned a smile toward him that brought a sour taste to his throat. "And I know you're too intelligent a man to mistake what happened back at Lodge's for anything but what it was."

Slowly, he withdrew his hand, letting the drag of his fingers over her arm sustain the contact.

"And just what was it, Kalli?"

She took up his mild question eagerly, twisting on the seat to face him fully to lend emphasis to her points.

"It was the past."

"The past," he repeated without inflection.

"Yes. It's natural, Walker. We're back here where we were kids and where we, uh, we, uh, learned to care for each other. And there are all the associations and all the emotions. It's like adults going back to where they grew up suddenly feeling—and acting—like they're eight years old again."

He'd felt a long way from eight years old when he had her lips under his, but the sour taste left his throat. He wasn't about to dispute her theory, since it seemed to make her feel more comfortable. Comfortable enough to look at him instead of in the opposite direction.

Not now, he wouldn't dispute it.

"And in addition to that element, that, uh, sort of conditioned response because of what happened before, we never really had closure on the past," she said.

"Closure?" He turned away as if checking the side mirror, just in case his face showed more than he wanted.

"Yes, a chance to finish off the past. To put a period at the end of it."

"You don't think a divorce was enough punctuation?"

She grimaced at his dry drawl. "That was a technicality, a legality."

Something strong and hot surged through him— How many times had he thought that very thing, that the divorce was a technicality and hadn't done a damn thing to change the heart of the matter? But he fought the sensation. Because just as many times, he'd realized that there were two hearts in this matter. And they no longer beat together.

"What I mean by closure is a way to finish up the emotions, in the way signing the divorce papers finished up the marriage, the legal contract. All those old feelings came to the surface just now, because we'd never really had closure on them. Actually this was good, and very natural. Very healthy emotionally. Now we've put the past behind us, *all* the past, and we can move ahead. We've closed off the parts of our lives when we, uh, when we cared for each other. And now we can be colleagues, we can cooperate for the good of the rodeo and for Jeff and Mary, and none of those feelings should shadow us anymore."

He could tell from her voice she'd about convinced herself of her words' truth.

It sounded to Walker like she'd been reading too many magazine articles, but he wouldn't argue with her twisting explanations. Maybe she was right. But he figured it didn't matter. Whatever the reason, whether the feelings carried over from the past or were something new, the result was the same. They wanted each other.

"Maybe so," he drawled.

She seemed satisfied with his response, settling back into the seat and looking straight ahead as they turned in to the rodeo grounds.

Yes, they wanted each other. But passion's survival didn't guarantee anything else had survived between them. Not liking or respect or enjoyment. Not love.

He knew that. But he also knew it was a start.

And he knew that sometimes you only got a start. Sometimes you got thrown as soon as the chute opened and the bull had room to make its feelings clear about being ridden.

The way Kalli had made it clear she wanted to put the passion firmly in their past.

He'd just have to see if he could hold on long enough to win this go-round.

Kalli had nearly finished the entries for two young cowboys she hadn't seen before, when Walker walked in the office, shadowed by Coat.

One cowboy nudged the other and she heard a muttered, "That him? Walker Riley?"

"Yeah, that's him."

Walker nodded to them in a general way as he came in. He cut a look at her that cut away just as quickly, sparing only a neutral "Kalli" in greeting, then exchanged good mornings with Roberta before making a beeline for the coffee.

He must have stopped at an outside spigot for a wash; the hair around his face and at the back of his neck shone darkly with captured water and his wrists and hands below the rolled-back cuffs of his shirt were devoid of the coating of dust he picked up from his usual morning work.

As had become habit, Coat came directly to Kalli, waiting for her to rub his ears. She always obliged, refusing to allow herself even a pang that while the dog stayed by her whenever she and Walker were in the same vicinity, Coat was at Walker's heels the second he made a move to leave.

Today she was in too good a mood to even have the pang.

Kalli was inclined to be indulgent over the note of awe in the young cowboys' whispered exchange and their shuffle-footed shifting of positions so they could keep Walker in sight without being too obvious. The pair of them couldn't be out of high school yet.

More important—and the cause of her good mood—they represented the fourth and fifth entries by newcomers they'd had in two days. She'd take that as a good sign. The entries hadn't returned to the level they'd been at before Jeff's stroke, but they'd improved. Word was getting out that the Park Rodeo was still a good place to compete.

"All set," she announced. "See you tonight, then, okay?"

"Huh? Oh, okay." The first cowboy flushed when Walker glanced up and started backing out of the office. "I mean, uh, yes, ma'am. See you tonight, ma'am."

"Yes, ma'am," agreed the second, wasting no time in following his friend. "Thank you, ma'am."

Mouthing the oft-repeated "ma'am" in utter disgust—you'd think she was ninety-two and frail!—Kalli stared at the closed door. The dual splutter of laughter from behind her spun her around to face Roberta and Walker.

"Oh, yeah, you think it's pretty funny, those two kids treating me like my own grandmother?"

"Sure do," Walker answered easily, one long leg extended from where he'd propped his hip comfortably on Roberta's desk.

Trying to maintain the semblance of anger, she turned to Roberta. "How'd you like it if they did it to you?" she asked, hoping for a more sympathetic audience. No such luck.

"Do it to me all the time. Even Matt Halderman. And ain't anybody can say he looks at you like you're anybody's grandmother."

Awkwardness flooded into Kalli. Some of the casualness seemed to go out of Walker's posture. But Roberta looked bright-eyed from one to the other. She'd done it on purpose, Kalli realized. Roberta had brought up the topic of Matt Halderman just to watch their reactions.

Deliberately, Kalli leaned against the counter, sliding her elbows behind her to rest on either side of her.

"Matt's a great guy." She'd started to say "kid," then realized it wouldn't strike the right note.

"Guess all these kids're making you feel older, too, huh, Walker?" Roberta turned her piercing look on him.

Kalli might have asked what made Roberta say that, but Walker apparently knew better than to give the rodeo secretary that kind of opening.

"Nah. What makes me feel old is cars I once owned being called classics. Or songs I used to listen to on the radio being 'discovered' by some new hotshot. Or realizing I've been out of school longer than I spent in it."

Kalli winced in amused sympathy at each of his examples. Roberta, however, was not to be diverted.

"So, your entering a few roping events this spring didn't mean you're about ready to give up on riding those bulls like you were still eighteen?"

An incredible surge of hope rushed through Kalli. She thought of his conversation she'd overhead, with the reporter, Jenny Belkin. Even if he wasn't prepared to retire quite yet, perhaps he'd give up riding bulls. Nothing in rodeo came without risk, but in the roping events, at least there wouldn't be nearly a ton of angry bull determined to get rid of him.

"Nope. Doesn't mean that at all."

And just that easily, hope washed away, leaving only a raw discomfort at acknowledging the strength of the brief emotion. Turning her back on the hope and its aftermath, refusing to analyze either, she also turned away from Walker and Roberta, finding a few final touches necessary on entries she'd previously considered complete.

Still, she had the impression Walker spoke directly to her when he added, "I'm going to keep riding bulls until my body falls apart. It's what I do. It's who I am."

The sharp silence lasted past comfort before Roberta asked, "Then why were you in roping events, if it wasn't because you wouldn't be the lone one with gray hairs entering?"

"I did most all the events as a kid, and worked roping now and again, all along. Way it turns out, it was good experience for doing this now, wasn't it? Gives me an appreciation of what those cowboys're going through, what they need in the way of stock and all."

Roberta made a scoffing sound, but said nothing. That restraint seemed to encourage Walker.

"Like now," he went on, and, although she kept her head down, Kalli could hear him moving behind her, going to the opening in the counter, coming around it and heading toward her. "It'll help me sort out tonight's stock. Soon as Kalli gives me that preliminary entry list."

He'd stopped immediately across from her, his hands resting on the counter between them.

"The list's right here."

He'd always had large hands. When she'd first known him, they'd seemed unwieldy, but he'd grown into them by his late teens. They'd always been nicked and callused. And so strong. Strong enough to hang on to a bull or a bronc. Strong enough to drive her wild. Yet gentle, too.

Now they looked more than nicked and callused. They looked battered, with evidence of harsh demands made on them, of broken bones imperfectly healed, of dislocations ignored entirely.

"Kalli?"

"Oh. Yes. Here's the list."

"Thanks. Soon as we get this stock sorted, Gulch and I are opening the arena so the newcomers can get accustomed to the setup. So if you need me, that's where I'll be."

So if you need me, that's where I'll be.

Skittering away from other implications of Walker's last statement, Kalli considered it in a practical light some time after he'd swallowed the last of his coffee and headed out the door.

There was a significant amount of time when she didn't know where Walker was. Not that she needed him, of course.

Most days, he and Gulch returned from picking up the day's fresh stock from the Jeffries ranch around noon or early afternoon. Some days, she saw him before he headed out to get the stock. Sometimes not. It seemed the "nots" held a majority lately.

He and Gulch would do a rough sorting of the incoming stock depending on the early entries, leaving the final ordering of bulls and steers and calves and broncs into pens until a couple hours before the events. Afternoons he spent finishing any repairs around the grounds left over from the morning, or sometimes he and Gulch would disappear on unspecified duties. But they were always back for the final preparations for the night's rodeo and the actual running of it. Afterward, one or the other of them would organize the crew that returned the stock to the ranch, where the animals remained until Walker thought them rested enough to have another run in the competition.

She'd sometimes wondered where Walker and Gulch took off on those afternoons they disappeared, but not enough to reveal her curiosity by actually asking.

So if you need me, that's where I'll be.

An innocuous enough statement. But it kept echoing as she and Roberta proceeded with the routine of taking entries and organizing the evening's rodeo.

Yet, when the call came from Mary, she didn't go out after him or take Roberta up on her offer to fetch him.

After all, he hadn't said anything about finding him if she had good news to share.

"...so they're moving Jeff up to Billings tomorrow—tomorrow!" Mary sounded so youthfully breathless on the phone that Kalli grinned even as a few tears of relief slipped free. "We thought it would be weeks yet, but ever since he started speaking, his progress has been so much faster, and they said his overall condition is strong enough now to go into the rehabilitation program, then, boom! This spot opened up. It's like everything just clicked along.'' Even Mary's sound of exasperation managed to sound happy. ''Everything except my packing. I'm going out to the house right now to throw a few things together, then I'll stay at the hospital tonight to go up early in the ambulance with Jeff. Once I get settled, if you wouldn't mind, I might ask you to bring a few things—''

''Of course, I don't mind, Mary. You just let me know what you want and when you want it. How about a car? Do you want us to arrange for you to have a car there?''

''No, no, that's all taken care of. My cousin Alice lives in Billings and I'll be staying with her and using her son's car.''

''Okay. How soon do you think I can visit Jeff?''

''I'll find out all that and let you and Walker know. But don't worry about coming up too often—that's a two-hour drive. And as much as Jeff will want to see you, you know he'll fret if he thinks you're taking too much time from the rodeo.''

Kalli laughed. It was so true; and it was so good to hear Mary happy, and to hear her talking about Jeff just the way he'd always been.

She was still smiling when she hung up after making a few more arrangements with Mary, and turned to Roberta.

''Great news!''

''I heard,'' the secretary said with an answering smile. ''At least enough to get the gist. You want me to go get Walker so you can tell him?''

Kalli's instinct for self-preservation took over, shouting a warning that seeing Walker Riley right now, sharing these emotions with him, would not be a good idea. She needed some time to restore her defenses.

"Uh, no, that's not necessary. I...uh, I'll go out later and tell him." Reverting to businesslike briskness, she picked up the stack of entries not yet recorded in the computer. "After we've finished this."

Roberta frowned, but didn't argue. However, when those tasks were completed, and they'd reached the lull before reopening the office for the evening, she wasted no time shooing Kalli out with orders to tell Walker the good news. "But take that sweater. Wind's kicking up cool."

Kalli stood by the arena fence, only mildly surprised to find enjoyment in watching all the activity. The memories, so sharp and painful at first, had eased over the past few weeks.

Maybe it was simply being back around the rodeo day in and day out— She now associated the sights and sounds and smells with her daily life instead of the past's hurts.

Or maybe, in facing the memories, she had weakened their power over her.

Coat appeared at her side as she watched two cowboys on horseback circling the arena at a leisurely walk, letting their horses get acquainted with their surroundings. Two others stood by their mounts near the chutes used for the roping events. Walker was talking to them.

Kalli rested her forearms on the top metal tube of the fence and propped her chin on her crossed wrists as she watched. By his gestures, Walker was explaining the fine points of the Park Rodeo's system. They listened with something close to reverence.

Walker's presence in the arena explained why Coat was not at his heels as usual. Dogs were kept out to avoid spooking a horse. Coat might be too savvy a rodeo dog to do that and Walker might have the authority to make his dog the exception to the rule, but Kalli knew he wouldn't.

For some stupid reason, that thought made her smile as she watched Walker vault to the top of the fence next to the chute, then swing one long leg over to straddle the narrow perch with the ease of long custom.

He was dressed no differently from the rest of the men in the arena, or even the adolescent railbirds watching from the far side. Boots, jeans, leather belt, long-sleeved shirt—though his red-and-denim stripe was the exception to the solid blues and whites—and cowboy hat. He sat quietly. The angle of his hat was neither jaunty nor mysterious, but simply in the optimum position to shade his face from the strong late-afternoon sun.

Yet he commanded attention.

She could see it in the way the others kept looking to him. She knew it in the way her own gaze kept coming back to him.

Perhaps it was as simple as reputation. But Kalli wasn't so sure.

Amid whoops and shouts of encouragement, one of the two young cowboys who'd been in the office earlier urged his horse out of the chute, chasing an invisible calf.

Walker's face remained impassive under the shadow of his hat, but his left hand tightened, eased, turned, and tightened again around the metal tubing, as if it were a horse's rein. As if he were the one out on the horse, guiding its path. As if... Realization kicked Kalli in the stomach. She straightened, her hands tightly wrapped around the fence. As if he were the one preparing to compete.

God, she could see the desire in every line of his body, so falsely relaxed. That cowboy cool, trying to mask what was going on in his heart. But she saw it. And fear gripped her.

He'd be leaving. As soon as Jeff and Mary could take control again, he'd be back on the circuit, gambling his body and his safety on the belief that he could outlast, outsmart and outmaneuver nearly a ton of bull.

Well, of course he would go back. She'd known that. Known it all along. That's what this was all about. They'd put their lives on hold temporarily to help Mary and Jeff. But only temporarily. And when Mary and Jeff no longer needed them, they'd each return to their lives. Hers in business in New York. His on the rodeo circuit.

Their real lives. Their separate lives.

He turned then, as if he'd felt her eyes on him, and she forced herself to raise a hand and produce a smile. He started toward her.

"Got some good news, Walker." She pushed every other thought away and made the smile real. "Mary called...."

It wasn't that she was lonely as the solitary occupant of the Jeffrieses' rambling ranch house. She'd scoffed at the idea when Walker had raised it after hearing Mary wouldn't be home tonight or any other night while Jeff was up at Billings. Mary had spent most nights at the Park hospital anyhow, and Kalli had lived alone for years. Besides, as she'd pointed out to Mr. Overprotective Riley, there were three hands and the longtime foreman two hundred yards away in the bunkhouse, so she wasn't exactly alone on the place.

No, clearly it wasn't loneliness that had her wandering the darkened house. More a restlessness that drove her from her room in the north wing, to the center of the house with its big kitchen, homey dining room, casual living room and cluttered den that doubled as Jeff's office. Then beyond that to the oversize master bedroom and sitting room on the south side. And back once more to the central part of the house.

The kind of restlessness that hit when she was tired, but couldn't sleep. When she wanted to stay still, until she stopped moving, then had to be back on her feet. The kind of restlessness she hated because she couldn't ignore it and didn't want to face its source.

The faint light in the den flirted with the face of a clock. She went in, drawn closer, though not really wanting to know the time. After one. She tried to block out the automatic computation of how much sleep she'd get if she went to sleep right this second. An exercise in futility. Both because her mind did the math in a blink, and because there was no way she was going to sleep anytime soon.

She went to the window, resting her elbows on the crosspieces that divided the panes and staring at the dark sky and darker form of the mountains, pierced by a solitary light that told of mankind's toehold on their majesty.

Turning away from that light, she ran her hand along the smooth edge of the wooden desk that had sat here as long as she could remember. On impulse, she dropped onto the leather seat of Jeff's big chair, feeling as oddly comforted as she had as a child wearing her father's oversize sweater.

The desktop's state of semicontrolled chaos informed her it hadn't been touched since Jeff's stroke. She felt a reminiscent half smile tugging at her mouth. Nobody but Jeff would know where to find things here, and he would know immediately if anything had been moved.

But Jeff wouldn't be back for a while. Perhaps a long while. If there was anything vital in all this clutter... She pulled the chair up to the desk and grabbed the first sheaf of papers, clearing an area to start forming piles.

And there were the ledgers.

Of course.

Why hadn't she looked here in the first place? A frown tightened her face. Why hadn't she kept looking after she'd discovered they weren't at the office? It was a basic she never would have overlooked in New York. How had she let herself get sidetracked?

An image of startling blue eyes looking back at her from under the brim of a well-broken-in cowboy hat provided an answer.

She hurriedly pushed aside the loose papers to grasp the ledger. Pulling out the heavy book set off an earthquake among the papers over, under and around it. She settled them to some semblance of stability, and opened the book.

An hour and a half later, her frown was tighter, her neck muscles were complaining and the scratch pad at her elbow was covered with figures.

Disturbing figures.

Figures that meant she wouldn't be getting any more sleep tonight.

"I've been looking for you, Walker."

He finished dropping the gate in place behind the last steer before twisting on his perch to find Kalli staring up at him from the aisle between holding pens, hands on hips, mouth tight. She seldom ventured to this area when they were sorting stock for the night's show. Whether it was because her fastidiousness suffered at the dust, smells and sounds the activity stirred up or, more simply, because he was always around, he didn't know.

But she was here now. Late-afternoon sun washed her hair with gold, brought even more warmth to her cheeks than the color she'd picked up the past few weeks. It also spotlighted a darkness and slight puffiness under her eyes that said she hadn't gotten much sleep.

God only knew why, but somehow that made him want her all the more. And his level of desire had already been sufficient to guarantee he hadn't gotten much sleep of late.

He said nothing.

"I've been looking for you all day," she repeated, clearly trying to hold her tone down to mere irritation.

"I was here dropping off the stock 'til round two. You could have found me then."

"I was at the bank. When I got back, you and Gulch had pulled your afternoon disappearing act. But I'd told everybody around if they saw you they should tell you I wanted to talk to you. You must have known I was looking for you before you took off. But you chose to ignore it. Where do you two go to anywa—''

"Maybe I just liked the idea of you looking for me so much, I didn't want to end it too soon. Wanted to savor it."

He'd deliberately baited her, which could have been dangerous. But this time it worked. Something flashed across her eyes, an awareness, a heat that had him gripping the metal tube of his perch. *Closure, my butt.* But whatever impact the flicker of that reaction had on him, it must have been as potent for her, because she shied away from the topic as if it was a rattler.

"We need to talk," she announced grimly.

"Okay." He turned to Gulch, an interested spectator to their exchange. "You can finish up?"

"Sure thing."

Walker swung his leg over the top of the metal fence in preparation to jump down, but paused when Kalli took a quick step backward. He met her eyes, knowing he was baiting her again, knowing he was gambling again. Her chin rose, and he couldn't resist.

He pushed off from the fence, adjusting his landing to within six inches of her toes. She leaned back, almost swaying, but held her position. This time, the flicker across her eyes closely resembled anger.

"Are you done playing games now?" she snapped.

Was she angry at him or herself?

"Yes'm." He made no effort to hide the amusement— He was living dangerously today.

"This is serious."

That slowed him some. She not only looked tired, she looked worried. "Okay, let's go to the office."

"No." She stopped abruptly, her outstretched hand bringing him to a halt, too. "I mean, let's go sit at the picnic table."

Neither said anything more. Sitting across from him, she silently handed him several sheets of paper, simply nodding at them when he looked at her in inquiry.

A quick scan had him frowning. The figures didn't improve any on closer inspection.

"The Park Rodeo is in debt." She sounded as if she couldn't quite believe it.

"Some," he acknowledged.

"But you know how Jeff and Mary always preached about never being in debt. They don't even use credit cards. They wouldn't even advance us our allowances just to teach us the importance of responsibility. Remember?"

She sounded so bewildered, he wanted to pull her into his arms. "I remember."

"You aren't surprised."

"Not particularly."

He would have left it at that, but she demanded, "Why?"

"Heard some things."

"And you didn't do anything about it?"

He'd give her that, considering the circumstances, but she was pushing it. He rested his forearms on the table and leaned forward.

"Heard about it after the fact. Last summer and the one before were pretty rough around here. Drought conditions two years in a row. Some folks didn't have the financial reserves they should have. I knew it was tough, but I was on the road so much.... Wasn't until Jeff's stroke and spending time here that I heard Jeff had bailed out folks."

"Oh. I see. The good ol' boy network passed you the word that this had happened, that Jeff had let his generosity go beyond his means, and you didn't bother to tell me."

"Wasn't anything that firm. More a worry than a word."

"And you didn't think I'd be interested in a 'worry'? Or was it that you didn't think my feminine little head could take the stress?"

"Not used to sharing worries." He spoke the words before he'd considered them. Once they were out, he didn't like leaving them solo. "No sense brawling about that now, anyhow. Once the chute's open, there's no sense trying to close it back up. You make the ride the best you can. That's what you have to do."

She jumped right on that. "Exactly. It's time to make the changes I talked about before. The first thing we've got to do is finish getting computerized. If the rodeo's books were on the computer, I would have known about this from the start and been able to take steps. And then, the special promotions to—"

"Hold on there, Kalli. These figures aren't that bad." He tapped the papers on the table between them. "If we just go day by day—"

"Still living only for today, Walker?" Kalli's voice, quiet as it was, cut. "Maybe you don't want to look beyond today in your life. But if we don't look beyond today on this, there might not be a tomorrow for Jeff's rodeo."

He leaned back, tilting his head to consider her.

"We got a rodeo to run tonight. And we both need some time to let this sink in. We'll talk about it in the morning. Ten o'clock in that room where we had the meeting before. You bring coffee, I'll bring doughnuts." He held up his hand to stop her words. "For once, Kalli Evans, give something some time. We don't have to decide things right this second. Not things that are going to have an effect for a long time."

Before she looked away, he saw the recognition in her eyes that he was referring to their past as well as the present situation. He waited until she looked back to him to finish what he had to say.

"I'll tell you this, Kalli. I don't just live for today. I look to tomorrow. But I'll be damned if I'll break my back trying to prove it to you."

Not used to sharing worries.

Walker's words, along with the emotions that had muddied the blue of his eyes for an instant—surprise, maybe a little regret, and something else she was even less sure of— echoed in her head as Kalli drove through the familiar darkness to the ranch. Odd how the landscape could be indecipherable yet still so familiar.

She glanced into the rearview mirror. Even the pair of headlights faintly visible there seemed oddly familiar.

She slowed down and looked again. A pickup. Walker's? There wasn't much on this road other than the Jeffries Ranch.

Did Walker intend to spend the night there?

A surge of something like panic hit her and she pushed it back with both hands. He had as much right to stay there as she did—more, since he was blood kin. At the start, she'd even braced for the possibility that he might arrive, claiming a room. But surely Mary would have warned her if Walker had decided to stay at the house.

Maybe he hadn't believed Kalli's assurances that she wasn't lonely in the house by herself. Or maybe he'd decided to talk about the rodeo's finances tonight instead of in the morning. Maybe he intended to stay in the bunkhouse.... But when she forked south onto the Jeffrieses' road, the headlights kept going. She slowed almost to a stop, but the vehicle that flashed past was no more than a vague shape in the night. It could have been anybody. She had no reason to believe it had been Walker.

Not used to sharing worries.

When she slipped into the soft sheets with only the sound of the stream that ran between the house and the bunkhouse to disturb her thoughts, the words stood out like an amplified declaration.

Walker Riley was a man not accustomed to sharing his worries. More, he was a man not accustomed to the idea that anyone would want to share his worries.

Lying here in the dark, she knew that the other emotion she'd seen in his eyes had been loneliness. A bone-deep loneliness that forced another acknowledgement.

The idea of Walker's being that lonely tore at her in a way she never would have expected. Especially since she wasn't a stranger to bone-deep loneliness herself.

Chapter Five

"The hell of it is..." Kalli's voice faded to a spurt of impatient breath.

Elbows propped on the table, she dropped her head briefly into her upraised hands. Walker noticed she hadn't touched the doughnuts, but was on her second cup of coffee. Trying to fill a sleep deficit with caffeine. He knew the feeling.

She pushed her hair back with both hands, and Walker stifled the curse that came to his lips. God, he'd like to have both his hands in her hair, stroking it more gently than she just had, or threading his fingers in it more tightly to hold her head still while he brought to her eyes a look so different from the worried shadow there now. To make them dark and lazy, the way they used to turn when she wanted him.

The way they'd looked after they'd kissed at Lodge's.

"The hell of it is," she repeated, "we can't implement the changes that would do the rodeo the most good because nearly every one of the ideas the group came up with would require some outlay of cash—which we don't have."

He'd wondered when she would recognize that aspect. It had been part of the reason he'd postponed their talk about the specifics of dealing with the financial situation until this morning. He'd figured even ten years wouldn't make a dent in that trait of hers— She'd much rather trip on the snag on her own, even if it meant a fall, than have him point it out.

The other part of the reason had been more personal, and less altruistic.

He'd wanted to postpone this meeting because this was Kalli's specialty, knowledge gained and honed into expertise after she'd left him. All this talk of business and profit margin and marketing and cost-effectiveness was an echo from her life in New York. With her throwing words like that around, how could her head help but drift back to that other life, even while her feet stayed planted in Park? And he didn't want her thinking about that other life.

He knew she'd be leaving. But she was here now, by God, and he wanted all of her, or as close as he could get, for as long as he could keep it, dammit.

Maybe he'd even been guilty of pushing aside the hints the rodeo's finances weren't rock-solid for the same reason.

And if that was selfish, then he was a selfish SOB. He'd been called worse, including by himself. And, as he recalled with absolute clarity, by Kalli Evans Riley not long before she removed his wedding band and dropped his name.

"There're a few things we can do that won't cost any."

She raised her head, met his look. Most of the bitter wariness her eyes had held had disappeared. He was glad, even though he knew not quite all of the bitterness and wariness was out of his system.

"Like what, Walker?"

He might be a selfish SOB about wanting to keep Kalli's attention here, but even selfish SOBs had their limits. He wouldn't let the Park Rodeo die just because efforts to save it might cause him some discomfort.

"Like me."

"You?"

"Me. Like you said before, maybe we can get some mileage off my name, my reputation. You seemed to think this angle of me coming back to where I started would get those reporters all fired up."

"You'd be willing to do that?"

"Yeah."

She still looked doubtful. "You'd be willing to talk to reporters—a lot of reporters? As many as I can get interested in the story, and not just from around here?"

"Yeah."

"I've got some connections, Walker, and I would hope to get interest from some of the biggest newspapers back East. Some radio and TV, maybe even the networks."

He didn't have to put much acting talent into his wince. "No need to tell me all the gory details, Kalli."

That drew the first thing resembling a smile from her since she'd found him sorting stock the day before.

"Okay," she said slowly, but he could tell from the determined glint in eyes she focused somewhere over his shoulder that she was already plotting ways to get his name and face spread all over the map along with the Park Rodeo.

At least one of them had started to cheer up, he thought sourly.

As if she'd sensed his mood, she turned to him. "I know how you dislike this sort of thing, Walker. It's very generous of—"

"There's one condition," he interrupted.

"Condition?"

"You be there for the interviews."

"But—"

"You're as much a part of running this rodeo as I am, and these are your connections you're calling on."

"But it's your story they'll be interested in."

He wouldn't debate this. "That's the condition."

He met her probing look and knew exactly when she decided he meant it.

"Okay. I agree to your condition, Walker."

"Good." He wasn't quite done. "You know there's something else we haven't exploited as much as we could."

He caught her slight wince at his use of the word "exploited." He felt satisfaction that her memory of using that word about him still caused her discomfort. He also felt an urge to apologize. He ignored both.

"What's that?" she asked.

"Guess you could say it's Jeff's connections, and some of mine—the goodwill toward the Park Rodeo and the network of rodeo hands going all over the country."

An uncertain tuck drew her eyebrows together. "You mean to draw more entries."

"Sure, more entries, and bigger names. We can get a quiet word out that we could use some bigger draws. But the traveling cowboys can also help us get more ticket buyers. We get them to take fliers along to their next stop, and the one after that, leave a few at the airports they fly through, the rest stops they break at, the motels and restaurants they use."

"It is another way to get the word out, isn't it?"

"Yep, and the folks a rodeo hand runs into are the ones most likely to be interested in seeing a rodeo."

"Jeff listed an expense last year for advertising fliers, but it looks as if less than half the fliers got used, so that might save us any expense. I wonder where they might be...."

She put down her coffee cup and picked up her pen to make notes on the pad she carried. He considered that a sure sign she was feeling better about the situation. Her weariness remained, and the worry hadn't disappeared, but a spark of determination had joined them.

"And it shouldn't cost any money for you to keep on dragging us rodeo hands into the computer age."

"You're right." She'd looked up at his dry tone, and he thought she might get defensive about his mild teasing. But he saw a bit of humor enter her eyes before she bent to make another note on the pad, muttering phrases as she wrote. "Keep updating entries system, get the books on, streamline the payroll process... May not have immediate effects, but it can't hurt."

With that, she straightened and smiled. He smiled back, and hers grew. A real smile, all the way to her eyes.

He didn't want to consider too closely what parts of his body reacted to her nearness while they smiled into each other's eyes. Or why, exactly, he was about to open his mouth and volunteer for another duty he'd rank a poor second to getting gored by a Brahman.

"I could take a stab at learning that computer stuff, too. Help you and Roberta out."

Silence.

"Close your mouth, Kalli." He handed her a doughnut. "Close it around this."

She smiled again, and then she did just what he'd asked with no argument. A first.

* * *

Kalli wasted no time in taking Walker up on his offer—
all his offers.

She started him on the computer that afternoon, much
to Roberta's delight.

The secretary teased unmercifully. It didn't seem to flus-
ter Walker's concentration, but Kalli figured her pupil's
frustration level had reached high enough without someone chortling at him that just because the little blinker was
called a cursor didn't mean he had to swear at it all the
time.

She distracted Roberta by putting her in charge of finding the rodeo fliers that Jeff's inventory indicated should
be around, somewhere.

For another hour, Kalli sat next to Walker, instructing
him in the basics of the keyboard, symbols and com-
mands. He seemed to wear a perpetual frown, but he listened.

She only wished her concentration was half as good.

A voice in the back of her head commented that her
concentration was fine— It was just concentrating on
Walker Riley instead of the computer.

The blinking cursor, lighted screen and detailed keyboard had to fight to hold her interest. Especially when he
turned to her, listening intently, and his deep, deep blue eyes
pinned on her face. Or when she stumbled on a phrase, had
to back up and try to regain her train of thought, and the
fan of creases at the corners of his eyes gave away his effort not to grin.

She stood, moving behind him as if that improved her
vantage point on the keyboard and screen. It did little good.
She found herself noticing the way his thick dark hair
lapped over the back of his collar. She wondered if the back
of his neck was still as sensitive as it used to be. She used to

be able to draw a shudder just by running a nail lightly up the center. . . .

"Kalli? Kalli!" His voice snapped her out of her reverie. "What the hell does invalid key mean? I'm hittin' the one you said."

"Oh. Yes, but you also have to hold down the Alt key for that function."

"Alt?"

"*A-L-T.* Here."

She leaned over his shoulder to press the key, and dived into the combined wave of scent and heat that surrounded him. The uncompromisingly crisp aroma of soap and shampoo, the lingering musk of leather and animal, the baking warmth of summer that seemed bred into his skin. But did the heat all emanate from him?

She sat down abruptly, determined to keep some distance and under no circumstances to touch.

It didn't help, because most disconcerting of all was the sight of his large, rough, tanned hands ranging uncertainly over the pale, inanimate keys. The endearing hesitation before an index finger pressed the next key, the impatient jerk of his right ring finger as it frequently went to the backspace button to delete a mistake, the confident tap of the thumb on the space bar.

Still, she might have been okay if it had been simply her physical senses involved. Her imagination did the real damage.

Breezing past the danger postings her mind kept raising, her imagination had a field day.

It produced images real enough to draw a flush, images of those same hands against a different pale surface. Not inanimate this time, but most definitely animate—and reactive. Her skin. Absorbing the sensations now bestowed on the unworthy keyboard, as well as movements never called for on a computer—sweeping, stroking, gripping, caressing.

"Kalli? You okay?"

She pulled her gaze from Walker's hands to take in his expression of mingled concern and puzzlement.

"I, uh..."

"You look kind of pale. Except right here—" A blunt, roughened fingertip brushed at one cheek, then the other. "You gotta fever or something?"

A fever *and* something.

The something being the unnerving realization—the most unnerving of all these unnerving moments—that these images were not memories of their safely distant past. Instead, it was the moment in Lodge's. And—worse!— moments she knew came from some vague vision of the possible future.

The door swung open with a muffled thunk against its wooden surface, a blow sufficient to send it hard against the wall with another clunk. Kalli started at the sound, but welcomed the intrusion by Roberta, carrying a cardboard carton. Both she and it were liberally dotted with smears of dust and cobwebs.

"Roberta, you found the fliers?"

"The fliers, the lost continent of Atlantis and Dr. Livingstone," the secretary grumbled.

Chuckling, Walker went over to take the carton from her. She released it, then gave his arm a slap for laughing at her disheveled state.

"I'll tell you, I had times I didn't think I'd get out of that storeroom alive. I don't care what that stubborn old man says, this winter I'm going to put that place in order, and Baldwin Jeffries is going to pay me for my time and effort, along with paying for the bulldozer I'll need."

She glared from one to the other of them as if daring a response. Walker put the carton down, turned away from

Roberta and gave Kalli a wink, his blue eyes laughing in a way that had her pulse stumbling. As he kept watching her, though, the look changed, slipping toward something more knowing. And more dangerous.

Kalli knew she should say something, should thank Roberta, should smooth the moment, should say anything to break the hold Walker's eyes had on her. She couldn't get a word out.

"Well, if that's all, I'm going home to get cleaned up and changed, then go into town for a real dinner at a real restaurant. And I might just take a whole hour for dinner. Of course if you need anything else," Roberta said with false sweetness, "you just let me know, Kalli."

What Kalli needed was some time to cool her imagination—a few months out in a blizzard might do the trick. But with a blizzard an unlikely occurrence in late June, even for Wyoming weather, at least she could put some distance between her and Walker Riley.

She scrambled out of her chair with more enthusiasm than grace.

"I'll come with you, Roberta. And dinner's my treat."

To be a good rodeo hand took timing, lots of practice, some tolerance for pain, an ability to sleep or eat anytime, anywhere and a combination of patience and rock-hard stubbornness.

The way Walker saw it, other than the eating and sleeping, caring for Kalli required the same things of him.

There was a saying that there was only one way to make sure the hours and weeks and months of training turned out a good horse— Have more time than the horse. He believed in that. Patience came naturally working with a horse. With Kalli, biding his time and using gentle persistence came harder.

It didn't take much figuring to see Kalli would have liked to keep their contacts to a minimum.

But she couldn't, thanks to his foresight in making her promise to be around for all his interviews.

She lined up as many as possible. Newspapers—the *Billings Gazette, Cheyenne Star Tribune, Denver Post* and, not to be left out, the *Rocky Mountain News,* plus a stringer from the *Los Angeles Times*. Radio—local at first, then a telephone hookup with his old buddy Sailor Anderson's stations in Texas drew more interest. And television—regional shows mostly, but there'd been interest from a local affiliate.

And he could see it paying off. The rodeo had drawn record crowds for the Fourth of July weekend. And he'd had the pleasure of Kalli's company a lot more than he would have had otherwise.

The pleasure of having her by his side during the interviews, of greeting people together, as a team. Almost the way a real couple might.

That made the interviews worthwhile.

"Hey, Kalli, you know where Walker is?"

The voice from behind stopped her in the act of opening the door to the Jeffrieses' truck.

"Hi, Matt. I'm just going to pick him up." She gestured in the direction of the opposite side of the rodeo grounds, where Walker and Gulch were fixing a section of livestock pen a recalcitrant bull had loosened the night before. "Then we're heading out for an appointment. Is there something I can help you with?"

"Uh, no. That's not . . . I mean, uh, you probably got to get going."

She checked her watch, though she already knew she'd left three times as much time as necessary for the trip to a local radio station. She didn't want to risk anything going wrong with this hookup with the network personality who'd carved out a reputation for warm, cozy "chats" amid the reports by hard-hitting journalists. She'd put in a lot of work to line this up. Giving in to a whim this morning, she'd replaced her simple white blouse with the jade one Walker had bought her that day at Lodge's, with some vague idea it might bring luck.

If she showed up now, Walker would probably give her that amused look, remind her they didn't have to leave a lot of extra time for traffic around Park and make her wait until he'd finished the job.

And she couldn't complain. Because, despite his dislike for being a public person, he'd accepted talking to reporters like a trooper. She couldn't help but be impressed by his willingness to do something he hated for the good of the rodeo. She also couldn't help but be impressed that he encouraged her to take the lead in dealing with the business side and being the spokesperson with the business community, and that he pointed out her role in each interview.

"It's okay, Matt. I've got time. Is there a problem?"

"Problem? No, no, it's not a problem. I just wanted. I mean... I wanted to ask Walker if he'd explain something. You know I've been trying the bulls some, along with the broncs. I've been practicing like he told me, going through things over and over on the practice drum, so it's natural and doesn't need any thinking when I'm on the bull. But there's this one move I saw that Trembler bull make last night, that real rank one?"

She nodded at his description of the animal who'd earlier taken exception to the pen fence.

"Well, he was spinning inside, and kicking his back legs out the same time. I wondered what Walker'd say to do in a case like that, when a bull has a lot of snap in him. I would have tried to draw my own conclusions, but Johnny

Prentice got thrown so early, I didn't have anything to go by."

"I can see your problem." Amused, Kalli also was touched by Matt's obvious regard for Walker and his ardent desire to improve his skills, even though she knew he'd been thrown himself the night before and had seen him earlier in the day walking with a gingerliness that spoke of aches and bruises. "But you're right, you would need Walker for that. Perhaps when we return from the radio station, or after tonight's events."

"Oh, yes, ma'am. That'd be fine. I don't mean to be holding you up."

As she turned to go, Kalli almost sighed at the respect Matt Halderman showed her these days. There'd been no harm in his slightly cocky flirtation at their first meeting, but Walker had definitely put an end to that. She swung back around almost immediately.

"Matt? Let me ask you a question."

"Ma'am?"

"Why do you do it? Why do you ride? You get thrown off and it's got to hurt, but you keep going back—you and . . . the others."

His brown eyes snapped with an inner excitement and his mouth tilted up slightly, but his brows drew down in an effort to explain.

"Once, when I was a kid, I was visiting my grandparents over in Nebraska, and a twister came through. A real big one. We could see it, way out across the fields, going this way, then that. And you never knew where it would go next. It was scary, but there was a feeling . . . you know, kind of under my skin. An excitement. And when it ended . . . Well, it's something you don't ever forget. Not ever. And that's the feeling, I guess," he added hesitantly. A slight flush stole across his cheeks at the effort to articulate, or perhaps at the self-exposure.

"Thank you, Matt," she said solemnly. "I appreciate your answer."

He tugged at the brim of his hat, mumbled a goodbye and hurried off.

But Kalli found the conversation lingered in her mind. Even as she picked up Walker. Even as she instructed him to wash off the worst of the dirt and put on the clean shirt she'd brought from the selection he kept in the office. Even as she tried not to react to the sight of his supple, bronzed back as he splashed water from a nearby spigot before drying off with a bandanna.

Even as she swallowed the dryness in her throat to smile at his halfhearted grumble that at least for radio he'd have thought he could stay in his work clothes. Even when she should have had all her attention focused on the taping. Even when the interview ended and they went back out to the truck.

"Well, that didn't go too bad, did it?" Walker fastened his seat belt and settled in the passenger seat with a satisfied sound.

Starting the truck and heading out the winding dirt road that led back to the highway, she figured he deserved to feel pleased.

It had gone great. The interviewer had blended Walker's achievements, the rodeo's current status and enough background information to pull in the uninitiated. Walker had also slipped in several comments about her contributions.

"You just liked the interviewer because he'd seen you win your second All-Around at the National Rodeo Finals," she teased.

"Hey, after all these folks you've had me talking to who don't know there's a difference between steer wrestling and bull riding, it was a pleasant surprise." She made a face at him, but it didn't dent his smile or erase one bit of the satisfied-with-the-world tone as he went on, "You know you're starting to drive like Wyoming again, Kalli."

"What do you mean?"

"When you first came back, you were still hugging the side of the road, minding your manners."

"That's what you're *supposed* to do."

"Maybe. But now you're driving down the middle where the road's better, like everybody else, until there's somebody around you need to share it with."

She glanced at his grin, then out the windshield to see that she was doing exactly what he'd said.

"The edges are rougher and there's nobody coming," she explained, perhaps mostly to herself.

"That's what I said. Turn right here."

"Here? Why? That's not the way back." She looked doubtfully at the rock-strewn road that seemed to make more vertical than horizontal progress, but turned. The vehicle took the new surface in stride. A pretty good road, after all.

"Different way back," he said complacently.

She grinned at herself. Maybe she was driving more like Wyoming if she found herself accepting as "good" any road with rocks as big as her fist. Hell, two months ago, she probably would have been horrified at the idea of driving on *any* unpaved road. Though she would have thought nothing of braving a pothole the size of a city bus.

She laughed out loud.

"Something funny?"

"Nothing I could really explain." How often had she laughed for no clear-cut reason in recent years?

"Okay." He accepted that easily, and she liked him for it.

She could feel his eyes on her as the truck gripped hard, then seemed to catapult over a final rise to a flat expanse where the road ended. She brought the vehicle to a stop, turned the engine off—it deserved a rest after this climb—unhooked her seat belt and looked at him questioningly. He looked back.

"Always liked the sound of your laughter." Walker's voice dropped so low, it seemed to rumble through her blood.

She grew breathless. His eyes pierced into her, leaving her muscles heavy, liquid and useless.

Then he turned away, was out his door, around the other side and gesturing her out her open door before she could replenish her oxygen supply.

"C'mon, I've got something to show you."

He took her hand before she could think to protest and strode ahead, leaving her to hurry to match his pace. Thirty yards away, she saw they weren't on a completely flat expanse. A sort of wide, natural stairway led down four feet to a flat rock set like a shelf in the side of the mountain. The earth fell away below that, seeming to open to the entire Big Horn Basin. The rest of the mountains stretched along the right side of the horizon, in front of them and behind them as far as the eye could see. The sun dropped lower, appearing about to be impaled on one of the sharp peaks. The sky stretched as wide as the world and as high as infinity, making everything below seem insignificant.

"Walker..."

"Sunset's something from here, Kalli."

"But—"

"The rodeo'll start fine without us this once."

She turned her back to the view and looked at him for a long moment, without anything as coherent as a thought forming in her mind. Abruptly, she turned again and sat down, her back propped against the wall of rock.

Wisely, Walker said nothing, either. Moving slowly, he came to where she sat, easing down next to her—close—

before he tipped back his hat and hooked one elbow around his bent knee.

They sat in silence as the sun began to slip behind the peaks, leaving the sky an inheritance of dazzling color. She was aware of him watching her, and she knew turning to face him would be an acceptance of sorts.

She turned to him.

His face was close. Close enough that she could see the variations of blue that made up the bright color of his eyes. Close enough that she could see his intention.

He dropped a kiss on her lips, then slowly raised his head, as if listening for a moment, perhaps to the wind that sighed around them.

With great deliberation, he took off his hat, removing its protection and its masking. Light flooded his face, eliminating the shadows that had hid what she saw now—hunger.

Then his mouth returned to hers, shifting and meeting, finding a new angle and pressure, tugging on her bottom lip with his teeth, then flicking her top lip with his tongue. He never pushed her to part her lips, but when she did, he took possession immediately, one hand coming up to cup the back of her head as he stroked and explored.

She could taste his hunger, rigorously restrained but stretching its leash as he sought her tongue, then enticed it into his mouth.

Clinging to his shoulders wasn't enough. She wrapped one arm around his back, guiding her fingertips to relearn, through the fresh cotton cloth, an individual topography of muscle and sinew. Her other hand more gingerly slid beneath his collar, then around to the back, to slip lightly up under the ends of his hair.

With something like a shudder, he released her mouth as they both pulled in air. His gaze rose from her lips to her eyes and locked with them for a moment, and she saw the pure, blue fire of desire there.

When his mouth slammed back on hers, she opened to him heedlessly, and knew the fire had reached her veins.

His hands never seemed to hurry, but they were everywhere. Everywhere she wanted them, and nowhere long enough to give her release. She knew he'd opened most of the buttons of her blouse and she could gather only enough wits to wish he'd hurry. His shirt was opened, and pulled from the waist of his jeans, so she could slide questing palms and fingers over the heat, strength and smoothness of his chest and back.

His mouth left hers and she felt the shock of separation, an atom of the loneliness of the past decade, before his warm, wet caress touched her jaw, then her throat, reuniting them. She arched into the hand he cupped over her breast, straining for the contact that through the sheer covering of her bra would almost satisfy a craving for skin against skin—his skin against her skin.

A sound came from deep in his throat as his mouth dragged lower, to the bones at the base of her throat— How could she feel such exquisite sensation through her bones? But she did. He slid his fingertips lightly over her nipple, so lightly it shouldn't have made her shiver, but it did. The fabric covering it seemed an abrasion against flesh he couldn't possibly make more sensitive, but he did.

His mouth covered her nipple, warm, moist, hungry. She felt his teeth's slight scraping and his tongue's lashing, then the strong, even pull.

And she knew blinding, instant fear. Sensation was pulling away her defense. Pulling away her safety. Pulling away the facade of her success and competence. Pulling away the pretense that she was over Walker Riley.

"Walker . . . no."

She couldn't have gotten out any more than that. If he'd ignored it, she would have crumbled into his arms, unable to resist the pull.

But he heard.

And he stilled. Along with her heartbeat, through tortured seconds, with his mouth on her, with her flesh carrying the imprint of his touch, with the power of him under her hands.

He sat up, away from her, with an abrupt jerkiness so unlike his usual slow grace.

"Walker, I . . ." Tears burned bright hotness behind her eyes, but she wouldn't let them fall. There was nothing she could say.

And there was nothing he would say.

In silence, with a return to his usual measured pace, he put his hat on, angling it low, then stood.

He watched her, without a word, without a readable expression on his face, as she adjusted her clothing. She overruled the temptation to turn her back on that unnerving regard as cowardly. Her fingers seemed numb and clumsy, but she rebuttoned her blouse at last, and stood, too near him in the limited space of their rock balcony. To hide her hands' unsteadiness, she brushed industriously at the dust on the seat and back of her jeans.

He made no move to button his shirt or stir the dust that clung to his clothing, but waited, watching and silent, until she finished, as the sun slipped completely behind the mountains. Then he simply nodded for her to precede him up the natural stairway.

Finally, a yard short of the vehicle, he spoke.

"I'll drive."

She didn't argue with him. She wasn't sure she could negotiate that steep road down right now, anyhow. She already felt dizzy from their intimate descent.

* * *

Kalli entered the room the woman at the front desk had identified as Baldwin Jeffries's with a bright smile. It sank to something near panic at the sight of the empty room.

Rushing out, she snagged a gray-haired nurse.

"Jeff—Baldwin Jeffries . . . No one's in his room."

The nurse consulted her utilitarian watch. "I expect he and Mary are still in the therapy room. He should be back in ten minutes or so, or you can go on down."

By the time Kalli had followed the nurse's directions, she felt considerably heartened. Jeff was already well enough to have therapy out of his room.

But her spirits dipped and she came to a sudden halt at the sight of Jeff struggling to stand by himself while a therapist and Mary watched. Kalli took an instinctive step to help him. Couldn't they see how much trouble he had coordinating the movements of one side of his body? The left side, the side Mary had said had some paralysis.

Jeff and the therapist were too intent on the task to notice her. But Mary, facing the door, must have caught the movement. She looked up, started a smile, then switched to a slight, warning shake. Kalli remained still.

Jeff laboriously straightened his spine, the aligning of each vertebra a seeming triumph of will. At last, to a murmur of praise from the therapist, he turned his head toward his wife. Mary smiled, a wealth of approval in her eyes. He slowly pushed back his shoulders to an approximation of his customary upright stance.

At the therapist's quiet request, he shifted his balance, swaying a little before holding the line, then doing it again. Another quiet murmur and he put weight on both feet, though Kalli thought his left leg trembled.

Then, just as slowly, just as laboriously, he began the descent. When he reached the chair, Kalli let out a pent-up breath and wiped her damp hands down the sides of her jeans.

With the therapist commenting, praising, fine-tuning and preparing Jeff for a repeat, Mary slipped away without being noticed, snagged Kalli's elbow and guided her out.

In the hallway, they hugged, then Mary reached up to take Kalli's face between her palms.

"If you show him that face, Jeff will think the rodeo's closed," she said in gentle scolding.

"He just looked so... so unsteady."

"He is unsteady," Mary said flatly.

"But couldn't that be dangerous? He might fall."

"That's not likely. They know what they're doing here and they aren't overly fond of having patients fall over. But it's always a possibility."

"It seems so dangerous."

"So's driving and flying and taking a shower and living in general."

"Couldn't they wait until he's stronger—"

"This is how he gets stronger, Kalli, by pushing his endurance," she said gently. "You're seeing him at the end of a session, and that's always harder. The way the therapist explains it, he's reteaching his muscles—especially on that left side—to follow orders. He pushes beyond what those muscles learned last time, so they rebel and he has to work even harder to get them to do what he wants."

An oath reached them through the open door. Not crystal clear, but most definitely Jeff's voice.

Mary gave a wry smile. "He also gets testier at the end of a session. Wait here a minute."

She returned in a moment and led Kalli to the stairs. "Annie keeps Jeff in line. Gradually, I'll be doing that. We'll let them finish the session and give him time to rest, then we'll see him up in his room. He'll be more himself."

Mary led Kalli to a bench outside, in a quiet corner protected by a wing of the building.

"Don't let him see you so worried about him, Kalli."

"I'll try not to. It's just... Don't you worry about him driving himself too hard?"

"I'd think someone gave me a fake Baldwin Jeffries somewhere along the line if he didn't drive himself."

Kalli's lips lifted in a small smile. "What if he tries to do too much? What if he gets worn down? He's already vulnerable.... Don't you worry?"

"Of course I worry, but I know Jeff, and I know how much he needs this. It's not just so he can do things—he knows he's not going to be striding around the way he used to, we've talked about that—but he has to prove to himself that he hasn't been licked. That he can fight back and come out more than fifty-fifty."

Mary took Kalli's hand between both of hers before she went on. "And because I love that man, what he needs is what counts for me. When you love someone, really love someone, what they want and need is more important than your own wants and needs. It's more important even than your worries and fears."

"...so Annie Slavedriver says trunk balance like mine... Tell you she said I was fastest from moving out of midline to standing without help?"

"No, you didn't tell me that, Jeff."

His words weren't precise, he left some out and the weakness in the lower left portion of his face was apparent, but Jeff looked so much better after a half hour's rest than he had in the therapy room, that Kalli felt great relief. And she positively basked in his enthusiasm.

Nothing could have healed her spirits better than a dose of Baldwin Jeffries.

"Told her—" he tapped his chest "—tough stock."

"That's true," Mary said. "We were very lucky the stroke wasn't worse."

"Some here real bad shape," Jeff said with a sympathetic shake of his head, as if he had no problems.

"The doctors say Jeff drifted in and out of a sort of light coma after the stroke. Once he shook that, they could see he'd come through better than they'd first thought."

Mary exchanged a smile with her husband. From the weakness on the left side of his face, Jeff's smile was slightly lopsided—reminiscent of Walker's now, Kalli thought, pressing her knuckles to her suddenly tight chest.

"Wrong, Kalli?"

Jeff's eyes certainly had regained their sharpness.

"No, nothing's wrong. I'm fine."

"Probably heartburn," Mary fussed. "You'll have an ulcer if you're not careful. All that stress you try to pretend you don't have. Better to face it head-on than swallow it and let it eat up your insides. Is that New York office of yours pestering you? There never has been a time you've come out here for a rest and they haven't called you every other day. Just keeping you riled up."

Kalli, oddly soothed by Mary's complaint, didn't point out that this time she hadn't come to Wyoming for a rest.

"My office has called a few times," she acknowledged. "But nothing I couldn't handle from here."

"Is it Walker? Is he giving you a hard time?" Mary demanded.

"No. Not..."

Not the way you mean. But being around him was giving her a hard time with herself. Since they'd watched that sunset, he'd been polite, cooperative and more distant than when she'd been in New York. Gulch and Roberta had given her odd looks that kept her tensed for one or both to demand an explanation, though neither had to this point.

She became aware of the silence, and the questioning looks from Mary and Jeff.

"He's working really hard," she said quickly, "doing everything he can for the rodeo. I couldn't ask for more cooperation these past weeks."

Which was the crux of the problem. Whatever fragile truce they'd built had cracked, but he not only carried out his regular duties, he continued interviews—blandly insisting she still accompany him—and he encouraged everyone to look to her as the rodeo's financial head. While Walker's attitude and diligence pleased her for the rodeo's sake, they also forced her to acknowledge he had changed. He wasn't the boy she'd known. So what did that say about her inability to quell responses to him reminiscent of when she'd been his hero-worshiping shadow?

"Rodeo?" Jeff jerked out the word in demand.

Kalli flicked a look at Mary. A frown tugged at her eyebrows, but the older woman nodded.

"Ticket sales have improved," Kalli said. "Not to where they were before, but better than when people were worried it would fall apart without you two in charge."

She tried to smile. Jeff still watched her intently.

"Go ahead, Kalli, what's the rest?" Mary asked, calm and even.

"If we stay at this pace, we'll fall a little short of last year. That wouldn't be bad, except..." She met Jeff's look, consciously trying to bleed the concern out of her eyes and voice. "I found the books, Jeff. I know you loaned money from the rodeo accounts to help people out."

"Do it again," he said doggedly.

"I know you would. And I'm not saying you shouldn't have—except from a business standpoint. There's no money coming in from those loans. In fact, I can't find any record of a repayment schedule for any of them...?"

She let it trail off as a question. Jeff simply looked at her, and she had her answer. There was no schedule, just a handshake between friends.

She sighed again. "There are virtually no reserves in the rodeo accounts to tide it over until next season. You know as well as I do, you need cash to get started the following season. I'm sure you could have produced enough revenue running the rodeo yourself to take care of that. But I'm not sure we can. Especially not with that dip in ticket sales when Walker and I first came. And what if we can't get them back to their previous level?"

"We'll take out a loan."

Kalli had been so intent on Jeff's reaction that Mary's pronouncement caught her off guard. "I'm not sure, with the management of the rodeo in doubt, that a bank would give the rodeo a loan."

"We'll get a personal loan. Or mortgage the ranch."

Kalli vowed right then that she would not permit these two people to take on that kind of debt at an age when they should be contemplating easy-living retirement. Even if she had to sacrifice the Park Rodeo.

But she was too wise to voice that resolve. "Before we borrow that trouble—or any money—let's see where we are at the end of the season."

Mary nodded in approval. Jeff considered her a moment longer, then spoke slowly, spacing his words with care.

"You and Walker will take care of it."

"Yes, we'll take care of it," Kalli agreed. She felt compelled to say it again, more clearly, with greater emphasis. "Walker and I will take care of it."

"And what about groups that maintain that rodeos are cruel to animals?"

Kalli went ramrod stiff, knowing how seriously Walker took his responsibility to care for his animals, and what he thought of those who didn't.

And this TV taping had been going so well.... The young woman interviewer had been enthusiastic, insisting she and her crew come to Park to tape on-site. The cameraman and reporter had followed Walker around for most of the night's rodeo. Now they'd been sitting nearly half an hour in the cleared stands, with lights glaring on Walker and the woman.

The reporter made it clear only a tiny fraction of this tape might ever see the light of day, but she'd also mentioned the possibility of a feature on her network's all-night news show. Seeing the ambition and determination in the woman's eyes, Kalli had felt hopeful.

Until now.

"I mean, with the straps used to make them buck—"

"You watch the animals and you'll know different. They buck because a man's on their back and they've been bred to it. If it was only the strap, why would they stop bucking when the man was gone but the strap was still there?"

"But these groups do maintain that rodeos constitute cruelty—"

"Baldwin Jeffries has never been cruel to an animal in his life and never tolerated anybody who was, and that's the way he taught me."

"But you would have to admit that not all rodeos are operated on the same high level as yours."

"As the Jeffrieses'," he corrected.

"As the Jeffrieses'," she agreed.

He gave the interviewer a long, serious look. "Guess every kind of operation could say that. Folks maintain some TV news shows aren't on the up-and-up all the time."

Kalli figured that would never make the final edit.

"I understand you've had your share of injuries." The woman's voice gave no indication she'd hit a brick wall.

"I haven't bought any spare teeth yet," he answered mildly.

"Were you prepared to when you got into rodeoing?"

"'Bout the same as a hockey player, I figure." He cocked an eyebrow at her. "You ever hear of Jim Shoulders?"

"Uh, no."

"Well, he's one of the best rodeo hands ever and he had more than his share of injuries—hunk of iron in one hip, broken bones. But he used to say as long as he didn't set off airport security scanners, he was fine."

The interviewer had been listening intently, but the bland finish drew a genuine laugh from her, as well as from the cameraman and another technician.

"What makes it worthwhile?"

His smile got a little sly, letting the camera in on the humor before he spoke. "I gotta quote another of the great ones there, too. Casey Tibbs said he kept rodeoing because he was winning all the money he could spend."

Kalli didn't realize she'd made a sound until Walker turned toward her, slitting his eyes against the lights.

"What is it, Kalli?"

At some level, she was aware that a man with a clipboard on the other side of the cameraman had started forward, perhaps to cut the tape, but the interviewer gestured for him to keep it going, never taking her eyes off Walker.

"What is it?" he repeated.

"Don't pass it off," Kalli blurted out, not sure why this was so important. "Answer it. Why do you do it?"

For long, silent seconds, she thought he might not answer. He kept looking at her as he spoke slowly.

"For eight seconds, you're on top of a force of nature. Riding it. Not trying to master it, but just trying to go with it. Because if you're not in sync, it's like slamming up against a truck. But when you are in sync... Lord, when you're in sync, for those eight seconds, you share the power. You're not just on top of that force of nature, you're part of it."

Silence ticked by while Kalli looked at Walker, knowing he was trying to make her out beyond the lights. That didn't change even when the interviewer spoke again.

"Aren't you frightened?"

"Of the bull? Of getting hurt? No. That'd be like being afraid of life. Only thing I was ever afraid of was loneliness."

Only after those words did he look away from Kalli, to focus on the interview. She barely heard the rest of it.

Chapter Six

"You look like you've been rode hard and put up wet, Kalli."

She mentally cringed at Gulch's comment. She'd been only half-conscious of turning away when the office door opened in order to be out of the direct line of sight. But she was fully aware of it now that the ploy had failed. She looked up from where she'd been checking entries and smiled wanly.

"I'm okay."

Gulch looked doubtful. Worse, he looked stubborn. And worst of all, he wasn't the only person looking that way.

Roberta stood right next to him with an identical expression and Walker was a couple of feet behind them.

"Don't look okay," disputed Gulch. "Does she, Roberta?"

"I've been tellin' her since she dragged in here first thing that there's no cause for her to stick around, specially not with her having a face that would scare a ghost."

Walker stepped around Roberta and sent Kalli a piercing look. But at least he didn't say anything.

"Thanks, Roberta." Kalli glared at the secretary from under her eyebrows, with no apparent impact on the other woman's equanimity.

"If you're thanking me for having a bit of sense, I'll say you're welcome. And then repeat that you should go home."

"I'm not going home. I'm fine," she said sharply, and rose, intending to go around the counter to replace the entry clipboard. And to escape this scrutiny in triplicate. She didn't get far.

Moving so quickly was a mistake. She could feel it in the clamp of discomfort at the small of her back and the squeezing in the pit of her stomach. It wasn't like this most months, but it was far from the first time she'd felt like this—or worse. When she woke up this morning, she'd immediately known both the symptoms and the cure—go to bed with a heating pad for a day. Or tough it out. She'd made her usual choice. She would live with it, as usual.

But she couldn't help leaning on the corner of the desk as she lowered herself to the chair.

Walker was standing beside her before she knew he'd moved. He placed one rough palm on her sure-to-be clammy forehead and wrapped the other hand around her wrist. She backed away from both touches but knew it was too late. Without looking, she knew he glared at her. She heard his expelled sound of exasperation.

Then she felt the earth give way as he scooped her up in his arms, one arm across her back, the other under her knees, and headed out.

"Walker, don't be ridiculous. This is silly. Put me down."

He ignored her. "Get the door, Roberta."

"You bet, Walker."

She sounded mighty pleased to follow Walker's curt order, as did Gulch, when he contributed, "I'll get the truck door."

"Good. And give those folks a call and tell 'em we won't be by this afternoon. Reschedule for tomorrow."

Already out the door, Gulch called back, "Sure thing."

Kalli wanted to demand to know what folks he and Gulch had planned to meet that afternoon and what would be rescheduled, but she considered being carried like a baby a very weak position for making demands. First things first. "Walker. Put me down. Now."

The words were right, but the voice lacked punch.

He kept going, out the door, down the two steps, across the few yards of dirt, to where Gulch held the red pickup's door wide open.

"Walker—"

He deposited her on the worn upholstery of the passenger seat and met her glare. His face was so close, she could see the dark centers of his eyes, could watch them expand, could absorb the warmth of his breath across her lips, could feel it sucking the oxygen out of her system, leaving her suspended, unmoving.

"Don't push me, Kalli."

He stared at her an instant longer, then backed away, leaving room for Coat, who jumped up with surprising nimbleness to the spot in the middle of the seat. Kalli's foot nudged at a brick wrapped with string, a contraption Walker used to need for wrist-strengthening exercises.

"Hook your seat belt." He stood and waited until she'd complied, then handed in her purse, brought by Roberta.

Walker closed the door with a controlled emphasis that told her he'd wanted to slam it. Ten years ago, he would have. But that thought was lost in others, more urgent, as she watched him circle the front of the pickup. Only by an act of will did she prevent herself from continuing to stare at him as he slid into the driver's seat, fastened his seat belt, started the engine and headed out of the dusty rodeo grounds.

Coat sat down between them with a gusty sigh of contentment.

Don't push me, Kalli, he'd said. There had been another phrase tagging along with those words, unvoiced, but clear. *Or I'll—*

Or he'd what? That's what she wanted to know. What had he thought as he'd bent over her so close, his mouth not even inches from hers, his arms still partially wrapped around her?

What would have happened if she *had* pushed? Would he have kissed her? Would he have slid his tongue in her mouth the way he'd taught her when he'd been the first to kiss her that way, the way he had at Lodge's and in the mountains watching the sunset? Would his arms have tightened around her? Would she have experienced the blessed weight of his body pressing against hers, felt the hot evidence that he desired her, as she had so often in that other time, that lifetime ago?

As she'd been dreaming of again?

Or would he have pulled away? Would he have said words that would rip apart the fragile barrier she'd erected between her scars and the present?

Swallowing, she closed her eyes against a burning, turning her face away from Walker and resting her cheek against the top of the worn seat back.

She didn't realize she'd dozed until she woke. And she didn't wake until the pickup stopped.

A leftover skill from those days on the rodeo circuit, this ability to sleep no matter how rough the road, followed by instant alertness upon arrival at the next stop. Strange that it lingered after all these years.

"Where are we?"

That, too, was a common refrain in the past. But this time, her question wasn't the idle curiosity of a woman so in love it didn't really matter where they were as long as they were together.

She rolled down the dust-dimmed window.

Instead of the well-established sprawl of the Jeffrieses' ranch she'd expected to see, she looked out at the wooden skeleton of a corral under construction, a new barn and a log house about half its size, all set in a semicircle of partially tamed landscape, the whole thing apparently cut out of the side of a mountain by nature's sharp hand. The mountain continued rising behind the buildings, not close enough to crowd them, yet giving a sense of solid protection.

Some distance in front of the buildings and the open space where the truck sat, the earth fell away to reveal the spreading tapestry of the valley—the hues of green where irrigation reached, the dusty golds and browns where it didn't, the dots of cattle, the silvered glimmer of cottonwoods tracing the path of streams or encircling the rarer blues or reds or whites of a house or barn. It stretched to the horizon, where she could imagine she saw the shadowed steps of the Big Horn Mountains some hundred miles away.

Walker had come around to the passenger door while she took her survey and now appeared prepared to scoop her up again. She slowed him with an arm to his chest while she unhooked the seat belt, then quickly climbed down herself.

"Where are we?" she repeated.

"My place."

"Your place?"

"Yep."

"But..." She clamped down anything else. This was where his money had gone. Money earned in dusty arenas, amid the smells and sounds of courage and pain and adrenaline. He'd turned it into this. This piece of land swept fresh by the daily wind.

"It's...it's beautiful, Walker."

He said nothing, and she risked a glance at his profile as he looked out over the valley. Behind the barriers he put up, she thought she saw pride and satisfaction.

He'd bought it, and he was building it. She guessed his hand had joined the logs into a house, his strength had raised the barn, his imagination had designed the corral.

"It's a wonderful place," she added. "And the view..." You could never feel closed in when you could look out and have the world at your feet like this.

"You can see Jeff and Mary's place." He sounded gruff, and she suspected it hid other emotions. "Down there, see?"

He pointed into the valley. She saw it, east and a little to the south. Shrunk by distance, but clearly recognizable. She also saw the twisting road they must have traveled to get here. A road reached by going straight along the main road after the drive to the Jeffrieses' ranch branched south. So maybe it *had* been his headlights behind her the other night.

"My land stretches down to Jeff and Mary's western border, then up the mountain almost to the top."

"All this?" Her eyes opened wider.

"Yeah. It's hard to tell from here, but there's some flat around the south side of this old rock." He pointed, and she saw that a branch of the road continued around the curve of an outcropping. Through the trees, she caught a glimpse of open space.

"I haven't been here enough to do much more than get the house and barn up, then keep them standing. But I'm running some stock with Mary and Jeff's. And a few head of horses I'm hoping to start breeding. Maybe next year. Then I can—" He broke off. "C'mon, get inside. You don't want to be standing out here listening to me and taking in the view."

Oh, yes, she did. When he got that dreamy look in his eyes and that deep note in his voice, she could have listened to him forever. But he clearly had other ideas. He cupped her elbow, his big hand spreading warmth above and below it.

"This is ridiculous, Walker." Her protest had less power than the breeze slipping around them. "I'm not really sick. I'm just...just not feeling great. I'm just—"

"I know what you're just. And I know what to do about it."

He hustled her up the broad wooden steps flanked by a pair of rather unhappy looking evergreens, across the planked porch, which held a trio of wooden rocking chairs, through the living room so fast she had no more than an impression of earth tones and a stone fireplace, and into a bedroom.

The room was almost painfully neat. A big, quilt-covered bed was centered on one white wall, facing a set of windows that looked east. She noticed a bookshelf, a dresser, a couple of area rugs, a bootjack by the hall door and two more doors. Living mostly out of a trailer or hotel room so many years had definitely taught Walker minimalism in decorating.

He opened one of the doors to reveal a closet as neat as the room. With no fumbling, he pulled out a flat box and removed a heating pad.

"If there's one thing old rodeo cowboys know, it's heating pads."

He aimed a dry grin somewhere over her left shoulder, moved quickly to the outlet next to the bed to plug in the pad, then disappeared momentarily beyond the other door. She heard water running. Must be the bathroom. Still, she stood stock-still in the middle of the room. He returned almost immediately with a glass of water in one hand; the other was closed in a fist.

"Here, take these."

She looked blankly at the pair of pills he deposited in her palm.

"Won't upset your stomach," he assured her as he turned down the quilt and positioned the heating pad. "If there's another thing old rodeo cowboys know, it's pain-killers."

He straightened, and she swallowed the pills quickly, for some reason wanting them down before he turned around to face her. For a moment, they looked at each other. His face had gone still, and when he took the glass from her unresisting hand, the movement lacked his usual slow grace.

"C'mon," he ordered, but he stopped short of taking her arm to guide her to the bed.

She sat on the bed, her initiative fogged by discomfort and a tremendous lethargy. He gruffly told her to take her boots off, and she complied. She also obeyed his gesture by pulling her stockinged feet up on the bed. On her own she curled around the warmth of the heating pad.

Coat came to the edge of the bed and surveyed her, as if assuring himself of her comfort, then headed out.

Walker issued one last command before pulling the hall door closed behind him. "Cover up."

She did, pulling the quilt's age-softened material around her chin. Its added warmth conspired with the heating pad, the pills, the quiet and, most of all, the permission to stop toughing it out, to bring relaxation to her cramping muscles and aching back. Her thoughts drifted.

Walker had been more awkward with her in the past few minutes than even in that first encounter in the rodeo office after a decade.

Could he be concerned about her opinion of his place? Clearly, he had a lot of himself invested in this piece of property. He seemed to be creating a haven here for himself. A place for tomorrow.

I don't just live for today. I look to tomorrow. But I'll be damned if I'll break my back trying to prove it to you.

Is that why he hadn't shown her this place before, the proof that he had looked to his future? Why he'd stopped himself just now when he came too close to telling her his plans?

Had her skepticism, born of their past, left him so wary that he didn't trust her enough to tell her of his future?

Or was it simpler? Did he just choose not to let her into this part of his life, a part obviously close to his heart?

Then why the hell did he bring me up here? she demanded belligerently of herself.

He could have taken her to the Jeffrieses' or left her to fend for herself in the office, for that matter, instead of bringing her to his home and tucking her away in his bed.

Her hand smoothed over the seams of the quilt, the rhythm of the ripples under her hand soothing her, driving out the worries and questions. And she let them go. Slower her hand moved, slower. For a little while, she would let the worries go . . . just for now.

A new rhythm took over as her hand stilled. A sliding kind of creak that never quite finished. A homey sound. Reassuring. Of course—the answer came without her searching for it—one of the rocking chairs on the porch. One of the chairs that looked out across the distance.

I thought I'd find myself a porch and a rockin' chair with a view of the mountains and tell everybody who'll listen 'bout my great career riding the bulls.

Had Walker found his porch and rocking chair? Was he ready to give up the life he'd lived for so long, that he'd loved more than her? Something pulled at her comfort, something that wasn't physical at all.

If he'd changed so much, what did that do to the careful presumptions she'd operated under this summer? How could she dismiss the physical attraction to him, how could she explain her feelings for him as passion somehow left over from the past, when he wasn't the same man?

He'd brought her here for the good of the rodeo, no other reason.

If she was too stubborn to see that she'd get more done long-term if she rested this afternoon than if she tried to push through the pain, then it was his responsibility to see she rested. She wouldn't give the Park Rodeo her best, otherwise, and that's all he wanted. The best for the rodeo.

He drained the last of the soft drink he'd stopped in the kitchen to pour and dropped into the rocker he always sat in, plunking his booted feet onto the rail and bending his knees just the bit needed to set the rocker moving.

He certainly hadn't brought her here because he'd wanted her to see his place, because he had any sort of wild ideas about her liking the house or the view or his dreams. He didn't have anything to prove to her. *He* knew he'd learned to look to the future. He had no need for her to know it.

And he certainly hadn't brought her here with the sort of impulsive optimism that had led him to take her to view the sunset. Optimism bought with her smile, and paid for by a painful reminder that she wasn't really his Kalli anymore. Not even for this summer.

No, he'd taken a glance at her pale skin, trembly hands and known what was called for—and it sure as hell wasn't sitting at that desk trying to pretend pain wasn't pain. It was getting into bed with a heating pad and somebody around to see that she didn't try sneaking back to the office.

It was easier to do that here. That was the reason he'd brought her here. The only reason.

It certainly had nothing to do with a foolish desire to have her to himself, even for just a few hours, even with her asleep on his bed and him out here.

He envisioned her head on his pillow, hair spread loose, quilt warming the curves that he'd felt heating and flowing against his body in a dressing room in Lodge's store, that he'd felt pulsing and shivering under his mouth for a few precious moments out at Sunset Rock.

Creak... Thud. He stopped the rocker and brought his feet back to earth.

He certainly hadn't brought her here to torment himself with thoughts like that, either.

Kalli's weary body won the battle over her uneasy mind, and she slept.

She woke once to find her way to the bathroom. The sound of a distant power tool had replaced that of the rocker, and she groggily wondered if Walker was adding to the corral.

The second time she woke, it was to quiet, and she realized that the pain had gone. She shifted to her side and stretched, curving her back, then extending it, just for the pleasure of moving.

Then she saw the framed photograph propped against books on the top shelf next to the bed. She leveraged herself up against the pillows. The picture was in her hands before she was conscious of reaching for it. Her hands trembled a little as she looked at it.

A snapshot, grainy from being enlarged and faded from the years.

Walker looked down at her with that old smile, and she looked up at him with that old love. God, they'd been young. So young, and so damn naive.

And on her other side . . . Cory.

The smile as bright as sunlight on a champion's gold buckle. The vitality so strong it reached out of a decade-old picture and stole her breath.

Clinically dead.

That's what the doctors had told them. Not at first, when no one would tell them anything. But later, when Walker had threatened to tear the place apart if they didn't tell him Cory's condition, family or no family.

Clinically dead.

The shock, the grief. And the soul-leaching guilt for that one unguarded instant when she'd thanked God it wasn't Walker.

Her head jerked up.

Walker stood inside the doorway, looking at her, his face expressionless. Why couldn't she read him anymore? Why couldn't she tell what he thought, felt?

"I, uh, saw this on the shelf." She twisted away from his gaze, returning the framed picture to the exact spot where it had stood.

He didn't answer, but he moved to the shelves and picked up the picture, holding it between his large hands, and staring down at it just as she had. She didn't want to know what he saw in it.

"Were you out working? What time is it? It must be getting late. We should get back to the rodeo grounds. Poor Roberta had the office alone all day. I've got to get back and give her a break."

Pushing back the quilt, she swung her legs over the side of the bed, but before she could stand, he replaced the photo, turned and walked out of the room.

She sat very still, as if moving might send the emotions welling up in her over some invisible edge. Relief, that's what she must be feeling. How could she possibly have wanted Walker to stay in the room and talk about that other time, that long-ago grief? How could she possibly be hurt that he had turned away from her? Again. How could she possibly want to put her arms around him and comfort him against the pain he'd never shown her?

Slowly, she rose and walked to the bathroom, not sure how long she'd sat on the bed. With great care, she washed her face, wiping away any trace of tears, and finger-combed her hair into some order.

She hung up the washcloth she'd used, straightened the bed, tucking the quilt in, then drew in a strengthening breath and headed out of the room.

Walker was nowhere in the house. Nor on the porch. Using a hand to shield her eyes from the afternoon glare, she studied the nearly complete corral. Not there, either. That left only the barn.

She spotted him as soon as she walked past the wide-open double doors, and was glad he hadn't heard her approach. He worked saddle soap into a strip of leather, sitting on a bale of hay by the narrower side door that opened into the corral, his back propped by the stall wall behind him. Coat sprawled at his feet. The horse in the nearby stall hung a companionable head over the half-door, contemplating Walker's handiwork.

Diffused light surrounded him, picking out the glint of a few threads of silver in his hair, casting the strong bones of his downcast face into a pen-and-ink drawing of pure line.

And Kalli looked at him and let herself see the man he'd become. Stripped of the shadows and shades cast by their past.

A good man.

A man who lived by loyalty and honesty and responsibility. He had a way with animals—always had. These past weeks, she'd seen he also had a way with people. Because they recognized they could trust Walker Riley. He was a man of his word.

She almost smiled at that thought. It sounded so old-fashioned. She knew her friends back East, even the ones who lived by it, would shy away from articulating the code that way. But not Walker. He'd say it straight out, with no self-consciousness.

Yes, he'd become a good man, this boy she'd once loved with all her heart. A man any woman would find sexy as hell. And a man filled with secrets.

"Walker, talk to me about Cory."

His hands stilled, but he didn't look up, and she wondered if he had already been aware of her presence.

He said nothing.

"Walker..." She didn't know how to ask this of him, or why it seemed so important now. "Please, Walker."

The leather strip disappeared in his clenched fist for an instant, then his grip loosened and he smoothed the piece absently.

Kalli wasn't sure if he would ignore her plea to talk.

"I still miss him." He spoke so low, she drew closer. His hands started moving on the leather again, broad fingers stroking and kneading the saddle soap into every pore and crevice. "Sometimes, heading to the next rodeo, driving late at night or trying to catch some sleep in some airport, I'll think I can hear him talking to me. Just the way he used to." He paused a beat. "Remember?"

"I remember." Wedged securely between two sets of broad shoulders, driving through darkness sometimes cozy and sometimes magical, with nonsense or philosophy floating through the small pickup's cab. The mood exultant or restrained depending on the previous stop, but always hopeful for the next one.

"Cory was half in love with you himself, you know."

She smiled slightly. Cory had done everything Walker had, so that was no surprise. Though his love had been strictly—sweetly—platonic, while the love between Walker and her... "I knew. And I loved him the same way."

"It was all a long time ago...."

He intended to close the door on their past. A chill ran through her, followed by a flame. No. No! She wouldn't let him do that. It was all she had of him, and she wouldn't let it go.

The thought left her slightly unsteady against the stall door, pretending a fumbling stroke at the horse's soft nose, trying to regain her equilibrium, at least physically. Her emotional balance might never return.

"But there's something I got to know, Kalli."

She froze, waiting, dreading, but unable to stop what was to come.

"Do you ever wonder what would have happened if you *had* been pregnant? Do you ever think maybe then you would have stayed?"

Chapter Seven

"Pregnant?" she whispered, not ready to face the second part of what he'd said. Not sure she'd heard the words right.

"Carrying my baby," he said roughly, still focused on the bit of leather in his hands. "That time you were late. The week before..."

The week before Cory Lloyd had been killed in the rodeo arena, riding bulls. Competing with his best friend in the world, Walker Riley.

She drew in a breath, hoping it would steady her. But it only allowed a muffled sob to escape, and Walker looked at her for the first time.

He was on his feet, before her in an instant. The leather slipped to the dusty floor of the barn, forgotten, as he swore under his breath, wiped his hands on his jeans, then took her face between his hands.

"God, Kalli, don't cry. I didn't mean to make you cry. Not ever."

He wiped away the trail of moisture with the side of his thumb, the rough skin softened by the infinite gentleness in the touch.

"It's okay, Walker. It's okay. It's just that I didn't know.... I didn't know...."

"You didn't know what, Kalli?"

Within his hold, she shook her head.

"I thought— I didn't think you'd even remember that. It was just a few days. And...and you didn't want a baby."

"Didn't want a baby," he repeated woodenly.

"I thought you were glad when it turned out I wasn't pregnant."

He laughed, a grating sound that matched the harsh lines of his face. But his hands stayed gentle as he dropped them to her shoulders.

"Glad? Glad to see you crying because for those few days, you'd been dreaming and planning, talking up a storm about our baby...then found out there wasn't one?"

"I'm sorry, Walker. I'm sorry. But you never said... You never told me."

"I never told you a lot of things." With the barest hint of pressure, his hands guided her to the bale of hay and induced her to sit. He dropped down beside her. His hands curved around her upper arms as they faced each other, knees bumping, but neither bothering to pull away. "Like I was scared spitless."

"But, why would you—"

A jerk of his head stopped her question. "And if we're being honest here, yeah, I got to admit that, mixed in with all the other feelings when we found out you weren't pregnant, there was a sliver of relief that I wasn't going to be revealed as a horse's rear end quite so soon. Hell, I didn't admit it to myself for a couple of years, but it's the truth."

"I don't understand."

"You were thrilled with the idea of being a mother, flying up there with the eagles. And you expected me to feel the same about being a father and I didn't know squat about it." He took his hands away, resting his forearms on his thighs as he stared straight ahead. "My own father'd been dead so long, I only had vague memories and some family stories. What did I know about being a father, having a family? A family! God, I was going to have a family to provide for and that scared me even more."

"You would have found a job." Leaning forward, she touched his arm, tried to see into his face. "We would have managed."

"I had a job. The rodeo. It's all I ever wanted to do."

The words were so simple. For all the changes, she knew that in this he remained the boy she'd known. The boy who had always dreamed of the rodeo, who had loved it long before he'd loved her. God, she'd been naive back then, thinking he'd give it up. Naive, or stupid. How could she ever have thought that if they were having a baby, he'd stop wanting to ride and suddenly develop a taste for the nine-to-five life and white picket fences?

He turned to look at her, moving only his head. "And it's what I knew. I figured I could provide for my family by jumping to the bigger purses—"

"That's why you entered that rodeo?"

"Yeah."

He said it almost with disinterest, as if the answer was obvious. He probably wouldn't believe her even now if she said she'd thought his announcement that he'd entered a bigger, tougher, more competitive rodeo with bigger, tougher, more competitive stock to ride had been his reaction to the fear of being tied down, brought on by the thought that she might be pregnant. That he'd been declaring a defiance of his own mortality and what she'd viewed—oh, with what arrogant naïveté—as the inevitability of quitting the rodeo and settling down. Getting a house in a suburb somewhere with a job in some city, an up-and-comer in an unspecified business. The two of them becoming . . . becoming her parents.

"That's why I entered that rodeo. And Cory followed. . . . And then you . . . and we weren't having a baby, after all."

But he'd never considered pulling out of the rodeo, not after he'd paid his entry, not after he'd signed up, not after he'd given his word.

"And then that night . . ." His voice grated with pain.

They looked at each other without touching, seeing the memories in each other's eyes.

An audience's cries, ambulance sirens, nurses' voices and doctors' orders slipped through her memory. The only constant was Walker. Walker with Cory, helping him set up in the seconds before the gate swung open with his friend— their friend—on the back of a ton of angry bull. Walker trying to clamber over the fence when Cory lost his grip and was shaken into an awkward tumble through the air, then lay there under the bull's hooves. Walker being held back by others so the rodeo clowns could do their serious, dangerous work in corraling the bull. Walker the first to Cory's side, while the spectators stood, hushed, fearful. Walker shoving aside the ambulance attendant who tried to keep him from riding with his friend to the hospital. Walker in those hours in the emergency waiting room.

His eyes.

The raw agony and—yes, she recognized it now, with the wisdom of another decade of living—the grief he'd never spoken. And something more.

"God, why didn't we talk back then?" Her question was a cry at the futility of all that pain.

She'd learned to accept what had happened—with Cory, with Walker. That couldn't change. But they might have spared each other a good deal of hurting if they'd only been honest. If she could only have told him what a failure she'd felt when she realized she wasn't pregnant. If she could only have told him how terrified she'd been when she saw Cory lying still and white in the churned dirt of the arena as the medics worked on him. If she could only have told him of that moment when she had thought that it could have been Walker, and for a split second that carried an iron weight of guilt, that she had been grateful it wasn't. If only...

"Talk?" He made a sound of derision. "Talk was the last thing I wanted to do. If I didn't talk to anybody about Cory's death, maybe nobody would have a chance to tell me what I already knew—that I could have prevented it."

She straightened at that.

"Walker, you couldn't have prevented it. No one could have."

"If I hadn't jumped to the higher class, if I hadn't tried going to a major rodeo, neither would Cory."

His words brought a realization that stunned her. She pushed at his shoulder, catching him enough off guard that a second push brought him around to face her. That was the other emotion she'd seen in his face that night, and the few days that had followed before she'd left.

Guilt.

"You've been blaming yourself. My God, Walker Riley, you've been blaming yourself all these years."

And he'd carried the grief and the guilt alone. Always alone.

He'd closed her off and she'd run away. God— What a pair they'd been. Old enough to hurt each other, but not wise enough to help each other.

But that was a long time ago. They'd changed. He'd opened himself to her now, and she wouldn't leave him to carry that guilt any longer, not if she could help it.

She took his face between her hands, and she spoke with all the conviction she had.

"Walker Riley, you listen to me. You are not to blame. Cory's not to blame. There *is* no blame. He made a decision. Things went wrong. We couldn't have prevented it, just as we can't change that it happened."

A sheen in his eyes betrayed him. Maybe he could have blinked the tears away; instead, he stared into her face, seeming to need what he could read there more than he needed to protect his pride.

One tear slid from the corner of his eye, across the lines sunk into his cheek.

As he had done for her, she wiped it away with the side of her thumb.

"All we can do is go on," she said, gently now. "We won't ever forget Cory or how it hurt losing him, but there's nothing to forgive. Not him, not each other, and not ourselves. You know Cory wouldn't have wanted you to feel guilty. Or me."

"You? What could you have to feel guilty about?"

"I...I..." Over the years, she'd made peace with herself, with Cory's memory, for her transgression, yet she'd never spoken the words aloud. But how could she deny Walker the truth now? "There was a moment, before you got to him, while he was lying there, not moving.... Before I knew it, I was saying a prayer.... Not for Cory, but...but thanking God it wasn't you."

She rushed the last words, sucking in a final breath to try to stop a sob. *Cory, Cory, I'm so sorry.*

"Oh, Kalli. Kalli, honey."

It was the most natural thing in the world to put their arms around each other, to seek and give solace. To come together in a meeting of soft to hard, instantly familiar and somehow *safe*. To put her head on his shoulder so her face sheltered against his neck. To feel his cheek against her hair. To hold on tightly enough that they exchanged heartbeat for heartbeat.

She felt his strength and his heat, but she also knew his pain and sorrow.

Enervated by the buffeting of memories and emotions, she held him and let herself be held.

He stroked her hair, the rhythm not perfectly steady, the rough surface of his callused fingers now and then catching on the strands.

He took a quick breath. Drawing in the air brushed his neck against her lips.

"What?" she asked softly.

Without conscious thought, she shifted slightly to maintain that bare contact when his expelled breath would have ended it. Under her lips, his pulse thrummed with life.

"All these years," he said.

"I know."

"We should have talked."

"I know." She wondered if he was thinking of how he had drawn into himself those days after Cory's death. Refusing to talk about his grief, refusing to listen to her demands that he give up the rodeo for good, refusing to acknowledge her ultimatum that he give up the rodeo or lose her. He'd looked at her with dull, unseeing eyes and gone off to compete.

She'd packed and left, ending their marriage. Telling herself that he had made his choice, and that giving it time, as Mary and Jeff had urged, would make no difference. Not in her, and not in him. He would never grow up, so she could do nothing else. She wouldn't stay around and watch him get killed.

Not acknowledging for years—perhaps not fully until right now—how scared she'd been. Scared that he was hurting and she couldn't make it go away. Scared that she had betrayed Cory with that relief it wasn't Walker. And scared—God, so scared—that someday it could be Walker.

If it had taken her years to get beyond that, how long had it been for Walker to come around? How long had it been before he'd wanted to open the door he'd closed, and realized he couldn't because she was gone?

"At least we've talked now," she said.

"Yeah, at least we have now."

He shifted, and she felt his lips against her forehead, then her temple. Not brushing caresses, but unhurried, luxurious kisses that lulled and relaxed.

Still, an instinct for self-preservation remained, warning her of defenses dangerously lowered. If he kissed her now the way he had kissed her the past two times...

Tipping her head back, she tried to look into his eyes, to gauge his intentions. His eyes weren't completely closed, but enough to hide their expression from her. And then his lips were on her eyelids, kissing one shut, then the other, and the need to read him became unimportant.

All that was important was the healing of touch.

Telling him, with fingertips that skimmed the new hollows and lines of his face, the same message that her words had held. The impossibility of blame. The necessity of self-forgiveness.

He answered with hands that cradled her head, stroked her back with regret for sorrows unshared.

And when his mouth touched hers, it was a sealing of the understanding.

With hypnotic slowness, their lips came together, parted, met again and clung. The deepening of the kiss seemed a preordained progression rather than a conscious act by one or the other.

Beyond where their bodies pressed against each other, providing warmth and support in solid form, everything else ceased to exist. Leisurely, thoroughly, they explored needs, leaving the explosiveness of desire to simmer under the surface.

But the surface holding back that desire was thinning. Kalli could feel it in the tightening of his muscles, in the liquefying of her own. She knew the warmth threatened fire and the leisure preceded urgency.

She broke the kiss with something like a gasp. They held there a moment, still wrapped tightly in each other's arms, both breathing hard as she stared into the startling blue of his eyes, lit from behind by a glow she remembered, and knew to be her danger.

"We agreed to be friends, Walker."

The glow flared to something hotter for an instant. "I don't recall agreeing to be friends."

He was right. She'd avoided using the word after that incident at Lodge's. It had seemed ludicrous to use such a tepid description for what was between them at the time. And after that evening watching the sunset, she'd avoided talking about it at all. The topic was too volatile.

These embraces had had such a different mood—of healing and comfort—so why did simple friendship still seem impossible?

"Colleagues, then." Still caught in the circle of his hold, she slid her hands from his back to his shoulders, and exerted a symbolic pressure. In common with most symbolic gestures, it had no effect. "Colleagues who are cooperating in trying to keep the rodeo going for Jeff and Mary. Nothing more."

"Don't recall agreeing to that, either."

But he loosened his hold some.

She resisted the urge to try to scoot away. Partly because she didn't want to engage in an undignified tussle; even loosened, she knew his hold was strong enough to keep her if he wanted to. She satisfied herself with straightening her shirt, and her back.

"I'm glad we talked, Walker. It's helped a lot, helped me understand a lot. But it's still the past." *We're still the past.* But she couldn't say those words out loud. "We have to leave it there. We can't change what happened."

He let her go then, though even in the act of releasing her, his hands bestowed a slow caress. His voice held a note in it that made her want to shiver when he finally answered.

"No. We can't change the past."

It was the future he wanted to change.

Did she have any inkling of how much he wanted that? No. She wouldn't be even this relaxed if she did.

And nobody would describe her as totally at ease. Walker took in the tense line of her shoulders as she talked on the telephone, keeping her back to him. She'd jolted like a bronc coming out of the chute when it rang.

He thought she might answer it, since she was about two feet away from the phone. He'd been at the other side of the kitchen, taking two glasses out of the cupboard for the cool drink he'd promised her.

By the time he turned around to tell her it was for her and handed her the receiver, he saw she was composed again, wrapping that reserve around herself.

Had to be a flaw in his character that made him itch to peel that reserve away. Make her forget it for more than a minute or two. The way she used to during those long, hot nights in that old trailer.

Friends? Colleagues? Bull.

She thought that was all there was between them? She thought the way their bodies ignited each other at Lodge's store and Sunset Rock, the way their hearts healed each other this afternoon, was simply a remnant of the past? Something gone but not quite forgotten? Bull.

Yeah, they'd dealt with the past this afternoon. And he'd never regret that they had. At least some of the shadows had been lifted from those earlier days. He would no longer have to shun the memory of them just to keep his hands steady and his mind clear. No, the past wouldn't be such a bad place to visit in his memory, come fall, back on the circuit with its long, blank travels from town to town.

But no matter what Kalli said, no matter whether she believed what she'd said or not, they'd also been dealing with the future.

Now, hips comfortably leaning back against the sink, arms folded across his chest, he unabashedly listened to her side of the conversation. It told him Roberta was relaying the news that Kalli's New York office had called.

Of course, he already knew that, because Roberta had told him when he answered the phone.

They probably wanted her to get back there as soon as she could, probably booking the next flight out.

Kalli hung up and glanced at him.

"We need to get back."

To New York or Park? he wanted to ask. Instead, he made a flat-out statement, "Not till you eat something."

For some reason, that seemed to relax her. She quirked a look at him that held amusement.

"I need to help Roberta."

"Not going to help her much by keeling over."

"I'm not going to—" She broke off and looked at him. This was the first time this summer he could recall she'd done that without looking as if she was preparing to run for cover or considering drawing a bull's-eye on his forehead. "You're not going to budge, are you?"

He allowed himself a small grin. "Nope. And I got the keys to the pickup."

She laughed then, a real laugh. "And it's a long, dusty walk back, huh?"

"Yep."

"All right. Do you want me to fix something?"

"No, you sit there—" he nodded at a chair at the small table by the open end of the U-shaped kitchen "—and I'll get it all ready."

He took a casserole dish out of the refrigerator, removed the foil covering it and put it in the microwave before rummaging in a cabinet.

"Uh, Walker? I don't want to insult you, but I remember some of the things you used to eat."

He fought to produce the frown her comment demanded. It wasn't easy when he wanted to grin at her comfort with pulling out a memory for them to share. "Are you disparaging my cooking skills, ma'am?"

"I don't think I'd call them cooking skills. More like can-opening skills."

He accepted that with a thoughtful nod, but defended himself. "I'll have you know my can-opening skills have improved a good bit." He ignored her murmured "Thank goodness," and went on. "But for your information, this late lunch is courtesy of Lolly Carmody. And if you've ever seen her sons and her less-than-slim husband, you'd know she's one of the county's best cooks."

The microwave dinged just as he finished emptying a can of applesauce into a bowl. He brought the casserole dish and the bowl to the table together, then returned for plates, glasses, forks and spoons and a paper towel each to serve as napkins.

"I guess microwaves have helped even you."

He nodded, deadpan. "I'm not above accepting a little culinary aid here and there."

She grinned, then inhaled eagerly. "I guess I am hungry. It smells wonderful. And applesauce! I love applesauce."

"I remember." Pretending to be intent on dishing up the casserole, he still saw the memory of a few really outrageous things they'd done with applesauce send fire up her cheeks. "And it's only natural it smells wonderful. I told you, Lolly Carmody—"

She latched on to that. "Ah, yes, the famous Carmodys. I did some checking after that day in Lodge's." He raised his gaze to hers without lifting his head, and watched the fire surge across her skin again, this time at a more recent memory. "I mean after Esther let that drop about you sending cowboys out to the Carmodys'. Turns out to be a very interesting setup."

"Nothing interesting about it," he disagreed.

"You sent several cowboys who were running short of funds because they hadn't won on the rodeo circuit in a while out to work for the Carmodys."

He shrugged and kept eating. "With Lolly laid up and their boys too young to do a whole lot, Nels needed the help. And the hands needed the cash so they could enter the rodeo. Just a matter of putting them together and everybody helping everybody else out."

"Except the cash didn't come from the Carmodys, did it, Walker?"

Under her soft voice, he heard the steel. *Wouldn't want to cross her in business,* he thought with more than a little admiration.

"No." He lifted his head to match look for look. "But it didn't come from rodeo funds, if that's what's worrying you."

"I know—"

He broke the look to reapply himself to Lolly's casserole, but his head snapped up at Kalli's next words.

"—I checked."

He glared at her. "You thought I was stealing from Jeff and Mary?"

"No! I never thought that. And it wouldn't have been stealing even if you had taken it from rodeo funds, because we both know Mary and Jeff would have done the same thing in a heartbeat, even with last summer's rescue operations leaving the rodeo in a bind. Though if you had, it sure as hell could have messed up my budget projections, so if the matter arises again, I want to know. Promise?"

"Promise."

"That came awfully easily." She cocked her head at him, considering. "Ah, of course... You can promise to tell me because you have no intention of ever using anything but your own money. And as long as you never use the rodeo's, you figure you don't have to tell me."

He shrugged. "If you'd thought that, you wouldn't have needed to check the rodeo funds this time, would you?" He caught her slight wince and didn't regret causing it; she'd laid a cut across his pride. But he had simmered down enough to wonder, "So why didn't you just ask me?"

And his wondering rocketed from mild curiosity to real interest at her obvious discomfort. She looked down to where she'd suddenly become very busy pushing the remnants of her food around with her fork.

"I thought you might not want me—anyone—uh, asking questions, uh, about your finances. I didn't know...."

He followed the progress of her gaze around the kitchen, not elaborate but modern, and toward the living room, then back to him.

"It doesn't matter," she said. "I just brought it up because I wanted to tell you I think it was a nice thing for you to do. Helping the Carmodys and those cowboys." She said it almost belligerently. "That's all."

"Okay."

He accepted it on the surface, but found this a good time to go get more of the pills he'd given her, to give him a couple moments to mull this over. With a mumbled excuse, he headed off to find them in the medicine cabinet.

Coming out into the hall without insight hitting in the two minutes he'd been gone, he could see her looking around his place again. That's when insight did hit him.

She'd thought he was broke.

She'd thought he was as down on his luck as his old truck looked, not knowing that its shoddy exterior hid an engine that could purr or roar depending on the demands he made on it.

That also helped explain that exchange over her green shirt at Lodge's. She'd thought he couldn't afford it.

And she'd been worried about him.

Or had she felt sorry for him?

"Here's a couple more pills."

He slapped the pills down on the table next to her plate, then went around to take his chair.

She pushed the pills away with one hand while shifting from her fork to her spoon with the other. "I don't want them, they'll knock me out again."

Reaching across the table, he pushed them back. "They didn't knock you out. You knocked yourself out. Your body'd been needing the rest a long time, but you just weren't giving it a chance. Take 'em, Kalli."

She looked at him, then apparently accepted what he'd said as the truth, and swallowed the pills. Another first. And some of the tension eased out of him.

What the hell, he was doing so well now, he might as well try another go-round.

"Trouble at the office?" He dipped his head toward the telephone.

"No, not really. Roberta's got everything under control."

"Meant your New York office. Trouble there?"

"Oh." She frowned as she swallowed two more spoonfuls of applesauce. "I don't know."

He waited.

"They called," she finally added. "Want me to call back."

"And want you to come back?"

She made a production of taking her plate, silverware and glass over to the sink. All of six feet away.

"I suppose so. They won't really need me until the fall, but it makes my boss nervous not to have everyone present and accounted for. Having anybody gone for a two-week vacation is about Jerry Salk's limit. Yes, I imagine he does want me to go back."

"Are you going?"

It cost to make the question sound disinterested.

"I won't leave until Jeff's back or the season's over." She glared at him over her shoulder, then turned the faucet wide open with a jerk of her wrist, deluging the dishes more than rinsing them. "I wouldn't pull out on Jeff and Mary. You know me better than that."

She turned the water off with less vehemence than she'd turned it on.

"I used to," he corrected.

"You still do."

She'd said the words without thinking, but then he saw her go still and he knew their import had hit her. And he waited for her to laugh them off or take them back or turn them around. Waited for her to do whatever it took to pull away from him.

She slowly turned to face him, her gaze going from his shoulder to his throat to his mouth and at last to his eyes. And she let him look into her.

"You still do," she repeated.

His lungs cried for oxygen, but he didn't dare breathe for fear of shattering the moment.

"You might have changed."

"In some ways," she conceded. "Not in that."

The moment suspended, drawing out in uncertainty of where to go from here.

At last, Kalli broke the silence, and Walker felt almost grateful when she gave her shoulders a little hitch and said, "Well, I'll get my things. And we can head back."

In a matter of minutes, he held the truck door open for her. She paused as she started to climb in.

"Thank you, Walker. For bringing me here. It was sweet." She flicked a look at him, as if afraid he might take offense at the description. "For taking care of me, and..."

Her words stumbled to a halt. He wondered if she thought of the unburdening they'd shared and decided that wasn't something to thank anyone for.

"You were right, you and Roberta. I needed to rest a while. I was tired."

"I know. You don't usually get that way unless you're pushing yourself too hard." He held her gaze an extra beat before he added quietly, "I *do* still know you well."

She didn't answer. The silence as they drove down the mountain, leaving behind the afternoon's isolation, had a different quality from the other silence that had stretched between them for so long.

The silence he'd started back when they were married and he was too scared to tell her his fear or his sorrow or his guilt. The silence that had helped drive them apart. The silence that had kept them separated.

Well, they were talking, really talking.

But he wondered if, unlike Jeff's situation, recovering their ability to communicate was too little, and much, much too late.

Chapter Eight

This was comfortable. Two old friends, sitting side by side on the top rail of the fence, boot heels hooked on a lower rail to balance. Two old friends watching the slow-paced afternoon activity in the arena. Two old friends chatting about this and that.

"This is comfortable," Kalli said out loud.

It *was* comfortable. Over the past week, she and Walker had worked together with an ease that rather surprised her. Maybe for the first time in all the years they'd known each other, their abilities could complement each other. Walker's low-key approach balanced Kalli's lightning-quick responses. Kalli's honed business sense gave structure to Walker's rapport with the rodeo community.

They'd made mistakes when they'd been married. Such basic mistakes. He hadn't communicated with her and she'd expected to remake him.

But they'd both grown up.

He'd certainly learned to see—and look forward to—a life after rodeo. And she knew marriage didn't require white picket fences and a nine-to-five existence. Having learned these lessons, they'd made peace with each other, which would now free them to perhaps find the right people to make their future lives with.

What felt like a vise tightening around her lungs at the thought of one or both of them finding new people was fear of the unknown. A natural reaction, something she would get past. Because now she was simply comfortable with Walker Riley. Nothing more.

"What's so comfortable, Kalli?"

Her mind had traveled so far that Walker's question almost startled her. He tipped his head back and regarded her under the brim of his hat and half-lowered eyelids. His dry tone and a slight lift of one corner of his mouth gave her the uncomfortable feeling he'd been watching her for some time and drawing his own, peculiar conclusions.

"This." A wave of her hand indicated the two of them, the arena, the bright sunshine and the freshening breeze. "Talking about your plans for the land, your own ranch… Hey, what are you calling it? You never said."

Walker shifted his position slightly. "Haven't quite decided yet. Waiting for the right name."

"Mmm. It's a very good investment, you know."

"Yeah?"

"Uh-huh. A lot of Hollywood types are buying up big spreads in Montana these days. I read about it in the *Wall Street Journal*. So, if you make a bundle again, that would still be a good place to invest."

"Did you also read they're driving up prices and taxes, too, so a lot of working ranchers are having a real tough time of it?"

"No, I didn't read that." Something warm and thick pulsed through her. Walker was a good man. Not fancy, not showy. But the kind of man who looked beyond how something might benefit him to how it might affect others.

"Besides . . ." She knew immediately from his tone that Walker had had enough of seriousness. "I'm so over the hill, the other hands'll start calling me 'sir' any day." She slanted an evil look for the reminder of being called "ma'am." He ignored it, adding with quiet amusement, "I'm not on anybody's list to be reaching Nationals, so I'm not likely to make a bundle any time soon."

"Oh, I don't know about that. I don't know about making Nationals, but you still have something that would be a good investment in New York."

"Yeah, what's that?"

"Your pants."

"My *what?*"

She grinned, idiotically pleased with herself for jolting him out of his cowboy-cool humor. He stared at her incredulously.

"Your pants."

"What pants?"

"The ones you have on."

The quality of his stare changed; he thought she'd gone nuts.

"They're dirty and—"

"All the better," she interposed.

"—worn."

She glanced down and her composure was rattled a little in her contemplation of one place they were worn, and by what. She swallowed hard.

"That's the way they like them. It's a hot item—pre-worn cowboy jeans. Yours would go over great in Manhattan." An image of how well the man inside the jeans would go over stabbed at her.

"Hmm." He stretched both long legs out in front of him, balanced on the thin top tube by his rump and his hands. "It might be worth it to go naked, then."

That image burned in her mind. And, Lord, wouldn't *that* go over great in New York.

"Hey, be careful," she scolded, her other emotions funneling into irritation as he theatrically teetered on the rail.

Instinctively, she reached out to steady him. He responded by twisting to wrap a large hand around each of her arms. For an instant, they hung there, looking at each other, caught between laughter and something more flammable. Then gravity tugged and they had no choice—to avoid falling, they had to jump.

Walker landed first by a second or so, and half guided, half caught her as her feet met the thick, loose dirt of the arena.

It seemed so natural for his hands to slide up to her shoulders, for her hands to slip from his waist around to where her palms felt the smooth, long muscles of his back through his shirt.

The heat enveloped her. His heat. *Their* heat.

She acknowledged that as she took the full impact of his hungry stare. He didn't mask the wanting. But was he aware of what else she saw? That if he kissed her now, they would take the final, dizzying step from the past to the present. And there would be no telling how much of the past, how many of its problems, how many of its griefs would be left behind. Worse, so much worse, there would be no telling what new problems they would face in the present.

She couldn't do it.

She released him and took a single step back.

Still watching her, Walker took another six heartbeats, then slid his hands over her shoulders and down her arms before they dropped to his side.

I'm not ready yet.

For an instant, when the blue of his eyes flared brighter, she thought she might have spoken aloud. Then every other thought was swamped as she recognized the import of inevitability in those words.

"I've got to get back," she blurted. Back to the way she'd thought when the summer started, back to when her heart hadn't been in such danger. "To the office. Help Roberta."

She turned on her heel, barely noticing his curt nod as he started off across the open arena in the opposite direction. She climbed the fence in record time and was nearly to the office before she considered the foolhardiness of subjecting herself to Roberta's eagle eyes right now.

An about-face and a snaking path between two stock pens and around the concession stand helped. She started a second circuit, away from the office and toward the arena, then took a left between the pens.

"Hey, Kalli."

She spun around at the greeting from behind her, and Jasper Lodge retreated a step. His hand flapped toward the office. "Uh, Roberta said I'd find you here. She said it was okay to come on out."

"Of course it's okay." Kalli had her reaction under control immediately. Jasper's face clearly said that this was business. "You just startled me. It's good to see you, Jasper. How's Esther?"

"Fine, just fine." His tone didn't match the words. And her abrupt reaction to his arrival didn't explain his unwillingness to meet her eyes. "Uh, maybe we'd better call Walker over here."

She raised her eyebrows, but before she could say that she could handle whatever needed handling—and it looked bad from Jasper's behavior—he continued, "Call him over here, too, so I can talk to the both of you at once."

And get it over with.

The implication was so strong in Jasper's manner that he might as well have said the words.

Kalli turned to where Walker now sat on the fence at the far side of the ring, and wondered if she would be heard over the noise. But Walker had spotted them. Almost as if he'd been waiting for her to turn to him, he jumped from the fence and started across the center.

Jasper headed toward the arena, leaving her no choice but to follow. They stopped at the fence, waiting for Walker.

"Hey, Jasper. How're you?"

As Jasper mumbled his reply to this greeting, Walker started over the fence, right next to where Kalli stood.

At the top, he paused. A hesitation that was, it seemed to Kalli, less physical than mental. As if he had some decision to make. She looked up, and he put a hand on her shoulder and squeezed.

A warning? A comfort? Kalli didn't know. Her hand reached to cover his, an instinctive response she stopped short. In the next instant, he released her and dropped down beside Jasper outside the fence, all in one motion.

"Now, Jasper, what've you got to tell us?"

"...So you see why Park needs the Park Rodeo to be running at a certain level. To be something we can count on, the businessmen, the whole community. I know I'm not telling you anything you don't know, but I'm the chairman and I'm the one who's got to say it."

"We understand, Jasper," Walker said.

Kalli wondered at his ease. She'd been in tough negotiations, but never one whose outcome meant any more to her than money and some prestige. This was different, and she'd had to fight to keep from cutting Jasper short, even though she knew the advantage of letting the other person have his say.

"And we're not hiding that the rodeo started off the season in some red ink," Walker went on. "We're working on remedying that, and we're making progress. But if that's what's worrying you folks, we understand, and I'll have the committee's lawyer write up something saying I'll personally guarantee the rodeo's finances."

Kalli stared at Walker hard, wishing she could read in his face the state of his bank account. Buying his spread and doing all that building must have cost a good bit. How much could he have won on the rodeo circuit? Would he have to mortgage his land? Mortgage his future?

But Jasper had started shaking his head before Walker half finished his proposal.

"That's not the sticking point, Walker. Think about it and you'll see. Sure, the Park Rodeo needs to run on solid financial ground, but there's not a member on the committee, not a..." He flicked a look at Kalli. "Uh, not a businessperson in town who doesn't believe it'll come around. And who doesn't know and appreciate what Jeff did."

He shook his head again, but this time in sad recognition that things weren't always fair. Only after he heaved a deep sigh did Jasper go on.

"It's the ticket sales we need. It's pulling in folks from other towns, other states, other countries, even. If you're selling tickets to those folks, they'll also be in town paying for motel rooms, gassing up their cars, feeding their kids, buying postcards and souvenir dish towels and—"

"Westernwear clothes?" Kalli couldn't keep the edge out of her voice.

Jasper met her look. "Sure, and buying clothes at Lodge's. I got a business, Kalli. I don't need the tourists as much as some, but I don't want to risk losing those dollars, either."

"I'm sorry, Jasper. That was—"

He waved it off. "It's natural. You're fightin' for what's important to you."

"You're right. It is important to us. And to Jeff and Mary. So tell us what the rules are of this fight so we can get started."

Kalli's brusque approach didn't seem to offend Jasper. In fact, he looked relieved to state the situation in plain words.

"The committee agreed to let you two run the rodeo for this summer, and we're sticking to that. But for the Jeffries Company to get the contract to produce the Park Rodeo next summer, it has to finish this season with higher ticket sales than last year. We need that growth for our community to keep growing. Hell, we need it to stay even."

Kalli's mind already grappled with the details.

"Whose figure is the committee going by on last year's ticket sales?" she asked.

Jasper looked surprised. "We hadn't gotten around to... Jeff's, I guess. From the report he gave us after last season. It's always audited, so those are the official numbers, I suppose." His face brightened as he remembered one detail. "But the wording on our motion does say real specific that the *sales* have to be higher, not including tickets given away or anything."

She nodded, two items marked off her mental list. "You said higher ticket sales— How much higher?"

"Now, that's an interesting question." He looked from Kalli to Walker and back, frowning. "Seems to me when we voted, we just said 'higher.'"

"So one ticket more will do it."

"Now, Kalli, I don't rightly know if the committee will—"

"If your committee passed a motion that simply said 'higher,' and that's what you were told to relay to us, the committee can't go changing the rules midstream."

"But, I don't know if the committee meant—"

"The committee should have considered what it meant before it voted. How would it reflect on the committee— and the town—if the story got out that you kept raising the ante?" Kalli guessed Jasper was thinking about all the positive publicity Walker and the rodeo had gotten lately, and worrying that she might generate as much negative publicity about him and the committee. Deliberately, she added another sting. "That would rank the committee right along with those sleazy loan sharks you read about."

Jasper's frown took on a pleading expression. Kalli stared back without giving an inch—or a ticket. He looked to Walker, clearly hoping for man-to-man sympathy. He got none.

"Kalli's got the right of it, Jasper. All we need for higher ticket sales is one ticket more than last year."

Jasper grumbled a curse under his breath, but Kalli didn't think he was all that upset. He had the attitude of a chairman who recognized his committee had been willing to vote tough because he'd be left to do the dirty work.

"All right, you two. But you got to have that one more ticket!"

Kalli nodded calmly, hoping the gesture hid her convulsive swallow. "I'll have Roberta type a summary of the points of this conversation, and Walker and I will sign it. It will be delivered to your office first thing in the morning, so there's no question about the rules we're working under."

"That's not neces—" Meeting her look, Jasper gave a deep sigh. "Okay. 'Afternoon, Kalli. Walker."

But Kalli had an addendum. "One more thing, Jasper." He stopped a few feet away and turned. "Tell the commit-

tee members there will be no more free tickets for them or
their guests.''

Jasper's mouth dropped slightly, then shifted into a grin
as he glanced at Walker. "You've got a tough one there,
Walker. A right tough one.''

Kalli didn't waste time wondering if she'd really heard a
chuckle from Jasper Lodge as he headed off again. She
simply watched him until he was surely out of earshot, then
turned to Walker, who still leaned against the fence, apparently completely at ease.

"I can't cite the exact figures without checking with Tina,
but I know we're behind last year's overall," she said. "It's
a question of how much." She caught the corner of her lip
in her teeth. "We have just over a month left. We have
to—"

Silently, he held up a hand to stop her words. He looked
at her hard, then deliberately turned. He rested his arms on
the fence's top rail, gazing into the arena.

Reining in the urge to hurry to the office and start *doing*
something, anything, Kalli breathed slow and deep, then
mimicked his pose as he had clearly intended her to.

The sun was starting to flirt with the heights to the west,
bringing a brighter blush to the cinnamon peaks. A truck
towing a horse trailer pulled in off the highway; a competitor arriving for the rodeo now two hours away.

A young barrel racer from Idaho, who Kalli had signed
up earlier in the day to compete in Park for the first time,
led her horse back toward the hodgepodge of trailers. Three
cowboys, also newcomers to Park, stood by the exit, com-
paring horses and exchanging news and affectionate in-
sults, while two of the youthful railbirds edged close
enough to listen and see, but not near enough to be shooed
away. Three more youngsters, in the absence of horses,
galloped themselves around the arena, obviously dreaming of competing one day.

She felt her mouth lifting, not quite a smile, but an easing of the frown, and when she turned her head, she met a similar expression from Walker.

He'd just wanted to remind them both of what they were fighting to keep. He was a good man, and sometimes a wise one.

"Okay, Kalli. What's the first step?"

She took a deep breath. "First, Roberta types up that summary, you and I sign it and we get it delivered to Jasper. Then, we make tonight's rodeo the best we've had yet."

He smiled at her, the one-sided smile that seemed so much a part of him now.

Still considering that, she wasn't prepared when he bent his head, swooping in for a kiss—a quick, firm, pressing of his lips against hers—then straightened immediately, never taking his eyes off her.

The impulse to touch her fingers to her lips—to make sure he really had kissed her or to hold in the light caress?—was strong, but she resisted it.

Willing her voice to stay steady, she said, "Then Roberta and I will run some figures and see how far behind we are and what we need to do to top last year's ticket sales. Then we get everybody together—Roberta, Gulch, Tina, the announcers, the stock hands, the ticket takers and everybody else we can think of—and we tell them what the situation is and that we need everybody's help. And then we start looking for answers."

He grinned, but something warmer sparked in his blue eyes, and in his low voice when he said, "That's my Kalli."

His Kalli.

Walker braced a hand against the porch column and considered the lone light in the Jeffrieses' ranch house below, ignoring the cool night air trying to work a chill in where he'd unbuttoned his shirt before coming out for a last look tonight.

The light came from the last bedroom on the right in the north wing. Kalli's room.

They'd stayed at the office late, going over the figures so they'd know where they stood when they met with the staff in the morning. The computer spit out numbers under Kalli's competent fingers. Figures not as bad as they might have been, maybe, but not great.

They'd made up ground the past month, but not nearly enough to offset the losses in June. If they stayed at this pace for the rest of the season, they'd be real close. But close wouldn't satisfy the committee. So Kalli would drive herself relentlessly to get those ticket sales high enough to keep the rodeo for Jeff.

Walker knew her, and he'd have to make sure she didn't go until she dropped. Already tonight, he'd had to put his foot down, threatening to physically tote her home if she didn't leave voluntarily. And if she hadn't believed he'd carry out the threat, his Kalli would still be in that little office, working away.

The temptation to smile that had teased his lips evaporated.

That was the problem, wasn't it? She wasn't his Kalli. Not anymore. Maybe she hadn't ever been. Or how could she have left him ten years ago?

He'd wanted to ask her that the day he'd brought her here. When they'd worked out the misunderstandings and doubts about Cory's death. He'd thought for so long that she blamed him for Cory's dying, but he'd believed her when she said he wasn't to blame. But that left the terrifying question of why she *had* left. God, he wanted to ask her.

But he was afraid he knew the answer.

Because if she hadn't blamed him for Cory's death, the only reason he could see for her leaving was that she didn't want him, or the life he led, which came down to the same thing.

And he couldn't take hearing that right now, because he'd started to dream. Started to see a future with her in it.

He knew danger. He knew the kind of courage it took to trust your luck and timing and skill to get on the back of a peevish bull.

But he didn't know if he had the kind of courage it took to see a dream get trampled.

It would be safer not to dream at all.

A twist in his gut answered that. Impossible. He'd held Kalli in his arms, he'd felt her body against his, he'd slipped his tongue into the sweet heat of her mouth, and he wouldn't stop wanting that—and more—until he stopped breathing.

But maybe he could hold his dream in by giving it a time limit, like the eight-second ride on a bull. He'd let his dream live and take him as far as it could, but only until the end of this summer. Only until the rodeo no longer needed Kalli and she went back to New York.

The light he'd been watching went out and all was darkness.

Two nights later, Kalli heard sounds through the open bedroom window as soon as she came out of her bathroom. The muffled thud of animal feet descending a trailer ramp and one low, male voice, uttering soft urgings.

Walker.

She'd tried to pretend she didn't wonder if he'd be here tonight—the only other person who would be anywhere around the Jeffries ranch for hours—all during the shower she took to wash away the long day's accumulation of rodeo dust. She couldn't pretend anymore.

After they'd told the staff yesterday about the committee's ultimatum, everyone had expressed absolute certainty that they would sell enough tickets for the Jeffries Company to keep the contract. But Walker had decided that a surprise birthday party planned for one of the timers tonight would provide a much-needed release. He'd insisted everyone go, including the crew that usually transported the livestock back to the ranch each night after the rodeo. Walker arranged that the crew would take stock back from early events, then he'd take the last load himself. Even Gulch had strict orders to go to the party in town and have a good time.

Kalli had made a quick appearance at the party, just long enough to wish Henry happy birthday and to see that Walker had been right—again. They did need this chance to party out some of their worries.

When she got to the ranch, there was no sign of Walker and she thought maybe he'd already finished. Refusing to examine her reaction, she barely took time to flip on a light in her room before taking a long, long shower. But now, standing just outside the bathroom door, she couldn't deny that she'd felt disappointment when she thought he'd left.

She snagged her bathrobe off the back of a chair, pulling it on over her short gown. Not taking the time to take her hair out of the clip that had kept it from getting wet, she headed out of her room and down the dark hallway.

She didn't even think about where she was going or what she intended to do. Then she heard the back door open and Walker's booted heels on the uncarpeted corridor off the kitchen.

She froze.

"Kalli? I saw light on in your room. You okay?"

He stood at the end of the hall, shadowy, but so solid. She swallowed, trying to form an answer.

"Kalli? You okay?" he repeated.

"I'm . . . I'm okay."

They stood there, neither moving, neither saying anything, neither able to see the other in the murky half-light.

"Kalli." A different note in his voice brought her skin alive and tightened her lungs.

"Yes, Walker." She found herself whispering.

"I'm tired of pretending I don't want you."

Her lungs couldn't take in enough oxygen. She breathed in quick, shallow spurts.

"Walker, we talked about that. The past... The past's very powerful. And we got beyond that—"

"That's right, we did. The first time I kissed you, maybe that was for the past. Part of it. But—"

"I know, Walker. That's what I said. It's understandable. After all—"

"That was the first time, Kalli. At Lodge's. That was the old anger and desire we didn't know what to do with." He spoke quietly, and he waited. Waiting, she knew, for her to argue, but suddenly she didn't have any more arguments. "The other times have been for now. At Sunset Rock— That was the start. That was our first kiss for now. Then at my place. Those were for now. And that's what tonight is, too. For now."

He took two steps closer to her, becoming less a shadow in the dark hall.

"I may be just a rodeo hand, Kalli," he said with a thread of amusement in his voice, "but I do know my tenses. I said I'm tired of pretending I don't want you." All amusement left. "That's present tense. Now. Right now."

They looked at each other. That was all. He didn't move any closer. He didn't say anything. But she could feel her heartbeat react to his presence. She could hear her breathing grow shallower and quicker.

When he moved, it was almost a relief. But the relief was short-lived.

He stopped in front of her, fractions of inches from touching. A deep breath could bring them together. He made no move to take her in his arms, no effort to kiss her. He simply stood and looked at her.

Heat seemed to roll off Walker, seeping into her bloodstream, where it ignited.

Kalli shivered and thought a little wildly that she hadn't known she could shiver from heat.

She swayed with the impact of that inner fire, brushing unintentionally against Walker. A sound escaped her, blending with his stifled groan. Still he didn't reach for her. The second time she brushed against him, it wasn't unintentional, and she reveled in the tremor of his muscles as much as in her own pleasure. Breathing became an adventure, rewarding her with small points of contact, punishing with separation. But when she eased back barely enough to separate their bodies, he locked his muscles and did not let himself follow.

And she understood. He waited for her declaration that she was tired of pretending she didn't want him.

And it *was* pretending. It had been for a long time. Maybe from the moment he'd walked into the rodeo office and back into her life. Maybe from the moment she'd walked out of his life.

Keeping her gaze on his face, she reached up and caught the brim of his hat in her hand. Deliberately, she eased it off his head, revealing his face as he had at Sunset Rock, lowering it to her side, then disposing of it by opening her fingers.

She opened the clip holding her hair, and let that drop, too.

Then she leaned in, closing those fractions separating them, brushing against him. And not pulling back.

As a declaration, it wasn't very eloquent, but she saw by his eyes that Walker understood it.

Chapter Nine

Never breaking the look, Walker leaned closer, closer. Until she could feel his breath across her lips and her eyelids became too heavy to hold up.

He didn't hurry. He didn't crush her mouth, but took it slowly and completely. He outlined her lips with his tongue once, then slid it inside her mouth, a possession.

She put her arms around his shoulders for support, and to press closer. His hands grasped the back of her robe at the waist in balled fists that rubbed from shoulder blade to hip and back.

The kiss deepened, tongues meeting, touching, retreating, thrusting. The press and movement of his chest against hers rubbed the material of her gown over breasts grown heavy and tender. When he dropped one hand to cover the curve of her buttocks and draw her lower body tight against his, the ridge under his jeans felt hot and stiff against her abdomen. Kalli's knees gave slightly, weakened by such pleasure. That weakness had a reward, for it brought them into closer alignment.

His hands dipped lower, under the robe and gown, dragging them up haphazardly so his broad palms and strong fingers spread across her buttocks. He moved against her—beyond suggestion to a blatant statement of desire. She answered by pressing against his hands, then more strongly against his groin.

She felt the heat flare in his body, like a fire fed by a splash of gasoline, and knew she would burn up in it. But she couldn't step away.

At last—too soon—their mouths parted, both of them gasping for air as if the fire had consumed all their oxygen. For a long moment, they looked at each other, regaining some measure of breath. But not of steadiness.

"Do you want to go to my room?" Her words came out in a curiously formal voice.

He muttered a curse, then rested his forehead against hers and drew in a breath. "Unless you want me to take you right here."

She leaned back enough to see his expression, and wondered at the atavistic thrill she felt knowing he meant every word.

Civilization won out. She took his hand and led him the few steps down the hall to her bedroom. Once across the threshold, he came up next to her with one long stride and they approached the bed side by side.

She hesitated, and he seemed to sense it, turning her into his arms almost before she realized she'd gone still.

One of his big, roughened hands rose to the wisps of hair that had curled from the shower's moisture. "You smell so good, Kalli. Clean and bright. I should take a shower."

She shook her head, all hesitation gone. She unbuttoned his shirt, fingers moving quickly despite not being entirely steady. He stood quiet under her hands, though she felt his breathing speed up. But when her hands went to his belt buckle and the backs of her fingers brushed against the hot skin that covered his flat, hard belly, the muscles there jerked and he sucked in a breath.

"No shower," she ordered, smiling a little at the sense of power he gave her. "You smell like you."

The quirk of his brows and the lopsided grin showed he was unconvinced. Still, he pushed her robe off her shoulders, and she cooperated, shifting her arms so it drifted down, over her hands, along the slick surface of her gown and to the floor.

"God, you're beautiful."

He kissed her, long and deep, the rhythm of it communicating to their bodies, until they moved against each other with the same tempo.

Backing off a few inches, he released her mouth. A breath of fear stirred across her at the separation.

Then he slid his hands between them, stroking his hands over her breasts through the silky material, and what stirred through her had nothing to do with fear.

"So beautiful," he murmured, then seemed to rouse himself. "Kalli, a quick shower—"

"No." She'd waited ten years for him; she wouldn't leave the fear any opening to drive a wedge between them now. "No, I like the way you smell."

His fingers found her nipples, circling them lightly, then with more pressure, then lightly again. And she wanted more. She wanted his mouth on them as it had been at Sunset Rock. And she wanted even more than that. She wanted him. All of him.

"Like a barn, you mean?" Even short of breath, his voice sounded wry. He'd dropped one strap off her shoulder and slipped his hand inside the loosened neck of her gown to resume his magical torment on bare skin.

Sliding his shirt down his arms, she deprived herself of the pleasure he gave to free him of the covering and to satisfy her own need to stroke her palms across the power of his chest. He made a slight sound as she pressed her lips to his collarbone.

"Like dust and leather and animal and sagebrush," she finally answered.

Her kisses traveled lower, until she pressed one to the skin where the back of her fingers had brushed before. With her tongue, she circled the area, just above the open belt buckle, while her fingers opened the snap.

"That's it," he said in a voice that declared he'd finished trying to make her see reason. A voice drained of patience and resistance.

She thought his muscles under her mouth clenched, as they had earlier under her touch, but she couldn't be sure, because Walker was in motion.

The gown came off her in a hurry. Her back met the mattress the same way as he tumbled her into bed. He stretched atop her, kissing her deep and long, but not nearly long enough, as he pushed himself upright.

"Don't move," he ordered as he yanked off boots and jeans. As if she'd had any intention of moving, when her lungs burned and her bones melted at the sight of his long, hard body, etched and molded by the years and the work to something so fine it made her eyes fill.

And then there was only the frenzy of trying to get enough of each other when it couldn't be done, no matter how much they kissed and touched and kissed again.

His mouth at the back of her knee. His palm caressing her calf and sole. His tongue tracing the curve of her neck and shoulder. Her fingers finding the flat brown circle of his nipple and drawing a groan from him. Her teeth pressed lightly into his earlobe, then soothing with her tongue. His knee between hers, spreading her legs so she opened a place for him. Her feet stroking against the back of his calves as he moved against her.

The only pause came when he shifted to draw on the condom he'd pulled from a pocket. Suddenly, she felt shy, of him, of the process. They hadn't ever bothered before. But the world had changed. Circumstances had changed. They had changed. And he was, indeed, a good man.

He bowed his back to kiss her waist, tasting her skin with his tongue and lips, then moving lower. Heat, such heat. And a fizzing in her muscles that made it impossible to hold still. But the last thing she wanted was to move away from this spot, this moment, this man, so she was left to small movements, shifting and squirming. His mouth moved lower still, pressing a kiss against her that made her gasp— an inarticulate sound she hardly recognized as her own.

"You taste so sweet, Kalli."

He straightened his back, dropping light kisses on her breasts. Then he took one nipple into his mouth, stretching across her body, giving her his weight for the first time. It felt so good....

Sucking lightly, he stroked his tongue over her nipple, then slid a hand between their bodies, pressing against her, slipping his finger slowly inside her.

"Walker..."

Arching against him, she held on, digging her fingers into his shoulders. So much, she wanted him so much....

She ran her hands down his back, savoring the feel of him the way she savored his scent. Over muscles clenched tight in restraint, her hands slid lower, urging him to her.

Poised to enter her, he held. She let out a breath in a sharp sound of frustration. But still he didn't move. Not until her eyes met his. Not until she was locked in their blue, blue depths.

Then he moved. Slowly, inexorably into her. She could feel her body adjusting to his presence, adapting, welcoming. He withdrew, nearly as slowly, then returned, the pace no longer measured. She lifted her hips, drawing him deeper inside her, tighter. He stroked into her again, even deeper. And again. She met him, and matched him.

Until the movements weren't small at all, but strong, powerful sweeps that drew them deeper and deeper into each other. To a place so deep, they were reaching up, reaching for something far above them and glittery, like the great orange ball of the sun, hanging above the peaks that came closer and closer together and grew higher and sharper, until the tallest and sharpest finally touched it and the sun burst. Showering them in a glittering stream of light and heat and brilliance. And peace.

Her fingers followed an idle path across his shoulders, chest and abdomen. It was a pleasant idleness, satisfying a lingering urge to touch, but not too taxing on her sated, exhausted muscles.

That changed when she realized the paths were not so idle, but often followed thin, raised lines mapped across his skin.

She raised herself on one elbow to get a better look.

Scars.

A dozen? More? Each thread of lightened skin was a testament to some injury he'd suffered, some pain he'd endured.

"Oh, Walker." An ache sounded in her voice; she shuddered at the vision that came too quickly to be ignored, of his being hurt. "I'm so glad you're not riding this summer."

The words came out before she could stop them, but maybe it was just as well. And maybe by being away from the circuit this summer, he would learn that he didn't need the competition the way he thought he did, didn't need it more than he needed her. Maybe this time, he would choose her.

Under her hand, she felt him hold his breath a moment. Then her hand lowered along with his chest as the air streamed out of him. And she knew he'd made some sort of decision; but she had no idea about what.

"Don't let these bother you. Every rodeo hand needs a few scars," he said.

His light tone made her feel as if a door had been closed in her face, but she followed his lead. She raised her head to quirk an eyebrow at him. "To prove how macho he is?"

He grimaced at her, then grinned, mischief lighting his eyes. "Nah, no need for that. Need scars to weed through all the women."

The abrupt, sharp slice of jealousy through her brought a spasm that tightened her fingers on his flesh. Almost as quickly, she tried to turn it into a tickling caress.

He wasn't fooled.

"*Ow!* What'd you do that for?" he asked. But the hint of satisfaction in his voice said he knew why she'd done it, and he liked it.

"Just disproving your statement about rodeo cowboys being macho," she said silkily, then continued, in order to show that his dealings with women between their past and now didn't concern her. "So, how do the scars help you weed through all the women?"

Since the question accompanied a deliberate trailing of the back of her fingers down his abdomen, over the hardness of his hip and down the front of his thigh, she was pleased that his answer, though still teasing, was delivered in a markedly lower, rougher voice.

"You know rodeo hands can have sensitive souls, too. They don't want to get chased for shallow reasons. A few scars eliminate the ones who're after you just for your body."

With her arm fully extended, she straightened her fingers, dragging the nails lightly over his flesh until the pads of her fingers stroked him, sliding temptingly up the inside of his thigh.

"Kalli..."

Did the warning or the hunger in his voice make her hesitate a fraction? It didn't matter. She continued.

She touched him with light, feathered strokes, eluding his hand when he tried to capture hers and deepen the caress. Ignoring his shifting to try to push himself harder into her hand. Instead, she continued the slight connections of skin against skin that could hardly be expected to explain the pulsing changes in his body, the clenching of the muscles in his thighs.

Except that these same light touches were producing such a strong effect on her own body.

Blindly, he reached behind his head to where one leg of his jeans had landed. He hauled on the denim until he could dig in the pocket and extract another foil packet. She watched the procedure with interest, assisting with more of those light, fleeting touches that had him grinding his teeth between promises of a retribution she was more than ready to withstand.

So when he let loose a curse, rose partway to grasp her hips and drape her atop him, she cooperated by levering herself above him until she felt him at her entry.

"Kalli..."

With the sound of her name on his lips, she took him inside.

He met her, one hand still at her hip, the other curving over her breast.

It was fast and hard, and they collapsed, still joined, too exhausted to move. She thought of nothing, long after their breathing returned to normal. Just lay on him, relishing the presence of him inside her, listening to the wonder of Walker's heartbeat.

"You're going to be the death of me, Kalli."

She smiled into his neck and shifted slightly against him. His instant response affected her most intimately.

"I wouldn't count on it, you know," she said.

His hands tightened on her lower back, pressing her more fully to him. "On your killing me?"

"Well, not that, either, since you already seem to be, uh, coming to life. But I meant I wouldn't count on a few scars keeping the women away from your body."

"Yeah?" It came out mostly a growl.

"Yeah."

"As long as they don't keep you away from my body, Kalli."

Then he moved against her again, and there was no more talking.

With memories of Kalli so impressed in his senses that holding the steering wheel awakened echoes of stroking her skin, Walker found the drive to see Jeff and Mary went by fast. Almost frighteningly fast. Not only from the aspect of highway safety, but of his emotional safety.

Physically, the pull between them was as strong as ever. Or stronger. The thought tucked a frown between his brows as he neared Billings. He'd been practically a kid when they'd been together, with all a kid's energy and hormones. But he couldn't deny that their lovemaking last night and this morning had taken him higher, rocked him deeper than he'd ever been before.

And that's what bothered him.

Because that meant a whole hell of a lot beyond physical was involved, and that's where they got in trouble.

The physical pull might not have suffered from ten years apart, but the emotional bonds were as fragile as a thread holding a bull. Those bonds had broken once when a couple of fool kids had stretched them too far. Or had they broken? Maybe they'd partially unraveled, leaving neither of them totally free, but not quite connected, either.

He and Kalli had done some mending this summer, but even if they succeeded in completely patching the bonds, would they be strong enough to keep her here this time?

Because that's what he wanted. Kalli by his side, for good.

No sense denying that. All those promises to himself about reining in his dreams to just the summer were no better than lies, he acknowledged grimly as he pulled in to the hospital parking lot. He knew what he wanted, and it didn't end with the last Saturday in August. It ended with gray hair, rocking chairs and enough children, grandchildren and—what the hell—great-grandchildren to carpet the valley.

But wanting didn't make it so.

He found a parking spot for the truck, turned off the engine and unhooked his seat belt, but he didn't get out right away. Enough breeze came through the open windows to ease the sun's warmth.

He didn't like not telling Kalli the whole truth of what he was thinking—dreaming—but could he risk it?

If—when, dammit, *when*, he corrected himself viciously—she left come September, he'd have a hurt to bear worse than anything he'd gone through before, even worse than her leaving the first time. But if he told her he wanted forever and she pulled away from him before she left . . .

No, he couldn't risk scaring her off.

He adjusted his hat and climbed out, trying to shift his mental gears to visiting with Jeff and Mary.

He wasn't entirely successful.

Walker certainly took in the fact of Jeff's improvement, and the news that the staff had mentioned letting him leave the hospital, though he'd have to stay in Billings a while longer. He and Mary would live with her cousin while Jeff got in-home care and continued intensive therapy.

Jeff might even be allowed one or two overnight visits to Park during that phase, as a transition to the next step, when he became an official outpatient, living at home and commuting two or three days a week for therapy.

"And I bet you're just itching to come by the rodeo and check up on us, aren't you?" Walker asked with a grin.

He and Kalli had agreed to wait until he saw on this trip how far along Jeff had come before deciding whether to tell him about the committee's ultimatum.

"First stop," his uncle promised, laughter and determination glinting in his eyes. His expression grew serious then. "But promised Mary it won't be last stop. Promised myself, too."

Walker looked from one to the other. He'd known them all his life, spent every summer and most holidays with them growing up after his father died. And as long as he'd been on the rodeo circuit, when he thought of going home, it was to the Jeffries ranch. Until he'd built his place, it had been the only home he'd had after his mother died. And in all that time, he couldn't remember ever seeing them look at each other with more love than they did right now.

That's what he wanted with Kalli. That was his dream.

"What..." He cleared his throat. "What do you mean, Jeff?"

"We're going to take some time. Enjoy things, that's what I mean."

"Not give up the rodeo," Mary explained, her eyes studying Walker in the quiet way she had. "But we're talking about getting more help. So we can go off and do things without being tied to it all the time. And take things a little slower than we have been. Not just with the rodeo, either.

We've been saying for years we might lease off some of our land. Now seems like a good time to do it."

That pronouncement dropped heavy in the air. They'd talked about leasing it off to him, so he could run more stock while he got his own place going full speed. But all of that was supposed to be for some distant time in the future, when he quit the rodeo circuit, when he'd be around all the time to work his place and their land. He couldn't do that while he was rodeoing.

Not yet. I'm not ready to quit.

The cry from his heart was followed almost immediately by one from his head. Would he ever be? Would he ever be ready to let go of something he loved so much?

"Nothing firm yet," Jeff said. "Maybe try that south section."

"Nels Carmody has asked about leasing that section now and again," Mary agreed, contributing to the effort to smooth over the moment of silence.

Walker did his part, too, and the conversation drifted to less perilous waters, until Jeff started to flag and Mary gave Walker a subtle sign.

He took his leave and she followed, kissing her husband and promising to be back soon.

"Not too soon," Jeff said sleepily. "Get a good meal out of this boy."

Walker, who'd insisted on taking Mary to lunch, grinned at both Jeff's admonition to his wife, and his calling a thirty-three-year-old beat-up rodeo hand "boy."

Jeff was already nodding off when they eased the door closed behind them.

"He's looking good," Walker said when he had Mary settled in the truck, heading for a small restaurant he knew. "Almost like his old self."

"He's doing better, that's for sure," Mary said, then let a silence fall.

Caught up in other thoughts, he barely noticed. But he noticed her next statement.

"They won't forgive her this time."

"What?"

"They won't forgive her a second time."

He supposed he should have asked who, just for form's sake, but he'd never had the heart to play games with Mary, especially since they never worked. But how the hell could she know the shift that his and Kalli's relationship had taken? Did the desire ooze out of his pores? Was passion so clearly imprinted on his face?

"What do you mean, Mary?" His throat tightened some around that because on some level he knew he wouldn't like the answer.

"Folks 'round Park, folks with the rodeo won't forgive her for leaving you a second time."

What if she doesn't leave? Thank God, he didn't say it out loud. He knew better than that. It would show too damn clearly just how far-gone he'd gotten in no time at all.

"Even if you make it clear you'd known all along that she'd be leaving in the fall..."

He *did* know that. No matter what his dreams. He'd known from the very start that come fall Kalli would return to the life she'd created back East. And he'd stay here, with his life. Still loving her.

So why did it feel like a bull's horn had just gutted him to hear it said out loud?

"... they won't forgive her. They protect their own, and they'll shut her out. Even with Jeff and me loving her, it won't be enough. So if folks see what's happening, see how you two still are, you'll be making sure that Kalli can't ever come back here again. Don't do that, Walker. Don't do it to Jeff and me, because we love her, too, and we need to have her coming here. And don't do it to Kalli. Because she needs this place. She needs the peace it gives her."

Grimly, he hung on to the wheel and the words that shouted in his head.

What about me? What about what I need?

He didn't say the words. He didn't say anything as he parked the truck and escorted Mary into the restaurant. And Mary didn't allude to that subject again, not during the meal and not later, when they said goodbye outside the hospital. Though he did catch both worry and mistiness in her eyes when she gave him a strong hug, a kiss on the cheek and her usual order to take care of himself because they loved him.

But her words never left his head as he drove back toward Park for that night's rodeo.

What if he'd told Mary he needed Kalli the way he needed to breathe, the way he needed to ride? Would she have understood? Would she have believed him? Would she have looked sad and shook her head at his folly?

What if he'd told Mary he couldn't give up this remaining month with Kalli, no matter what it cost any of them? Because it would have to last him the rest of his life.

Dammit all to hell.

He slammed his palm against the steering wheel.

"Then I'll just have to make sure folks don't see what's happening with us." He curled his hands around the wheel, holding on tight, as he added harshly, "Because I'll be damned if I'll give her up before I have to."

Chapter Ten

Kalli took a customary scan to make sure everything was in order, clicked off the lights and locked the office door from the outside.

The night air sifted around her, and she raised her face to the breeze and moonlight. After the bustle and noise of the evening, the rodeo grounds seemed preternaturally quiet, and utterly deserted.

Until a shadow detached from the darkness in the vicinity of the ranch station wagon. Urban instincts tightened her hand around her keys, points bristling out.

"Didn't think you were ever going to call it a night."

Her hand eased, but her tension didn't evaporate entirely.

She hadn't seen Walker since this morning. She'd awakened to the sound of her shower running. He'd come out almost immediately wearing one towel around his hips and rubbing another one at his hair.

When he saw that she was awake, he paused a moment, then walked slowly to her side of the bed. Without a word, he dropped the towel he'd been using on his hair.

Then he dropped the other towel.

Almost an hour later, as she headed to the shower, Walker kissed her a final time and said he was going up to Billings to see Jeff and Mary.

She knew from others' passing comments that he'd arrived at the rodeo grounds in midafternoon, but he hadn't made an appearance in the office at all.

"Had some things to clear up," she said.

"So, you finally ready to head home?"

She could feel the thud of her heart against her ribs. "Yes."

"Good. You go on ahead, then."

She looked at him, trying to see his face in the irregular illumination from the moon and the security lights, then quickly turned away. "I see."

But before she'd gone three steps, he spun her around with a hold on her arm. "No, you don't see, Kalli." He took two deep, impatient breaths. "You go ahead to Mary and Jeff's. I'll come by later. I'll be there."

And this time she really did see.

"Don't you think it's a little late for discretion? The ranch hands aren't any different from anybody else around here. News of your truck being at the ranch all night probably reached the café two hours before you left."

"Nobody saw the truck. Parked in the garage."

"Oh." She didn't know how she felt about that precaution. "Okay, Walker. If that's the way you want it."

In the gloom, she thought he winced, but his voice was normal when he said, "It's best, all things considered."

For the solitary ride back to the ranch, the brief, refreshing span of her shower and in the minutes waiting in the dark of her room, she wondered what things he'd considered in deciding to keep their relationship secret. Propped up by the pillows, she plucked a fold in the mid-thigh silk gown she hadn't worn since leaving New York.

But then, a shadow filled the open doorway, and all that was forgotten.

"Kalli."

"Yes. I'm here."

Something about the way he moved in the dark, sitting on the edge of the bed with a tired sigh, made her move up so she knelt just off his right hip. She put her arms around him from behind. One of his hands came up to pull her arm even farther around him. With her cheek against the thickness of his hair, she tightened her arms' hold while her hands stroked softly.

He gave another sigh, but this time she could feel tension go out of the muscles she pressed against. And just that easily, she knew his mood had shifted.

"Take your boots off, cowboy."

He responded to her mock sternness with a humble "Yes'm."

He bent to yank off one boot with a grunt. Straightening, he let it drop to the throw rug. Before he could bend down for the second one, she leaned over his shoulder to kiss the side of his mouth.

He held utterly still a second and a half before he turned his head to meet her lips fully.

"Open your mouth, Kalli."

She parted her lips, and he slid his tongue along them before slipping inside. Their tongues met lightly, retreating and circling. Without releasing her mouth, he made another demand.

"More, Kalli. More."

She gave him more.

The kiss grew deep, rhythmic, intoxicating. The sleek friction of his tongue against hers—sliding in, withdrawing, delving again—created a new pulse in her, commanding the opening and closing of her heart, the movement of her blood. All to his beat.

Dipping his shoulder and twisting, he brought his knee up on the bed so he nearly faced her. She started to drop back on her heels, but his powerful hands at her sides held her. Instead, he used the one knee on the bed to balance with her as they kissed again and again, until their bodies swayed together in the same beat.

He broke away from her mouth and dropped back to a half-sitting position, but again prevented her from doing the same by his grip on her sides.

Even in the shifting shadows, she could see the way he looked at her. The way his eyes traveled over her. No hurry. No pretense. His gaze touched her skin through the thin barrier of silk. And he enjoyed it.

So did she.

It was the reason she had put on this gown, with its thin straps and its skimming fit. The way she felt right now, she wouldn't have argued if someone told her it was the reason she'd packed it back in June. She could almost believe she'd bought it on a rainy March day all those months ago in New York with this moment in mind.

And then Walker did more than look.

At first, it was no more than a slow sweep of his thumbs across her midriff. His thumbs reached nearly to the top of her hipbones before starting up, almost meeting across her waist, then continuing up to brush the undersides of her breasts.

Again and again he created an arc of sensitivity on her body, until she had to hold on to his shoulders for balance.

By the time he moved his hands up, her breasts were aching, the nipples straining against the silk. When he finally touched them, sweeping his thumbs across their tips with the same movement as before, she swallowed a moan.

"Walker."

"Lots of time," he murmured. "Lots of time, Kalli."

He rose briefly to fit himself against her, as if to both give her support and let her know the state of his body. As he pulled away, she slid her arms inside the curve of his so she could unbutton his shirt, though she had to fight the distraction of his lips on her neck, the curve of her ear, her throat.

She finally succeeded and started on his pants. Before she could do more than open the belt buckle and the snap at his waist, he'd shrugged out of the shirt and come to her again, his hands roaming her back and buttocks, contributing to the slide of silk caught between her skin and his, while still holding her upright.

His fingertips traced the back of her thighs below the gown's hem, then the sides, then the front. Breathless, she forfeited more breath with a deep, lingering kiss that earned a sound from him that she cherished.

Openhanded he started a path up her legs, gathering the loose gown in folds that floated across his bare forearms. His thumbs lazily skimmed her inner thighs, across her stomach, her midriff, lingered tantalizingly on the fullness of her breasts, pausing to circle the hardened tips, once, and again.

Finally, his fingers reached her shoulders, his thumbs meeting where they rested at the pulse point at the base of her throat. Unable to stay even this far from him, she leaned into him, needing the feel of his hard chest against her aching breasts. She heard his sharp breath, and felt it.

She withdrew only enough to see his face. It was drawn, tight with the emotions she'd felt in his body, but also with something else less easily defined.

"Kalli, I never meant to hurt you."

"I know, Walker."

"I won't do anything to hurt you now. You can trust me not to hurt you."

She slowed her response this time so he knew the words weren't simply automatic.

"I know that, Walker."

His thumbs still a gentle pressure on her throat, he kissed her. Not harshly, not deeply, not ending the kiss until the need for air broke them apart.

Some dark mood in him seemed to have broken. He scooped the gown over her head, flung it away with a whoop, and bore her down to the bed with his weight, holding her there for a series of kisses that wandered from her mouth to her throat to her collarbone, to her nose, to her cheek, to her shoulder, to her ear and back.

He felt heavy and oh, so right, cradled against her body. When his knee parted her legs, she cooperated willingly. That left just one problem.

"Ow!"

"Wha— Oh, sorry."

He sounded so sheepish, she couldn't help but tease him.

"If you're not going to hurt me, you better get that belt buckle out of this bed, cowboy."

"Yes'm." He propped himself on one elbow in order to slide the open belt through the loops and toss it aside. The heavy metal of the championship buckle clanged on the floor by the bed. The change in position ignited a new course of fire through her system.

Her voice dropped low on the next command. "And you better get all the way out of those pants."

He shifted so he loomed over her, staring directly down at her. Even in the shadows, she could see the glint in his eyes.

"I can't."

"You . . . can't?"

"I've still got one boot on, Kalli." The half of his voice that wasn't laughing rasped with desire.

"Then you better hurry up and get it off, cowboy."

The sound he made combined a chuckle and a growl. He rolled off her and the bed lithely, and in less time than it took to blink, she heard the boot clunk to the floor.

"Have to get a bootjack in here, lady, so we don't have these kinds of delays anymore."

Then she heard another sound, a harmony of denim dropping to the floor and a rustling of foil, in the instant before he returned to her. In his arms again, she shivered at the heat of his nakedness against her. And firmly put aside the voice that whispered a sliver of disappointment that he wasn't quite totally naked.

Hot and urgent, he pressed against her. But he paused for another kiss, a union of lips and teeth and tongue. His mouth still pressed on hers, he slid his hands under her hips and lifted her as he joined them with one, deep stroke.

And she gave herself up to the heat and the touch and the blue, blue eyes that she had carried in her soul even through the darkest nights.

They took the ranch pickup and drove together to Billings the next week, leaving with the light still new and tender. It reminded her of some trips they'd made the year they'd been married, following the rodeo circuit.

Except this time Walker had asked if she wanted to drive. Ten years ago, she'd driven only when he'd been too exhausted to withstand her arguments. She smiled slightly to herself as she glanced over and saw he'd leaned his head back and pushed his hat forward and fallen asleep. Maybe some things hadn't changed all that much.

But the reason for this trip was different. They'd discussed it with Roberta and decided the Jeffrieses should know about the rodeo committee's ultimatum.

The early start allowed them to catch Mary at her cousin's house, before she went to the hospital. She could decide how best to approach Jeff.

When Alice ushered them into the roomy kitchen where Mary sat finishing her breakfast, she started to rise, a reflex of alarm.

"It's okay, Mary," Kalli said quickly, going to her side. "Jeff…"

"We haven't seen Jeff." Kalli had argued to Walker that they should ease into the conversation, but now she saw the benefit of giving Mary the facts fast instead of letting her wonder. "There's a problem with the rodeo. We're working on it, but we thought you and Jeff should know. And we thought we should tell you first, and let you decide how to tell Jeff."

Mary settled back, though her look missed nothing. "What kind of problem with the rodeo?"

Kalli took the lead explaining the situation, what they'd done to meet the goal and how close they were, with Walker filling in now and then.

When they were finished, silence held for a moment.

"You keep saying 'we,' Kalli. Who do you mean?"

It wasn't the question she'd expected. "Walker and me. And, of course, Roberta and Gulch and Tina and all the rest. Everybody's pitching in. But it's really our responsibility."

Mary followed the movement as Kalli gestured from herself to Walker, then she released a long sigh that sounded to Kalli like acceptance.

Looking at Walker, Mary said, "I suppose I knew all along it would be this way."

"But we're not giving up, Mary," Kalli protested, a little alarmed at Mary's fatalistic reaction. "We're a long way from finished. I think we can still top last year's ticket sales, and then you and Jeff will have the rodeo back next year just like before.''

"Not quite just like before," Mary murmured enigmatically.

"People being what they are," Walker started slowly, meeting Mary's eyes, "I suppose you're right. But I promise you—you and Jeff—I'm doing the best I can."

Kalli frowned. Why did Mary seem to be blaming Walker for this? It didn't make sense. "We're both doing the best we can," she inserted, sharing the blame if there was really blame to be taken.

Mary gave a nod that seemed to be directed solely at Walker, then looked over at Kalli and put a hand on hers. "I know you are. I know. And I'll be praying that will be good enough."

Then she stood up and her tone altered, as if she'd just changed the subject.

"Now, don't you worry about the rodeo. I'll take care of telling Jeff, and soon, but he'll agree that we know you'll do everything you can. And if that's not enough..." Her eyes glinted with a martial light. "Well, we still have a string or two we could pull with that committee."

Back in the truck and headed to Park, with Walker driving this time, Kalli studied his profile.

"Did you have the sense Mary was talking about something beyond the rodeo?"

He looked out his side window at a passing car, watched it move safely into the lane in front of them, then glanced at her.

"Mary always did see the big picture."

Kalli got nothing more out of him on the topic. Feeling dissatisfied and even slightly alienated from him, she stared out her window for a good ten minutes.

Then she felt Walker's hand sliding up her shoulder, under her hair and around the back of her neck. He released a long breath and said, "You have to sit way over there?"

He sounded like the loneliest man on earth, but when she looked over her shoulder at him, she saw humor and mischief mixed in his eyes. Unable to resist the combination, she slid across the seat toward him.

After that, it was hard to feel dissatisfied or alienated with Walker's arm around her shoulders, her hand resting lightly on his thigh and their sides pressed together.

Kalli leaned against the arena fence and indulged in a moment's satisfaction.

True, they still lagged on ticket sales, but they were making up ground. Inch by painful inch. She studied the projections every day. With slightly more than three weeks left, today's had indicated that if they kept at this pace, they would top last year's figures by three tickets. Not much of a cushion if something—anything—went wrong, but considerably better than coming up several hundred short as her first projections had shown.

And everything else kept clicking along fine. The competitors' lot held a hodgepodge of trailers, trucks and campers, with a good mix of out-of-state plates showing they were drawing entries from distances, which meant tougher fields, which meant better shows, which meant bigger crowds.

As if to prove her point, two newly arrived cowboys sauntered up to the fence, off to her right, looking over the layout with practiced eyes and starting to easily stretch their legs and backs.

Yes, everything was going fine. Including her and Walker.

She missed him.

She felt a little foolish making the admission, even in her own mind. After all, he was only gone for the day. He and Gulch had gone for a weekly visit to Jeff up in Billings. He—they—should be back anytime. In fact, she'd expected them by now. They could have gotten hung up in the traffic from the daytime rodeo being held at a county fair midway between Park and Billings.

The possibility of that rodeo cutting into their business had worried her for a while. Roberta, Walker and Gulch had all said it wouldn't work that way. But until she'd seen that they'd received more entries than usual—as cowboys took advantage of the proximity of the rodeos to pack in two competitions in one day—she hadn't been convinced.

But the figures she and Roberta had totaled before they closed up for the break didn't lie. And the bits of conversation drifting to her from these two new cowboys confirmed it. So she would let Walker say I-told-you-so... if he'd just get here. She wanted to share this with him.

She wanted to share everything with him.

The thought burned across her mind, and she shied away from it. She wanted to share everything about the rodeo. It was only natural, they'd worked so hard together on this. She knew from her business experience that on an intense project, a sort of camaraderie developed, like with a military unit or a group on a tour. An esprit de corps built on reaching for the same goal, on seeing each other a dozen times a day, on laughing together. She and Walker did all that... and more. They made love. Sweet, passionate, consuming love.

And she'd worked desperately hard during these days at not letting herself think about what it meant to her.

Oh, God, was she falling in love with Walker Riley all over again?

Twisting around, she faced into the arena, lessening the chance anyone might notice her, might read her emotions from her face.

She latched on to the conversation of the nearby cowboys like a lifeline sent to rescue her from her own thoughts.

"Hell of a ride," the cowboy in the blue shirt said. "Didn't think he'd get much when I saw he'd drawn that chute-fighter Impact."

"Looked a little rusty to me," answered the one in a red bandanna print.

"If that's rusty, coat me in iron and turn on the water."

"I just meant—"

"You just meant he whipped your butt today, Jack."

Bandanna-print grimaced. "Yeah, he did. Wish he'd retire."

Fingers of cold crept across Kalli's skin, as Blue Shirt said, "There were rumors he might be, what with cutting his summer rides back like this."

"Yeah. What I don't get is why a champion like him is picking some of these small places to ride and not taking advantage of being right here. Having his own rodeo."

She didn't want to hear this, but the cold flashed across Kalli, freezing her immobile.

He was riding bulls. When she thought him safe, he wasn't. He was risking his life, her heart.

She'd been a fool to believe there could be something for her and Walker. Something beyond the purely physical. Even as she framed that thought, her heart and mind rejected it. It wasn't just that between them; it might be easier if it were. Because whatever they had, it wasn't enough.

They'd gotten past the hurts from the past, but that hadn't changed anything in the present. Not anything basic.

Unknowingly, Blue Shirt echoed part of her thoughts. "Whatever his reasons, it's working, because he hasn't changed from when I first went up against him six years ago. Walker Riley still knows how to get the most out of a dud, and when he's got a real rank one . . . Well, there's nobody better at sticking to 'em like a burr."

"Speak of the devil," murmured Bandanna-print.

At some level, she heard the two move away from the fence, toward the parking lot, pausing to exchange greetings with a newcomer. And she knew that newcomer had to be Walker. But she couldn't move. Couldn't think. Could barely breathe.

"Hey, Kalli."

She didn't turn, but she pushed the two syllables of his name from between numb lips. "Walker."

He came up beside her. "Mary and Jeff send their love." He dropped his voice to a more intimate level. "I'd hoped to find you in a less public place. I wanted to say a proper hello. Along the lines of the good-morning we had in the shower. It's been a long day since then—"

"Just long enough for you to get your fix of riding bulls in a rodeo, right, Walker?"

Abrupt and absolute, his stillness seemed almost painful.

"Kalli, I—"

"Don't bother. I already heard. You had a great ride." Images of what could have happened to him in another kind of ride, the kind Cory had taken that last day, inundated her mind, sweeping away logic and reason, leaving only the bile of fear.

"I didn't—"

"You won, I'm sure. And impressed a few more young boys like Matt Halderman with what a great hero you are. I suppose congratulations are in order, but I'm sure you got plenty of that from everyone else, so you won't feel deprived if you don't have mine."

"Kalli, listen to me—"

She backed away from the fence and brushed her hands together, as if to rid them of dust, but really to try to get feeling back into them.

"Did you even bother to go see Jeff, or was the whole day a lie?"

His head snapped back as if she'd hit him, and that seemed to revive his ability to move. He grasped her shoulders in a tight squeeze.

"All right, if you won't listen, then talk to me. Get it all out."

"I have nothing more to say to you."

Jerking out of his hold—and knowing she'd succeeded only because he'd let her go—she spun around and headed down the path. Passing faces blurred; she gave automatic answers to the greetings, and kept going.

The office door seemed to promise sanctuary, if she could only get inside it in one piece. If she could only be alone...

But even before the door clicked shut behind her, she heard someone hailing her.

"Hey, Kalli. Can you sign me up for tomorrow? Roberta's on the phone and I've got to get into town."

"Sure, Matt." How could a few words be so difficult to produce? "Just let me get some coffee."

Grateful that the telephone occupied at least some of Roberta's too-perceptive attention, Kalli raised the hinged portion of the counter, wincing when her hand's unsteadiness let it slip the last few inches with a slam.

The coffeemaker sat at the far end of the counter, against the wall where the tiny bathroom extended into the main room. That way, both those behind the counter and visitors on the other side could help themselves to the coffee.

She poured half a cup, pulling in breaths she hoped might contain composure somewhere in their depths.

Damn Walker Riley. Damn him, damn him, *damn him!* And damn herself for hoping he could change so fundamentally.

A last breath and she turned to Matt, half-filled coffee cup in hand. She hoped he wouldn't notice it trembling.

"So, Matt, what can I—"

The door imploded, its rubber-tipped stop encountering the wall with a sound like a muffled shot.

Kalli jerked, sending a coffee wave to the lip of the cup. Roberta and Matt spun around, openmouthed at Walker's entrance.

She'd thought when he let her go, when he didn't follow her, that that would be the end of it. Now she saw he had simply been building up steam.

Two long strides took him to the counter. He slapped the hinged portion up with enough force to shudder down the wooden length, and this time the liquid in Kalli's cup slopped over the edge onto her hand, causing her to jump and send even more coffee across the counter.

Her curse got swallowed by a spurt of voices.

"What the—"

"Get out, Matt."

"Don't be ridiculous," Kalli snapped, anger thawing any numbness. "Matt and I have business—"

"Now."

She spun on Walker. "You have no right—"

He ignored her. Didn't even look at her. "Roberta."

The secretary had already hung up the phone and now calmly retrieved her purse from the desk drawer.

"But...but—" Matt gawked from Walker to Kalli and back.

"C'mon, Matt." Roberta shepherded the young cowboy toward the door. "You give me the events you want to enter and I'll add you to the list a little later. Then you go off to town like you planned."

"Lock the door, Roberta."

"Don't you do any such thing, Roberta," Kalli countermanded. "These are office hours and the office will remain open."

"Lock it," Walker barked.

Kalli heard the bolt click home from the outside, the sound cracking a silence that burned into her lungs and eyes like smoke.

Walker had stopped four feet away from her. As far as she knew, he still hadn't looked directly at her. After her first glance, she'd been disinclined to look at him, either.

"You have no right to burst in here like this and close up the office during business hours. As hard as we're working to keep this rodeo going, trying to build the entries and ticket sales, this—"

"Talk."

His single word cut across hers with precision.

The fear that she might meekly follow his order, might do anything Walker Riley ever asked her to do, drove her to action. Turning away, she opened the door to the tiny bathroom in search of paper towel to mop up the shallow lake of coffee on the counter.

"You can't—" The small space seemed to smother her words, so with her back still to Walker, she started again, louder. "You can't come in here throwing orders around like that." She snatched two paper towels from the holder next to the sink. "I don't have to follow your—"

She hadn't heard him move, but Walker crowded her in the confined space of the bathroom, his grip hard on her right arm, anger charging the atmosphere.

She was too angry to be frightened. Or maybe she recognized at some level that for all his fury, he used only enough force to contain her, never to hurt her.

"Leave me alone, Walker." She succeeded in prying herself away from him, then tried to get around the narrow opening between the sink and the edge of the open door, hoping to get out into the main office. Maybe she'd be able to breathe there, where the essence of Walker wouldn't be quite so concentrated. "Who do you think you—"

He blocked her escape. Slamming the door, he braced it shut with their combined weight. A hand to either side of her head caged her.

"Don't you ever walk away from me again, Kalli. Don't you ever leave me without a word."

His face loomed so close she had nowhere to look except his eyes, and once she looked into them, she couldn't look away.

Desolation. Such desolation.

She hadn't known anyone could look so lonely, so lost. Except for the person she'd seen in the mirror sometimes.

"Don't you ever walk away like that again."

She saw it then, with the same shock and clarity that she'd finally recognized his grief and self-blame over Cory's death. She saw how much she had hurt him. How in her effort to protect herself by getting away as quickly as possible—a decade ago and minutes ago—she had hurt him so desperately.

"Walker."

Fingertips trembling, she soothed the scar by his mouth, the one that had robbed him of his smile.

"We're not going to waste ten years this time," he swore. "We're not going to regret not having it out and getting this clear. Not this time."

He'd been wrong to lie to her today, but she'd given him no chance to make it right. As, ten years ago, he'd been wrong to close her out, and she'd been wrong not to give them a chance to make that right, together.

"I'm sorry, Walker. I shouldn't have. I'm so—"

Even as she spoke, she knew her words weren't what he needed. His mouth crushed the words coming from hers, and asked for what he did need.

To know that she was here, that they could still hold each other. That she wouldn't walk away from him this time.

She opened her mouth to him, and gave.

Chapter Eleven

"Kalli..."

He pressed against her, his face buried in her hair, as she held him, caressed him.

"I'm here, Walker. I'm not walking away."

Her fingers had barely freed the last button of his shirt before he dragged her hand lower, pressing it against himself. She made a sound deep in her throat at the imprint of that heat on her palm, and he echoed it, arching more deeply into her grasp.

"Let me... Walker..."

She had to fight him to get her other hand between their bodies, to get enough room between them for her to manipulate the intricacies of belt buckle and fly.

Even when he understood her intention, he made it no easier, drawing the fabric even tauter with his efforts to dig out a foil packet from his back pocket at the same time he scrambled her nervous system with soft bites and openmouthed, dragging kisses along her throat, under her chin, into the valley between her breasts. Without hesitation, he bunched her short denim skirt around her waist and tore off her panties with one quick yank.

The moment she freed him from the constriction of his jeans and cupped him in her hands, he held her briefly away to pull on the protection, then shifted to pull her close again. She gasped at the speed of his move, opening her eyes wide an instant, before closing them in the intensity of sensation. Holding her hips high, he dipped to get his legs between hers, spreading them as he straightened his legs and brought them into full contact.

And there he held her.

Breathing hurt, so she stopped. She waited, suspended, for the final movement that would unite them. But it didn't come.

She gave in to her lungs' demand with a released breath that did nothing to release the tension of being held just at the edge of fullness.

She opened her eyes with some reluctance. His face stark, he held her look, unwavering, relentless, allowing no escape, as he came into her.

But it wasn't his motion alone that joined them.

She met him, not halfway, but beyond, somewhere so deep it was as if they melded. Slowly, deliberately, each withdrew to repeat the motion. And again. Still staring at each other. Almost like two combatants not taking their eyes off each other... or two people making a pledge.

The end came fast, explosive, disorienting for Kalli. The world seemed to tip, spin, shatter. And all that remained solid in it was his body. His shoulders that she clung to, his face she saw, his hips driving against her. And that was all she needed.

"Kalli!"

Her name burst from him as he arched, held stone-still an instant, then shuddered into release.

She held him, pinned by the weight of his limp body against the door, his face pressed against her neck as she stroked his hair with short, feathery touches where the thick ends lapped the collar of his loosened shirt.

She stroked him in silent assurance that she was here. She was here now, and she was his.

When they reached the spot where Walker's road forked off from the one to the Jeffries ranch, Kalli waited for him to flash his lights as always, a sign that he would park his truck, then come back to her. But the lights stayed steady.

She made the turn, her gaze pinned to the rearview mirror, then twisted around to be sure the mirror hadn't deceived her. No, he had definitely made the turn into the Jeffrieses' road. Openly following her.

When he pulled in, she stood by the truck, waiting. Not sure what she waited for, or what it might mean.

There'd been no time to talk before the night's rodeo; there'd barely been time to adjust their clothes and assume public masks that would get them through the evening. He'd said only that they would talk tonight and apologized rather formally for the damage to her underclothes.

Now, leaving his truck running, he got out and stood in front of her. He didn't touch her but she felt the tension in him. His first words came out short.

"I was rough with you."

"Yes."

"Did I hurt you?"

"No."

He absorbed that in silence a moment. His stance didn't change and his voice didn't mellow, but it didn't carry as much pain when he spoke again.

"Come home with me, Kalli."

She felt a burn in her chest.

"I—"

He cut off her answer before she could give it. "No sense pretending people aren't going to know what's going on between us after today. If it ever was a secret, it isn't now."

"No, it isn't." She recalled the looks she'd gotten tonight in the office—interested, but not in the least surprised. It probably never had been a secret.

"So come home with me."

"Okay."

That was it. He handed her up into his truck from the driver's side, holding her next to him when she might have slid farther over, and he drove them to his place. To his home. To his bed.

"I tried to tell you, Kalli."

"Not very hard."

"No. Not very hard. I wasn't looking forward to your walking away—just the way you did."

She turned to him in the thinning dark of predawn. They'd made love several times during the night, dozing between, never speaking of anything but their desire for each other and their pleasure. Until now. "You can't blame this all on me, Walker Riley. You can't—"

"Not all. Half."

"Half? You sneak off and—"

"Can't hardly call it sneaking off when you'd known about the trip all week."

He rolled onto his side, then propped his head on his hand, looking at her. The move slid the sheet and quilt down to his bare hip and sent the excess into the valley between them.

"You *sneak* off to go bull riding, acting as if you can just pick up riding after two months away from it like you were still nineteen instead of thirty-three. Risk your neck and with it, this rodeo's welfare and possibly Jeff's recovery and it's half *my* fault?"

"Yes."

That's all. No explanation, no defensiveness, just the statement.

She pushed up on her elbows to put her on a level with him.

"How do you figure that?"

"I would have been working out and competing more than I did—" He cut a look at her and pieces clicked together in her mind of Walker's disappearing for chunks of afternoons, sometimes longer, often in Gulch's company, occasionally returning with a slight gingerliness in his movements, always returning freshly showered. She should have guessed. "—if I could have told you."

"Well, next time, damn it, tell me!"

The words were out before the implications of a *next time* hit her. A next time of his riding a bull. A next time of her having any right to know what he did or where he went. *Next time* edged them dangerously close to the uncharted expanse of time beyond this summer.

"I'll tell you." No fanfare, no oaths, but she knew Walker had just made an unshakable pledge.

And had asked nothing in return.

But he needed something in return. Or perhaps she needed to give it.

"And I won't ever walk away like that again, Walker." The words came quiet, firm.

He looked at her a long moment, then nodded.

"Good."

He twisted around, reaching for something. But she didn't pay much attention to what. She sat up straighter, half wanting to make him see what a step she'd taken with that promise, half afraid to.

"That's all you have to say? Good?"

He straightened, the lopsided grin tugging at his mouth. A slight sound drew her eyes to his hand and she saw another shiny packet.

"Thought I'd express myself another way," he said.

In one motion, he pressed her back to the mattress and covered her body with his. She opened to him, and he found his place in her.

"Four days of rain. My God, this is Wyoming—not Seattle, or Ireland or the Brazilian rain forest. What is going on?"

Neither Roberta nor Walker answered Kalli's tirade. She didn't expect them to. They'd done their share of griping about the weather the past four days. For the second time in four nights, they'd taken the rare step of calling off competition because the morass made it too dangerous for human or animal participants. The other two nights, the rain had made it too miserable for anybody but contestants' relatives to come watch.

Kalli stared out the office window at the relentless rain that was pounding the grounds, heedless of the constant drumming on the roof.

"You go on ahead home, Roberta," Walker said. "I cut Gulch free, too. No sense in you staying."

For all its quiet, his voice deepened the uneasiness Kalli had felt since he walked in a few minutes ago. With the water still streaming off his hat, he'd stood in the doorway, looking at her. There'd been something in his eyes, something she hadn't wanted to see. That's when she went to the window.

But she'd been very aware of his gaze on her, even as he'd told Roberta that he and Gulch had gotten all the stock back to the ranch and everything squared away for the night.

Another night without a rodeo.

Another night without selling a ticket.

"There's no sense in any of us staying." Roberta gathered up her oversize purse, spare sweater and umbrella.

"Go on ahead home," Walker repeated.

From the corner of her eye, Kalli caught Roberta's glance in her direction, and Walker's nod. The secretary put up no argument, leaving with brief good-nights.

The office was quiet except for the rain. Then she heard the sound of Walker's boot heels on the wooden floor, coming to a stop behind her.

She delayed a little longer.

"It rains like this sometimes in the East, like it's never going to quit, but I don't remember it ever happening before when I've been in Wyoming."

He waited long enough for the sound of rain to fall between them again.

"I'm riding, Kalli."

She kept her back to him, concentrating on keeping her head and shoulders up.

"We're too close to not matching last year's sales," he said.

At that, she faced him. "We should make it, Walker. I told you that."

"I'm not risking this rodeo on a 'should.'"

She backed away at the harsh tone in his voice. Without changing position, he reached for her, cupping one hand around her elbow. Touching her but not holding her.

"Kalli, if the figures are a little off, if it rains a couple days, if a tour cancels, if any of a hundred things happen... If we fall short, we won't have another chance. The rodeo'll be gone, out of Jeff's hands. For good. Neither of us wants that."

The thought flashed through her mind that he expected her to keep backing away, to walk away. Deliberately, she took a small step closer to him, and thought she detected an easing of the lines around his eyes and mouth.

"But your riding won't guarantee—"

"No, it won't guarantee anything. But I'm a champion, Kalli. Folks don't forget that in rodeo. They'll come. Some because they cheered me on then, some because they want to see what all the fuss is about, some to remember, some to see if I'm washed up."

"That's awful. How can you let them use you—"

"The same way we're using them—to hold on to the rodeo. Having a champion riding will help sell tickets. It's as simple as that. Besides, you said yourself that using me's good PR. And you proved it. If my being in the ring sells ten, twenty extra tickets each of these last seventeen days, that'll give us some—"

"Seventeen days! The championship is one thing, even the final weekend, but seventeen days—"

"Is what we need to give us some margin on the tickets. Besides—" The corner of his mouth lifted. "You were the one who pointed out last week that I'm not as young as I used to be. I'll need the other rides to get in competition shape for the final. We're planning some real rank stock for that show. I'll need to be sharper than I am now. Seventeen days ought to about do it."

Seventeen days. Seventeen days waiting for him to go out that night to pit himself against eighteen hundred pounds of bull that didn't want him clinging to his back. Seventeen days of wondering.

"You said to tell you before I rode the next time. Not a week ago you said it."

The rumble in his voice shuddered something through her body that went beyond the fear.

"Yes." She swallowed, trying to keep up her end. "Thank you."

"Maybe you can call some of those newspeople you know, give 'em a new angle on the story, a sort of update."

"Yes. I could do that. It's a good angle." She would do it—for Jeff, and because Walker had offered a kind of gift by suggesting it—but she couldn't think about it quite yet.

"There's another aspect, you know," he said.

"Oh?"

"At my age, I gotta stay limber, work on my moves, keep moving all the time. Even all night long."

She looked into his eyes and saw the desire and the humor glinting in them, mixed with a pleasurable excitement at the prospect of two and a half weeks of steady competing. He didn't try to hide it.

He slid his palm along her cheek until his fingers delved deep in her hair.

"I could use some assistance on that. Do I hear any volunteers?"

She went into his arms, wrapping hers around him, holding him tight, trying to keep the fear at bay.

"Sure thing, cowboy."

Another day passed before he could ride, as rain wiped out another night's rodeo.

It was hard to wait. He hadn't competed in front of his hometown crowd in a long time. And he hadn't competed much at all this summer. The eagerness hummed through his system like high frequency through a wire.

It was hard to watch Kalli, too. All that next day, her uneasy glances bounced from him to the rain-peppered window and back.

Lying in bed, with her head tucked under his chin, her cheek on his chest, he considered that.

She hadn't been nervous about his riding when they were kids, when they were married. Not until Cory died, and she suddenly demanded that Walker give up the rodeo. Immediately, and for good.

He'd been in too much pain to even really hear her at the time. And after she left, the new pain had kept him from seeing what her motives might have been—other than to get away from him.

She'd seen rodeo as a kid, but she hadn't grown up with it, not the way he had, not from inside. She hadn't felt the bumps and bruises, hadn't taken the knocks and learned from them the danger was real. Until she'd learned—in one heartbreaking blow—that the danger could be deadly.

Was it a lesson she hadn't recovered from?

With his free hand, he stroked her hair. Whatever the reasons, whatever her motives, he knew his riding put a strain on the fragile emotional bonds they'd re-formed these past months. But he couldn't *not* ride. It was in him, it was who he was, it was what he wanted. Just as he knew he couldn't stop wanting Kalli beside him like this. That, too, was in him, was who he was, was what he wanted.

He'd always known he wanted Kalli back, but never as much as these past weeks, having her at his side. The nights he stayed with her or the nights she came to his bed—even when they didn't make love, sleeping with her warm and soft against him—had left no doubt. He loved her. Again or still? It didn't much matter.

Maybe they could get past this. Maybe, if nothing else frayed at those bonds, maybe if they had no added strain to bear, maybe then Kalli would stay this time. And he could dream a little longer of a future.

Kalli picked up the sheet of paper from the seat of her chair—a perfect spot to make sure she didn't miss it.

The paper had a clipping taped to it. The clipping stated an insurance company's findings that statistically, driving qualified as more dangerous than competing in a rodeo, even bull riding. Someone had underlined the last line.

Walker might have left it. Or possibly Gulch. But Kalli suspected Roberta.

It didn't really matter, though.

She knew her fear was irrational. After all, Walker had been pursuing this occupation for years, with some injuries and scars, true, but no irreparable damage. None of that eased the hold fear had on her— She couldn't shake it.

She also couldn't change his mind.

So, weren't they back where they'd ended a decade ago?

Not quite. Because this time, she couldn't run away. And while that bothered her, it also relieved her of trying to decide if she wanted to run away. At least until the summer ended, she would continue to be with Walker—though she refused to watch him compete.

Each day, he did interviews or took care of the stock or whatever needed to be done for that night's competition. Each evening, he disappeared into the camper behind his pickup and changed into riding gear—tough jeans, crisp new shirt, fancier hat and the gleaming belt buckle that proclaimed him to be what everyone already knew he was, a national champion. He would put on the protective chaps and the special glove and spurs just before he entered the chute and lowered himself onto the bull's heaving back, but he'd already made the transformation from rodeo producer to rodeo hand.

Each day, she ran the office with Roberta, worked on promotions and did whatever else needed doing. Each evening, she carefully stayed in the office, watching the ticket sales gain steadily against the previous year's total. Pretending she couldn't hear the loudspeaker announcing that Walker Riley would be the next rider, blaring his scores and most often proclaiming him the winner.

And all the while, she tried not to visualize a ton of bull doing its damnedest to dislodge Walker.

The phone rang, and Kalli answered automatically. "Park Rodeo."

"Kalli? Kalli, that you? Kalli! How're you doing? Still whooping it up out there in the Wild West?"

Her office. Again. Only this time, Jerry sounded as if he were pulling out all the stops. "I'm fine, Jerry. How are you?"

"Fine! Great! Everything's great!"

Oh, she knew that tone. "What do you want, Jerry?"

"I call to ask how you are and this is what I get?"

"I told you, I'm fine. So what do you want, Jerry?"

The phone line went silent, but in the office the door creaked open. Kalli jammed the newspaper clipping into her top desk drawer just as Walker stepped in. He gave her a smile, then turned to the results clipboard on the far wall.

Did she imagine it, or did he move more stiffly today? He'd certainly shown no sign of that last night.

Her sigh was masked by a gustier exhalation from New York. "So, when are you coming home, kid? We miss you."

"I've told you."

Kalli thought she'd keep her tone neutral, but Walker slowly turned around and eyed her, with no hint of a smile.

"You've told me what? That you're going to be gone all summer nursing this horse opera? That you're going to stay out there maybe even longer? What does that mean?"

"As long as I'm needed, that's what it means."

"What, I don't need you? The clients don't need you?"

She'd avoided using Jerry's name, but from Walker's expression it was a pointless subterfuge. He knew very well who was on the line, and at least suspected the gist of the conversation. She turned away to speak into the phone.

"Jerry, I told you from the first day that I'll stay here as long as I feel I'm needed. If you aren't comfortable with that, if you feel you can't wait until I'm satisfied that things are under control, you are certainly within your rights to terminate—"

"Terminate? Terminate? Who said anything about terminating? I call and ask you how you're doing and you start talking about terminating. What kind of talk is that after everything we've been through? Who took you in when you were still wet behind the ears?"

"Wet behind the ears? With two degrees, two internships to my credit and—if I say it myself—a good number of job offers," she objected, with a stir of humor.

Jerry didn't miss a beat. "And we've done some good things together, haven't we? That's why I want you back here, so we can do more."

"Jerry—"

"Just for a few days. That's not so much to ask—"

"Jerry—"

"Not for me. For Lou Loben. He's been working with us all summer on putting together the deal for that aluminum recycling business. We're close. Real close. But you know how he is. He needs a little hand-holding. Now, it's not that I can't do it. But with everybody else off taking vacations and having babies and running rodeos... If it weren't Lou Loben and if you hadn't worked so well with him... Well, you know."

She knew. She knew that even as Lou Loben admired Jerry's business acumen, his habit of not listening to other people grated. Jerry was smart enough to assign Lou to her. "I can't, Jerry," she said with some regret. "There's a situation here, and I need to be here."

"Is this so much to ask? After all these years? And your working so well with Lou. Is that too much to ask?"

"No, it's not too much to ask, but—"

"You going?"

She spun around to Walker's voice. He leaned on the counter, making no bones about watching and listening.

"What?"

"What what?" Ignoring Jerry's confused question, she tried to interpret the shifting shadows in Walker's eyes.

"You want to go? Go."

"I heard that," Jerry said. "See? They'll take care of those rodeo things. They can get by without you a couple days. And that's all I need—a few days. Just long enough to get Lou fixed up. Five, six days. A week, tops."

"Be quiet, Jerry." He obeyed. She covered the mouthpiece. "What are you talking about, Walker?"

He repeated his earlier question. "You going?"

"I don't know."

"You want to go?"

What sort of question was that? She wanted to help Jerry. She wanted to get Lou Loben settled in the business she'd found for him. She wanted to do what she had trained to do, what she excelled at. But was that an answer?

"They need me," she said, carefully neutral.

He nodded, and not only couldn't she read his reaction, she couldn't even make out her own.

Maybe, in addition to getting Lou over the hump, a few days away would help clarify her feelings.

She uncovered the mouthpiece, not taking her eyes off Walker's. "I'll give you two days, Jerry. Next week."

"Well, two days—"

"Two days, Jerry." She kept her voice steady and strong because she knew if Jerry Salk heard any doubt, he'd attack it. But it was difficult with Walker turning away.

"That's so close to when you said you were coming back, you might as well stay here from then on and—"

"I'll come to New York for two days, then I'm coming back to Wyoming, Jerry."

"When you get back here, you might—"

"Jerry, listen very carefully to what I'm saying." And she hoped the man heading out the door was also listening. "I am coming back to Wyoming."

Walker slapped his hat against the coating of dust on the seat of his jeans. He didn't mind ending up on his rear in the middle of the arena, not if that came after the eight seconds ended and after a wild ride sure to pile up points.

The clowns seemed to have the bull contained near the exit gate, but Walker kept a watchful eye in that direction as he headed toward the fence amid the crowd's cheers.

Gulch, wearing a glare, met him as he came over the fence. But before the older man could say anything, they were joined by one of the veterans who'd stopped by Park for a few days when the word got out the rodeo could use some aid.

"What kind of hospitality is that, Riley? Makin' it tough on the rest of us with a ride like that. Nice score."

"Stupid ride, if you ask me," Gulch muttered vehemently.

"Nobody did," Walker snapped.

It didn't stop Gulch. "Stupid and reckless. When'd you go back to thinking you got a duty to give the bull a good chance to stomp you? Thought you got over that a long time ago."

Feeling as if he'd gotten a blow to the gut, Walker bent over to loosen the fastenings on his chaps.

Gulch was right, he hadn't ridden like that in years, and he'd done it then with the help of a couple pints of brain anesthetic. He hadn't ridden like that since the last time Kalli had walked out of his life.

Two days, she'd said. Two days she'd be away.

Two days as the start of forever.

What he'd feared all along, rushing at him ... not someday, but now.

Well, he'd survived it before, he'd survive it again. And just like last time, when she left him, what he would have left would be the rodeo.

"God, what a ride, Walker!"

Walker straightened and looked into the admiration-bright eyes of Matt Halderman, and felt like an ass.

Avoiding Gulch's I-told-you-so look, he swore under his breath, then gave a succinct description of the ride, elaborated only by a few trenchant, profane adjectives, and watched Matt's expression turn thoughtful.

"And if I ever catch you riding like that, Halderman, you won't be back in rodeo anytime soon, you hear?"

"Yes, sir."

Walker's mouth twisted in grim humor. So, it really had come to the point of being called "sir." Well, he just hoped he'd been listening to his own advice.

"Got a surprise for you."

The opening of the office door hadn't drawn Kalli's concentration from the computer, but Walker's voice did. The smile on his face wiped away any lingering interest in the machine. There hadn't been so many smiles between them lately that she would ignore one.

"A surprise?" It was afternoon, way too early to know the ticket count, so it couldn't be that.

"Uh-huh." He swung the door wide, following it in with a flourish, and there on the steps were Jeff and Mary.

"Jeff! Mary! You're here! When did you get here? Why—I mean how long will you—"

"I think that about covers all the questions I asked, too," Walker said, grinning. "They said they'd answer when they had us together so they'd only answer once."

Jeff got around well with a quad-cane, but he gave a little sigh when he settled into a comfortable chair. Mary took Kalli's chair, darting interested looks at the computer, while Kalli drew up a folding chair and Walker levered himself to a seat on the counter.

"Now," Kalli demanded, "answer the questions."

"Doctor said yesterday that Jeff could take a little overnight visit if he wanted to."

"Field trip," Jeff said, with a grin.

"We drove down from Billings this morning and—"

"But why didn't you tell us? We could have gotten everything ready for you," Kalli interrupted.

"We didn't know for sure until this morning. Had to see how Jeff felt after yesterday's session. We went out to the ranch first thing, had lunch and a rest. As for getting ready, the house looked fine. In fact, it didn't look like anybody'd been living there much."

Kalli flashed a look at Walker, and if Mary and Jeff caught the heat of his return look, they had confirmation of what they clearly suspected. "I, uh, haven't spent much time there."

"Figured." Kalli had to fight to keep her jaw from dropping when Mary said no more on the topic. "So, we looked around, checked in with the hands and caught up on news. We thought we'd stop by for a little talk now, then come back later to watch the rodeo. We'll stay at home tonight and head back to Alice's tomorrow."

"Everyone will be thrilled to see you. We'll have to make sure you don't get trampled by the hordes," Kalli said.

"What sort of little talk, Mary?" Walker asked. "You said you wanted to stop by for a little talk. What about?"

Jeff tipped his head toward Walker and Kalli as he said to Mary, "Tell 'em."

When Mary hesitated, dread whispered across Kalli's mind. Was Jeff not recovering as well as they thought? He looked so much better, but . . . "Tell us what?"

Mary gave her a sharp look. "Now, don't go leaping to worries and churning up your insides. There's nothing wrong. We've been talking, Jeff and me, and it's time to let the two of you know what we're thinking." Mary sat forward. "A thing like this gets you thinking."

"Stroke," Jeff clarified.

Mary nodded. "Makes you realize your time's not unlimited. And you want to start making plans. Now, don't get that look, Walker." She returned frown for frown. "This has got to be said. We *want* it to be said."

Kalli shot a look at Walker and he gave a palms-up gesture of acquiescence—with no promises of liking it.

"Some plans we want to make for while we're still living." Mary exchanged a look with her husband. "Some are for after we're gone. We're not going to talk of funerals and cemeteries and all. We're settling that ourselves so nobody else will carry the burden."

Tears and a smile surfaced together in Kalli— It was so typical of the Jeffrieses' practical compassion.

"But some things can't be settled that way. The two of you—" Mary looked from one to the other with such clear-sighted love that Kalli felt the tears press "—are the closest we could ask to having children of our own. More than we ever expected once we knew . . . We've loved you most of your lives, and what we have, we want to pass on to you."

"Mary, that's—"

"You hush, Walker," she scolded, then repeated more softly, "just hush. We worried about it until this summer, but with you two, uh . . ."

"Mending fences," Jeff offered into a silence as Kalli carefully avoided looking in Walker's direction.

"Yes. Well, now we've got it settled. Most of the land will go to Walker. It'll match up with your place real well. And the house, Kalli, will go to you."

She opened her mouth and got no further.

"Now, don't you start," Mary ordered her. "Walker doesn't need a house, he's got one, and you need a place to get away to. So you'll always have the house, if we're here or not. With a bit of land so you don't feel closed in."

Kalli guessed that Mary and Jeff's idea of "a bit of land" would make her a real estate mogul in most eastern states. But there was no arguing with them; they so clearly had it arranged to their satisfaction. Besides, from Mary's expression, that had been the easy part. Now came the hard.

"But the rodeo's not so easy to divide up."

"Still ours." Jeff's expression of fierce determination eased when he caught Mary's look. "Partly."

His wife nodded. "You two got thrown in this year. But it's not like this, not most years. We wanted you both to see what it's like in a regular season. To see if it's something you could like...."

Mary looked from one to the other again. "So, we're hoping you two might come back to run the rodeo next summer. With us. All four of us working together."

Dead silence.

Kalli turned to Walker for his reaction, but he stared straight ahead, at a blank section of wall.

"Walker? What do you think?"

Kalli held her breath at Mary's question, fearing he would say there might not be a rodeo to come back to. Mary and Jeff had given them a vote of confidence and, at least for now, she wanted to believe they were right.

"Kalli's got a life in New York. You can't expect her to drop that and come out here."

His harshness surprised everyone. Kalli watched Jeff's eyes narrow and Mary's mouth tighten with hurt.

"I could—" She stopped, then regrouped and tried again. "I might be able to work something out."

"Like what?" Beyond challenging, Walker's tone dripped with disbelief.

His reaction seemed so strange. He certainly wasn't thrilled with the suggestion that would bring them together another summer. Maybe he wanted to be free to resume competing full-time. Or maybe he didn't want to be tied to a permanent relationship between them. Even the kind where the rodeo tied them together. Much less the kind she'd foolishly allowed to creep into her dreams.

"Like summers."

The words came so quickly, they must have been brewing in the back of her head for some time. It might work. She could live in New York nine months and spend the summers in Wyoming.

And it might not make Walker feel crowded by her.

"Summers," he repeated in an odd, flat voice.

"Yes. It's the quiet time because so many people are out of the city. That can make it virtually impossible to finalize any deal until September. I might need to go back now and then during the summer, but . . ."

"That's the idea," said Jeff, approving. "All of us working, everybody'd have time off. Mary and I could kick up our heels, Kalli tend to business. You could rodeo."

Kalli shot a look at Walker, to see if that resolved his problems with the proposal. Apparently not, judging by his scowl.

"Well, we'll let you think about it," Mary said soothingly after a thoughtful look at Walker. She laid a calming hand on her husband's arm when he would have pursued the subject. "We know you're not ready to give up the circuit, Walker, and Kalli would want to work it into her career. We thought, this way, you could both get to know the business better before you had to be making decisions of a more *permanent* nature. So just think about it, that's all."

Kalli said she would. With all eyes on him, Walker gave a short nod.

That evening, she watched Walker accompany Jeff and Mary to the press box, above the Buzzards' Roost, where they would watch the rodeo. Word was out in town that the Jeffries would be here, so Gulch would stand at the door of the press box and keep the flood of people wanting to say hello to a manageable flow. Walker insisted on getting them settled himself. He angled a shoulder, unobtrusively warding off overexuberant greetings to Jeff, and Kalli felt something swell and lift inside her.

For the first time, she faced the prospect of returning for good to New York after the season ended in less than two weeks—leaving Wyoming, leaving the ranch, leaving Walker.

Jeff and Mary's offer provided an alternative, but was it one she could accept?

Could they part, then come back together next June and pick up where they'd left off—emotionally and physically as well as professionally? How could she adjust to being without him for nine months, then adjust to being with him again? And what if she came back but he chose not to? Could she survive that?

Jeff's hand caught Walker's sleeve as he started to turn away after getting them seated. Reluctantly, Walker met his uncle's look. Only then did Jeff speak.

"One thing I learned with this— Don't waste the time you've been given."

Jeff's blue eyes, faded, but no longer with the lost, unfocused look they'd held in the hospital, bored into Walker's for an instant, then his uncle released him—hand and look—and turned to greet Jasper Lodge.

"I heard you and Mary were here," Jasper said, beaming. He tried unsuccessfully to frown at Walker. "And you tell that Kalli Evans of yours that I *did* buy a ticket. In fact, I bought two. Esther'll be along any minute."

Walker manufactured a smile. "Sure, I'll tell her." Then he made his escape.

His Kalli Evans? Not for long—if she was his at all. Jeff had said to make the most of the time he'd been given, but that time would run out in twelve days. And she'd already promised two days of that to someone else.

His Kalli Evans gave her time to that boss back in New York, and she'd give her summers to Jeff and Mary, but what about him?

He didn't know if he could take having her only summers. He wanted all of her, all the time. If he couldn't have that, would he be better off with none?

"Walker? Walker, are you in there?"

Kalli could hear sounds from inside that might have drowned out her voice. Still, she hesitated before knocking on the camper's door. She'd stayed away from it so carefully, so long, it seemed strange to go there of her own volition with only seven more nights of the season left.

The summer, which had stretched so long and forbidding ahead of her when Tom Nathan told her the committee insisted she work with Walker, had nearly run its course.

Today was Sunday, and the last rodeo would be this Saturday. She would leave in the morning for New York and the two days she'd promised Jerry, then return to get ready for the championship rounds Friday and Saturday, the end of the season.

Then what?

She pounded on the door.

"Hey!" Walker's voice protested from inside. "Don't knock it down— It's open. C'mon in."

She swung the door open and stepped in. Walker, turning from the tiny sink where he'd just washed his face and hands, stared at her an instant, obviously surprised to see her here. Then he started forward.

"Kalli? Something wrong?"

"No, something's right!" She put her arms around his neck to kiss him. "We did it, Walker! We did it!"

Though clearly puzzled, he scooped her into his arms.

"Tina and I just finished double-checking the whole season's tickets," she said. "And as of tonight, we'll top last year's attendance!"

The half grin that had become as dear to her as the full smile she'd once loved lit his face as he lifted her off her feet and spun her around.

"Hot damn! We did it!"

"We sure did." She punctuated the agreement by tightening her arms around his neck and kissing him emphatically.

The kiss ended only when a breathlessness that started as exuberance and transformed to something more intimate demanded an infusion of oxygen. But their arms remained locked around each other.

"So the Jeffries Company will be running the Park Rodeo again next year. How about that? There'll be some fine partying tonight, Kalli. Nothing like a little job security to bring out the wild in folks."

She laughed, even as she considered that job security didn't necessarily go all the way to the top. Would she or Walker help run the rodeo for the Jeffries Company next season? They'd carefully avoided that topic.

"Have you told Jeff and Mary yet?" Walker asked.

"No, I wanted to tell you first."

His hold tightened fractionally. "We could tell them when they come for the final."

"We could.... No, I think maybe we should call beforehand. There's going to be so much excitement for Jeff, he should have a chance to assimilate this."

"You're right." With a final kiss—quick, yet conveying promises of more leisurely kisses to come—he released her and turned to the bunk, unbuttoning his shirt as he went. A satchel sat there. Through its gaping zippered opening, she saw the tapes, bandages and ropes, chaps, gloves and spurs he used when he rode bulls. A clean shirt, hat and one of his championship belts sat beside it. "I'll finish getting my rigging set, then we can call them."

"Your rigging? But...you're not going to compete now."

He stilled, then straightened and pivoted slowly. "Why wouldn't I? I'm entered. Folks who bought tickets tonight are expecting to see me. The other riders are hoping to beat me. Paying my entry fee's a promise to all those folks, and I'm keeping it. I'm riding."

Keeping his word.

She knew she couldn't win against that, but she tried.

"You don't have to compete. The rodeo's secure. We don't have to sell a ticket the whole last week and we'd still have the rodeo back next year for Jeff. And the last week's usually one of the best, so there's absolutely no need for you to ride now."

"Maybe not to save the rodeo or for Jeff. But there's still a need—for me. I need it, Kalli. I love it."

Suddenly, she was more frightened than she'd ever been. Even more frightened than when she'd seen Cory lying so still in the arena. She'd been horrified then, but she hadn't known how much pain would follow. She hadn't known what it could feel like to lose Walker, too. Now she did.

"And me? Walker, if you care for me at all, please—"

"Don't do this, Kalli." His voice sounded raw. "Care for you? I love you. I want us to have a life together. The rest of our lives together."

He said it so simply. Not as if he'd spent days, weeks, months wondering if he truly felt what he thought he felt, as she had. He said it as if saying the words, acknowledging the emotion was the most natural thing in the world.

I love you.

Looking at him, she knew it was true. She looked away.

He let out a long breath, a sigh that made her want to cringe. Neither moved for a moment, then she heard the soft swish of material that said he was taking off his shirt, sliding into the clean one...continuing his preparations.

Staring at the bunk, her gaze latched on to the length of leather lying there, one end carrying a sparkling emblem of what he'd achieved.

Too buffeted by emotions to demand, she asked, "Is it for the glory, the gold buckles, the championships? Is that why you ride?"

"No."

"The thrill?"

Make me understand, Walker.

"Some."

He reached out for the belt, and her eyes stayed on the buckle as he threaded the leather through the loops on his jeans. When he finished, his hands went to his hips, and he let out another sigh, shifting the buckle to cast a metallic light.

"It's like I said that day with the TV interview. It's not for the glory. It's not for anything but the doing of it, Kalli. To enjoy those seconds that seem to swell up with life like a balloon pumped full of water."

She looked at him, not sure why she couldn't accept it.

"Are you trying to kill yourself?"

"No." He returned her gaze steadily. "I'm trying to live."

"And you can't live without it."

Her tone made it an accusation.

He shook his head. Hands still on his hips, he turned half away from her. His frustration seemed tangible.

"Yeah, I could live without rodeo. Someday soon I'm going to have to. At least the part in the ring. And I know it. But until I have to... Why would you want me to? That's what I don't understand. Why would you want me to live without it when it's something I love?"

"What if I said I think I love you, Walker?"

The words came before she could consider if they were true, or if they were wise. Hearing them, she still didn't know if they carried truth. But Walker's tense stance and taut jaw proved they hadn't held wisdom.

"All right, you think you love me. Well, you said that before, and then you walked away, didn't you, Kalli?" She winced. "Only you were more positive about it then. You said you loved me, and you said you wanted to spend the rest of your life with me. But you didn't love *me,* you loved what you thought you'd turn me into. And when I wouldn't be what you wanted, you walked out. If that's what you're meaning by love this time, Kalli, I've got to warn you. This is who I am."

His gesture took in his rodeo gear.

"I can try a computer for you, Kalli. I can talk to reporters. I can step back and let you head the business. I can look beyond today to what the future's bringing and maybe, eventually, I could accept you giving us—me—only your summers. But I can't let go of rodeo. It's who I am as much as it's who Jeff is. And I don't understand how you can think you're loving me when you're wanting me to be a different man from the one I am. That's what I don't understand, Kalli. Don't understand at all."

Because the thought of your getting hurt scares me to death. What would I do if anything happened to you?

Each word came crystal clear into her head, but something stopped her from speaking them.

She caught the gleam of precious metal at his waist. The championship buckle. The emblem of all those times he'd risked his body, and her heart.

"I just want you to be a man who wants what I can give," she said, fighting the fear. "I can't give you what the rodeo can. I can't make you a champion, like rodeo can. Someone for boys like Matt Halderman to idolize. Someone for strangers to cheer when you make a good ride or to gasp and cluck when the bull wins the go-round. All I can do is love you. I can't give you gold buckles or make you a national champion!"

"You think this is what the rodeo gives me? You think this is what it's about?"

He unhooked the massive buckle with one jerk of his hand and yanked the leather belt through the denim loops. With a curse, he slung it onto the narrow bunk. Her eyes followed the arc of its movement as if her life depended on watching.

"Then you still don't know me, Kalli. Dammit, you still don't know me."

The door banged shut behind him, but Kalli couldn't take her eyes off the buckle. Weighted by the heavy metal, the belt lay twisted and curved, like a dying snake. The buckle, faceup, innocently blinked at the ceiling.

You still don't know me, Kalli. Dammit, you still don't know me.

Why did he have this need to climb on the back of a nineteen-hundred-pound Brahman when he knew how it scared her? When he knew how she felt about it? How...

How it scared her. How she felt about it.

The phrases dinned at her until she sank under their weight, slipping to the bunk, one hand outstretched for balance. Her fingers encountered the buckle and held on.

How it scared her. How she felt about it.

Even greater than her fear for him had been her fear for herself. What his injury—or worse—might do to *her*. All these years, the fear had been for herself. Because she couldn't take it if something happened to him.

The truth became a roaring in her ears, a slicing pain in her heart.

The edge of the buckle bit hard into her palm and fingers. She tightened her hold.

Because the thought of your getting hurt scares me to death. What would I do if anything happened to you?

Scares me . . . scares ME . . . ME.

Now she knew what had stopped her from speaking the words—an instinct that recognized that the words revealed her selfishness. Showed that her fears for *herself*, for her own feelings if he should get hurt, were more important to her than having Walker do what he loved.

As if Mary sat beside her now, Kalli felt the older woman's hands clasping hers, and heard the quiet, certain words.

When you love someone, really love someone, what they want and need is more important than your own wants and needs. It's even more important than your worries and fears.

She understood now, in a way she hadn't even when the evidence was in front of her eyes, the love and strength Mary had shown all these long weeks by encouraging Jeff to fight the limits left by his stroke—because that's what he wanted and needed, and his wants and needs were more important to Mary than her own.

Did Kalli love Walker? More important, did she love him the right way, the way that would help her put his wants and needs ahead of her own?

The pounding on the door barely penetrated Kalli's consciousness.

"Kalli? Walker? You two in there? If you're doing something you don't want the world to see, you better stop, because I'm coming in." Roberta's face in the open camper door followed her words.

Kalli looked at her without moving.

"Oh, you're alone."

At another time, Kalli might have found some humor in the disappointment in the secretary's voice.

"Yes, I'm alone."

Roberta's look sharpened, but she asked no questions.

"Well, get a move on. There are tickets to sell, money to count, results to figure. We've got a rodeo to run."

Trying to push aside questions she couldn't answer and thoughts that only troubled, Kalli tackled the nightly routine. But for the first time, she made no pretense of ignoring it when the loudspeaker announcement came:

"And now, out of chute two, the first bull-riding competitor in our final event of the evening—two-time national bull-riding champion, one of the legends of the sport, Park's own—Walker Riley!"

She knew her stillness had attracted Roberta's attention, but she didn't care.

Eight seconds until the ride was over. Eight seconds to get through.

Beneath the crowd's roars, she could almost imagine she heard the faint *chunk* of the chute gate opening, allowing the bull to bolt into the arena where he'd have full freedom to buck and whirl, spin and kick, with Walker on his back.

One second passed. Two. Three.

Her eyes went to the wall clock, watching the second hand tick its way toward Walker's safety.

Six, seven, eight. The horn.

The ride was over.

Then came the crowd's gasp, a chorus of dismay condensed into a single sound that said something had gone wrong. Horribly wrong.

Chapter Twelve

"Kalli, wait..."

"Kalli, you can't..."

"Kalli, don't..."

The voices, the orders blended. She moved too fast from the office to the arena, and cared too little for what they said to pay any heed.

She reached the fence and climbed it before anyone could stop her. The clowns tried to corral the bull at the far side of the ring, but she hardly noticed. She focused only on the figure in denim and white, sprawled just this side of the arena's center. Even as she tried to sprint across fine dirt that gave under her feet like sand, she felt the terror rising, the urge to turn around and escape.

She kept going.

Closer, she saw a splash of red. Blood.

Her heart seemed to stop, and she gasped for the oxygen she needed to keep running.

Then she realized he was moving, and her heart tripped. His head turned toward the bull, Walker levered himself up, favoring his left leg, where the blue of denim opened to tanned skin and the red of welling blood.

Seeming to catch the different quality of the crowd's noise as it reacted to her arrival, he turned once he got upright, and she saw his face grimacing, but also grinning.

A light brightened his eyes, the light of a man who'd ridden the tornado, who'd shared the power of a force of nature. And didn't mind that he'd paid for the privilege with his blood.

Then he saw her, and the light changed.

"Kalli! What the— Get the hell out of here!" He limped toward her.

She ignored him and kept going over the irregular ground that tried to suck her down.

She saw him glance at the other end of the arena, where the clowns had now herded the still-uncooperative bull, then limp faster toward her.

"Walker! Are you—"

"Kalli, will you get out of here?" He tried to grip her arm, but she eluded his hold, instead slipping her shoulder under his arm and wrapping hers around his waist in support.

"Fine," she said as calmly as she could. "Let's go."

He cursed under his breath, but didn't stop to argue. He sent a couple of looks toward the bull, which she suspected he wouldn't have taken if she hadn't been with him, and when helpful hands opened the gate, he gave her a firm-handed push on the back to make sure she went through first.

But as soon as the gate closed behind them, she slipped her shoulder back under his arm.

"Where's the first-aid van?" she demanded of Gulch.

He jerked his head toward the square-bodied vehicle that dispensed cures for cuts and bruises, and doubled as an ambulance in an emergency.

"Let's take a look at that." The retired doctor who attended each session to provide medical services ambled up.

"It's nothing," Walker said. In case his words got covered by the grunt the doctor gave as he squatted and poked at the raw flesh, he repeated louder. "Nothing."

The word didn't mask his grimace as the doctor's fingers probed.

Kalli didn't need the doctor's diagnosis. "You're going to the hospital. Gulch, get ready to drive the van." She looked up to see Roberta's concerned but calm face in the circle. "Call the hospital and let them know we're coming."

"Okay, Kalli."

"You got it."

Gulch and Roberta disappeared in opposite directions.

"Aw, hell, Kalli. I don't need the hospital," Walker protested. "Doc here can clean it up and stitch it. Tell her, Doc."

"Well, he's right it's not that bad, Kalli. But," he continued, turning to his patient, "you ought to take that ride over to the hospital. Doctors there will take neater stitches than I could here."

"You heard what the doctor said. Get in the van, Walker."

He protested more, but Kalli simply didn't listen. And with everyone cooperating with her, he didn't have much choice.

The doctor cut the rest of the jeans leg away, gave the wound a preliminary cleaning that had sweat popping out on Walker's forehead, laid a temporary covering over it and pronounced the patient ready to go. Since Walker already sat on the cot in the back of the van, all that was required was for Gulch to start the engine and Kalli to pull the door closed after the doctor had climbed out.

They sat in silence the first few swaying minutes as the van negotiated the dirt-packed parking area and gravel drive before lurching onto the paved highway.

"I'm sorry, Walker, if I insulted your manhood by insisting on basic medical attention and by going into the arena after you, but—"

"My manhood!" He added an obscenity that made her blink. "I was worried about getting your little butt out of that ring with a ton of angry bull still roaming around. Don't you know it could have been dangerous for you?"

Reaction rushed through her like a hurricane, bandying fear, anger, caring, fury and adrenaline around like so many feathers.

"Dangerous? Dangerous for me! That bull tossed you in the air like you were a rag doll. You were lying out there bleeding, maybe bleeding to death with that bull on the loose. And you're telling me it could have been dangerous?"

She knew she was shouting, but she wasn't aware of the tears streaming down her face until she automatically dashed them away.

"You were worried."

It should have surprised her that his soft words could be heard over the roaring in her ears, but it didn't.

"Worried? Worried, you unmitigated ass— I was scared to death! It could have been an artery that got slashed. It could have been your head he trampled. It could have been one hoof to your temple. It could have been you, just like Cory.... Oh, God, it could have been—"

And then the tears and fear took too strong a hold to be denied. And when he put his arms around her, she accepted the warmth and solace.

"It's okay, Kalli. It's okay, honey. I'm all right and we'll work this out."

He said other things, but she heard only the tenderness of his tone, felt the warmth of his arms and most of all, the strong, steady beating of his heart under her ear. He was so undoubtedly alive.

The van came to a stop and the doors swung open. An orderly stood at the opening, looking from one to the other, both smeared with blood and dirt.

"Two of you? They only said one."

"Just me," Walker said.

Half expecting him to try to weasel out of the medical care, given such an opening, she looked up, surprised.

"Might as well get this over with," he said to her with a ghost of a smile. "And then you and I are going to do some talking."

"Are you sure you're okay?"

He stifled the urge to growl at her. She'd fussed around his bedroom for half an hour now. And on top of the fussing at the emergency room, on the drive back and during the time before they could get Gulch and Roberta to leave his place, he'd about had his fill.

She'd gotten him to lie in bed, his back propped against pillows, his leg throbbing no worse than various parts of him had throbbed a hundred times before. Then, just when he thought she would settle down next to him, she'd started flitting around the room, pretending to pack some of the things he'd encouraged her over the past weeks to leave at his place.

As far as he could tell, she hadn't put anything resembling clothes into the carry-on bag that was all she said she'd need for New York. Guess nothing from Wyoming would do for New York City, he thought sourly.

"I'm fine. Now come to bed."

"I am. I just wanted to finish." She zipped the bag closed and looked around the room as if searching for another project. "Are you sure you don't want another pain pill before I—"

"I'm sure. Kalli, get in bed before I get out and put you in bed."

She was so worn-out she could hardly stand, but only when he tossed back the top sheet in preparation for making good on his threat did she switch off the lamp on the dresser, leaving the room in the soft glow of the bookshelf lamp. And, finally, she eased into the bed next to him.

He gave out a sigh of satisfaction as she slid partway down against the pillows behind her.

His relief was premature. She hadn't finished.

"I think you should stay in bed tomorrow," she announced.

"No way, Kalli. The emergency-room doc said—"

"The doctor doesn't know everything."

"That's not what you were saying before. Changed your tune, huh, once she agreed with me? Besides, who'd run the rodeo with me in bed and you off to New York City?"

She sidestepped the edge in his voice. "I could postpone my trip a day."

"No. I'm not keeping you that way, Kalli."

She sidestepped that, too. "I just want you to be sensible."

"I am being sensible. I'm used to this, remember?" She winced. Oh, hell, he'd never figured to win any championships when it came to tact, anyway, so he might as well say what he thought right out.

"Look, Kalli, this should make things easier between us if you look at it right."

Apparently, she was only prepared to look disbelieving.

"The worst's happened from your standpoint," he explained. "I got thrown. I caught a horn a little bit, but—"

"A little bit?"

"But," he repeated, overriding her protest, "I came through fine. That emergency-room doc says I can ride tomorrow—"

Her eyes jerked up to his, then away. It made it harder to finish, but he did. He wouldn't lie to her.

"And I will. So why don't you come watch tomorrow?"

Almost absently, she reminded him, "I won't be here tomorrow."

"That's right, you won't."

Something in his tone must have caught her attention, because she turned to look into his eyes. He had the uncomfortable feeling she saw more there than he would have liked.

"I'm coming back, Walker." He almost winced, himself. He hadn't wanted to be transparent, for God's sake. "I told Jerry two days. I'll be here Wednesday night. Thursday at the latest."

"Rodeo season ends Saturday." Pointing out what they both already knew served as a setup, so he could tack on the question he couldn't ask outright. "Doesn't seem real practical if you're coming back for just two days."

"I don't know how long I'm coming back for. I don't know how we'll work that out, but I promise you, Walker, no matter what, I'm coming back."

He shifted, uneasy with the intensity of her gaze, or maybe with the idea that she could see in his face how pathetically eager he was to believe that. He couldn't crawl. Not even for Kalli.

"Well, if you come back—"

"When."

He took the risk and conceded, to her certainty and to his own desire. "Okay, when. When you come back, why don't you come watch me ride instead of sitting in the office imagining things? Your imaginings are a load worse than the real thing, ninety-nine times out of a hundred. Besides, you're stronger than you know, Kalli. Just take tonight—the worst happened, and you handled it fine. Except if I catch you coming in the ring like that again, I'll—"

"The worst?"

The quaver in her voice stopped him. It had been a long, wearing night for both of them. But her tone had sounded more than tired.

He ducked his head for a better look at her face. And he felt a clutch at his chest. From beneath her closed eyelids tears gathered in her lashes, then slipped down her cheeks, over her chin and down her throat.

"The worst?" she repeated, still with her eyes closed. "This wasn't the worst. The worst would be losing you. For... forever." Her voice broke, but she went on. "Losing you. Like Cory."

He was stunned. By her pain. By his stupidity.

That bull tossed you in the air like you were a rag doll. He'd heard her say the words tonight, but he hadn't stopped to argue with them. Because the bull hadn't tossed him. He'd already dismounted and started to back up, to clear out of the clowns' way, when the crafty Brahman gave a feint, then twisted his massive head to catch Walker a slashing blow with his horn.

But Cory *had* been tossed like that the night he died.

And that's what his Kalli saw in her mind every time she thought about him going up on a bull.

He should have known. Hell, she'd even said something about Cory during the trip to the hospital.

God, he hadn't even come close to it when he said her imaginings were worse than the real thing. Cory's death was the worst thing he'd seen in nearly twenty years of rodeoing. He'd heard old-timers who'd said the same thing, only doubling the years. If that's what she thought every time he rode...

He took her in his arms. The tears still falling, she resisted a moment, then leaned into him. Letting him hold her, letting him rock her. He felt powerful and invincible. And humbled.

"It's all right, Kalli." He kissed the top of her head and smoothed her hair back. The stream of tears wetted his fingertips. "Aw, Kalli. Kalli, honey. It's all right. It's all right."

He kept murmuring assurances, until the tears slowed. She took in a deep, cleansing breath and released it in the only sob he'd heard since she'd started crying. Then she took another breath and released it slowly.

That's when he kissed her, feeling the wetness on her mouth, tasting the saltiness that had tracked her lips. She responded. When they were both breathless, he followed the salty path over her chin, down her soft throat, past her collarbone. Opening and pushing aside her button-front sleep shirt, he found a tiny pool of droplets between her breasts. He licked it dry, then kissed the spot, anointing it with a new wetness.

"I want you, Kalli. I want to make love with you."

He needed her now. The need might eat at him when she was gone, but for now, she was still here.

"Your leg... No..."

But she helped his questing hands, shrugging out of her sleep shirt, reaching for him. He'd heard the need in her voice. The same kind of need he'd felt that day in the office, after she'd walked away from him. And he realized a little more just how scared she'd been.

"My leg will be fine."

"Walker," she protested again. But by then they were both naked. And their skimming, stroking, dipping touches showed they were both ready.

"It'll be fine." He put on the condom with hands not entirely steady. "You're going to make love to me."

He positioned her astride him, and plunged into her before she could voice another protest. He watched as her own needs took control. Her need to prove how real, how alive he was under her. He understood that need, and met it.

He watched her face as she rose above him, concentrating to hold back his own release until hers was complete. Caressing her breasts, he gripped her hips, arching up into her in movements that tormented him and drove her nearer to where she needed to be. Where he needed to take her.

"Walker? Walker!"

"I'm here. Right here."

The brightness of the clock's electric numbers was beginning to fade against the coming daylight when she shifted in his arms and found him awake and watching her.

She said the words weighing on her heart.

"I don't want you getting hurt, or worse."

He moved his head so they were looking straight into each other's eyes.

And she saw again what she'd seen earlier— He wasn't convinced yet that her leaving wasn't for good.

"And I don't want you walking out of my life."

He kissed her, and she answered. A deep, lasting kiss. But in it, she tasted the knowledge they'd both acquired over the past ten years: you don't always get what you want.

He drove her to the airport, grinning at her fussing about his driving with that gash in his leg.

"At least I don't have to be a witness to your competing tonight," she grumbled. "It's probably just as well I'm leaving."

That wiped out his grin, and suddenly she felt nervous and awkward about the whole situation. About being here. About being with him. About leaving him.

The rest of the short drive was made in silence. As they waited at the gate, the conversation consisted of her last-second listings of rodeo details he should handle or remind Roberta to see to and her urging him to call New York if he had to, and his stolid assurances.

When the clerk called her flight and the other passengers had started out toward the small commuter plane, they looked at each other, glanced away and stood.

Two steps from where the attendant waited to take tickets, Walker's hand on Kalli's arm turned her toward him. Without preamble, he wrapped his arms around her and kissed her, sliding his tongue into her mouth with deep, slow thrusts that brought memories of their lovemaking to an immediate blaze in her body.

He released her mouth, but still held her against him, their bodies fully prepared to complete the union their mouths had intimated.

Under the brim of his hat, his eyes showed blue around desire-dilated pupils.

"Come back to me, Kalli."

Then he let her go and strode away. Like an automaton, she handed her ticket to the goggle-eyed attendant and made her way to the plane and her seat. But all she saw was Walker's face, and all she heard was his voice.

Come back to me, Kalli.

Two days.

Two days, she'd said. Thursday at the latest.

She'd left Monday at first light. Now it was Thursday night. No, make that Friday—by the clock and soon by the sun.

Walker stood on his porch, leaning against the post, looking down at a house where no light showed in the last room on the north wing and calling himself every kind of fool.

He shouldn't have let her go. If he'd kept her here—somehow—he could have fought her fear. But now the fear had a clear field again. The same fear that had kept her away ten years.

Not learning from your mistakes in rodeo was a sure path to failure, and a possible route to getting killed.

Seemed like loving Kalli could be just as deadly.

The blaring car horn didn't make her jump as it had her first day back in the city. She glared at the driver who'd expressed his outrage at being denied an opportunity to run a red light by pedestrians daring to cross with the green.

So, her New York skills had not all disappeared. She'd begun to wonder since arriving three days ago.

The sounds had seemed louder, the lights harsher, the buildings grayer, the air denser, the sky farther. Even her own apartment seemed alien and severe.

Not that she'd spent much time there, she thought with a wry smile as she entered a restaurant. The maître d' seemed slightly taken aback, then returned her smile and led her through the maze of tables.

Jerry Salk had plunged her into a whirlwind of activity, finagling her into dealing with two other clients in addition to Lou Loben "as long as you're here." From power lunches to tense conferences to late strategy sessions to breakfast negotiations to—finally—this celebratory late-night drink, where she would join Jerry and Lou in self-congratulatory toasts, every minute had been full. But work hadn't kept any demons away this time, because every moment had also been empty.

Empty without Walker Riley.

She missed him. Missed him with an ache and loneliness that surpassed even what she'd felt when she first came to this city ten years ago, a refugee from her own fear. Perhaps she missed him more now because she missed the real Walker, the man he'd become.

The man she loved.

"Kalli!"

She barely heard Jerry's exultant greeting. She sat hard in the chair the maître d' held for her because her knees had stopped holding her up.

She missed the man she loved.

She loved him. Absolutely. Unreservedly. Loved him more than anything else in this life.

This time with a love stronger than fear.

To protect herself from worrying day by day, she'd lost the chance to love him and be loved in return hour by hour, minute by minute, and in the end, she'd lost years. No, *they'd* lost years. Because he'd had his fears, too. To protect himself from wondering second by second if she might leave, he'd presumed she would walk away again.

I don't want you getting hurt, or worse.

And I don't want you walking out of my life.

Their fears had almost led to what they feared most—losing each other.

"Are you okay, Kalli?"

Her surroundings came into focus. Lou Loben watched her with puzzlement and faint concern, Jerry was talking—as always—and she had a half-empty glass of champagne in her hand she didn't remember accepting, much less drinking from.

"Okay? She's riding high. And now that this deal's wrapped up, you can talk to Arliss Rand tomorrow. He's got questions on that hardware store chain."

"No. I stayed an extra day and a half, but—"

"A day? What's that matter when it's a team like us?"

"No, Jerry."

"What do you mean, no?"

"I mean, no, I can't talk to Arliss Rand because I am leaving in the morning."

"Leaving?" he repeated blankly. Lou began to smile.

"I'm going back to Wyoming and—"

"Going back? For what? A couple days, that's all. Then you're back here. You might as well stay, save yourself all that flying."

"There won't be much flying, because I'm going back to Wyoming for good."

His mouth opened, closed, then reopened immediately. "So you go back a few days, okay, finish up what you want, then you come back. I'm not an ogre. You finish up that rodeo, then you come on back. Arliss Rand will wait."

"He'll have to wait a long time, because I am not coming back, Jerry. I have another month of vacation time, so consider that your notice. I officially resign."

"Resign? What are you talking about, resign? We can work this out. We won't talk about it now. Tomorrow—"

"Tomorrow I'll be on a flight to Wyoming." She made the next words as solid as a few square miles of the Rocky Mountains. "The decision is final."

"I don't understand," Jerry said a little plaintively.

Lou leaned back, his smile full-blown. "You know, Jerry, there's a country-western song I think wraps up what Kalli's trying to tell you."

Jerry looked as if he wanted to pull his hair out. Or perhaps Lou's and hers. "A song? What's this?"

"It's called, 'Take This Job and Shove It.'" Lou lifted his glass to her in a toast.

"What? What are you talking about?"

Ignoring Jerry's demand, she grinned back at Lou. "I didn't know you liked country music."

"How could you not like a sentiment like that?"

"Wyoming!" Jerry bleated. "You'll come back, just you wait and see. You'll miss the excitement, you'll miss the deals, you'll miss the life. You'll be back, begging me."

"You should come to Wyoming, Lou," Kalli said, enjoying herself. "I'd invite Jerry, too, but he doesn't seem interested. But please, come out and see the rodeo."

Even as Lou said he'd love to and Jerry muttered himself into silence, she considered her final words and made a slight adjustment.

"Come out and see *our* rodeo."

One flight canceled. Another caught by thunderstorms over Chicago and diverted to Detroit for an hour's wait, and more pacing. A missed connection. By the time she caught the commuter flight from Denver to Park, Kalli thought the pioneers might have had an easier time in covered wagons.

When she finally landed, she knew everyone would be hip-deep in running the Friday-evening rodeo—the second-to-last of the season. She tried the ranch, but got no answer; they were probably all at the rodeo. She rented a car, ignoring a tiny, practical voice nagging about the extravagance for someone soon to be unemployed. If she waited a few hours, someone on the rodeo staff could pick her up.

She wasn't waiting any more hours.

Still, when she got to the rodeo grounds, the events were in full swing.

She went straight to Walker's camper.

It was empty.

She stood in the doorway, numbed for a moment. She'd been so sure she would find him here. She would explain what she'd realized these past few days, and then tell him she loved him, too. But he wasn't here. Which probably meant he'd gone to the bull chutes to wait, among the other competitors, to ride. Not exactly the most romantic spot for telling a man you loved him and wanted to marry him—again.

The powerful arena lights streamed through the open door over her shoulder and glinted on something metallic on the bunk. Walker's championship buckle. Left where she'd dropped it five nights ago.

Staring at it, her mind began to function again.

Maybe the bull chutes provided exactly the right spot for this declaration of love.

Smiling, she pulled off her belt and threaded the heavy leather of Walker's championship belt through her jeans' loops. The buckle felt cumbersome, but she could almost imagine a warmth emanating from the metal. Positioning the buckle at the front of her waist, she wrapped the leftover leather far to the side, well beyond the last hole.

After thirty seconds of rooting in a drawer in the kitchenette, she found a roll of tape. With an awkward but effective wrapping motion, she secured the leather and bit off the tape, tucking in the end.

Then she went in search of Walker Riley.

The routine soothed him. It offered no solace, no easing of the pain. But it did provide the comfort of familiarity.

He'd taped up. Put on his chaps. Strapped up the bull he'd drawn. Checked his rig. Now he waited. Until the moment came when he would lower himself, working his glove into the strap, getting it just right, flexing his hand to check it, tightening his hold, retesting it. Then giving the signal to open the chute. To let two thousand pounds of bull free to try its damnedest to rid itself of his relatively inconsequential weight.

He could feel the adrenaline, familiar, welcome and necessary. But he could also feel the drag of his heart.

God, he loved her.

But she couldn't love him, at least not this part of him, not when she let her fear stand between them. And though he knew—and accepted—that the moments like this were dwindling, it was still a part of him. It would never lose its hold on him. Even when he no longer competed.

A chute opened down the line, the crowd roared and a rider held on for dear life. One more to go before his turn.

He didn't even try to still the thoughts, though he knew the danger of letting anything intrude between him and this moment. He couldn't stop thinking of Kalli any more than he could have stopped loving her from the time she first smiled at him, all those years ago.

"Walker?"

Gulch's voice sounded odd, as if he knew Walker's mind wasn't where it was supposed to be. Walker didn't bother answering. Last thing he needed was a lecture.

"Walker!"

He growled a curse without looking up from where he flexed his hand in the skintight glove. "What?"

Gulch punched his arm. "Lookit. Look over there, you sorry son-of-a-gun idiot."

Walker did look up because it almost sounded as if Gulch was grinning. He was. As wide and as bright as he could manage. Walker gaped at him, but Gulch didn't pay any attention; he was looking over Walker's shoulder.

Walker started to turn in the same direction, but apparently not fast enough to suit Gulch, because the older man cuffed him on the shoulder to hurry up the process. "Lookit, will 'ya?"

Walker looked.

It was the prettiest sight he'd ever seen.

Kalli Evans was standing not four feet away. Smiling at him. A little tentatively and with a tear slipping down her right cheek, but smiling at him. And wearing his championship buckle.

The symbol of his rodeo success, also a symbol of their years apart. Now she wore it, linking past and future.

He started toward her on an instinct bred as deep as the need to breathe, and the urge to ride, but Gulch caught his arm.

"You're up next, boy. And by the looks of it, she'll still be here when you're done."

Kalli must have heard, because she gave a nod and her eyes promised she would be there when his ride ended. This ride, and the last ride. She said something, but the only words he caught over the announcement of the preceding rider's scores were "good ride." Then she backed up a couple of paces, leaving him to do what he had to do.

He looked at her a moment longer. "I will. I love you, Kalli."

He made no effort to make the words loud enough for her to hear over the noise of the crowd. They were words to be felt more than heard, anyhow. And by her eyes, he knew she'd felt them.

Then he turned all his attention to the bull. Centering. Clearing. Setting. Nodding his head and giving the terse, "Ready."

In eight seconds and the time it took to sprint across the arena, he came over the fence grinning, looped his arms around her waist and spun her off her feet before she could react.

Then he kissed her, there in front of his fellow competitors, the inordinate number of employees who happened to find an errand in that vicinity right then, the spectators milling in front of the concession stand and anyone who happened to look over the rail from the Buzzards' Roost.

He released her mouth, but didn't loosen his arms. The light in his eyes had turned serious.

"Are you back to stay?"

"Yes."

"Are you going to help me take some of the load for Mary and Jeff next season?"

"Yes."

"Are you going to marry me?"

"Yes."

The light in his eyes flared from serious to sensuous, asking another question that she let hers answer, also in the affirmative.

When the loudspeaker announced his score, he gave a disparaging smile. "Routine score for a routine ride."

"Routine? I think I lost a couple of inches of enamel from gritting my teeth." She hoped he couldn't see her hands trembling.

"If that's what it takes, I'll love you toothless."

She shook her head. "I'll learn to adjust to your riding the bulls before it comes to that point. At least I will as long as I can ask of you what you asked of me."

"What's that?"

"Come back to me."

He tilted his head, delving into her heart, seeing how much this meant to her. And he made a promise they both knew he couldn't guarantee, any more than she could have guaranteed that there would be no delay in her return from New York. Or that there would be no accident, no natural disaster that would have kept her from ever coming back to him. "I will, Kalli. I'll always come back to you."

"And I'll do the same."

He tensed. "What do you mean? You're leaving?"

"Sometimes," she said gently. "I can make adjustments, and I won't work out of New York, but I'll need to be gone sometimes in order to keep doing what *I* love. Mary once told me that really loving someone means putting their wants and needs ahead of your wants and needs—and even your fears. I'm learning to do that with the rodeo for you,

Walker. Because you love it, and I love you. Can you love me enough to let me go, Walker?''

How long? How often? Greedily, he wanted the answers to ease his fear. But he knew the only real way to deal with fear was to tighten your grip on the one thin rope that connected you to that force of nature, hold on for all you're worth, then tell them to open the chute, and just take that ride.

''As long as you come back to me one more time than I let go.''

''That's a deal, cowboy.''

Epilogue

Spring came to the calendar long before Wyoming could be persuaded to give up cold winds, freezing dawns and occasional ankle-deep snows. The fire in the Jeffrieses' den drew the room's four occupants for warmth as well as cheer.

"How can we plan for the summer's rodeo when winter's never going to let go?" Mary muttered.

"Don't mind her," Jeff advised, his smile only slightly lopsided these days. "Mary's never been much for the benefits of a little bracing winter air." Ignoring her disgusted "Bracing?" he went on, "Tell you what, I'll take you to Florida next winter. Or Arizona—your choice. The whole winter, not just a month like we did this year."

"You've promised me that for forty-three years, Jeff."

The older man winked at his guests. "It's kept her around. 'Course, you two've been so busy, you probably haven't noticed the chill in the air these past months."

Turning, Kalli intercepted Walker's smile at the gentle teasing. "We have been busy," she agreed.

"Weddings have a way of keeping you busy," Mary said.

It wasn't the wedding—which they'd kept small and simple because they both wanted to get remarried as soon as possible—it was all the celebrations after. Her family had been protectively disapproving, until she and Walker flew to Connecticut for a long weekend and her relatives saw for themselves. Then they insisted on a belated reception at Thanksgiving for family and friends. There'd been a party thrown by the Park Rodeo employees, another by Jasper and Esther Lodge and, finally, one by Walker's friends from the circuit at the National Finals Rodeo in Las Vegas in December.

"Honeymoons, too," Jeff said with his old chortle.

Kalli pretended to frown. "I meant, we've been busy because of my work...."

She had agreed to free-lance for Jerry Salk on projects on this side of the country during the rodeo's off-season and was already building a reputation for a sharp eye for investment opportunities in the West. She'd made business trips, but kept them short—Walker hadn't said anything, but she didn't like being away any longer.

"...and everything Walker's doing..."

He'd worked hard on the KW Ranch, named by twinning their first initials the way he finally admitted he'd thought about doing all along. He worked outside when weather permitted, in the house or barn when it didn't. In addition, he'd been knee-deep in plans for a rodeo school for novices to start in May, a month before the rodeo opened, as a way to minimize risks for those just learning. Kalli thoroughly approved of that. Her enthusiasm had been less wholehearted when he'd entered a string of winter indoor rodeos to "keep his hand in."

But she'd gone with him—twice they'd worked it so she had a business to scout in the same city where he competed. She'd watched him ride. And she'd cheered him on. Because it was what he loved, and she loved him.

"Seems like you found time for some other doings," Jeff commented slyly.

Walker broke into a big grin as he often did at the mention of her pregnancy, and laid a protective hand on her abdomen, at two months barely showing any change. Though he checked every day, with kisses and caresses.

"Winter's got its benefits. Long nights," Walker murmured.

Kalli had never known the fierce peace she felt in those hours when he talked of their future, their family.

"I've had to keep him busy with the ranch and rodeos and school as self-protection," Kalli said as lightly as she could around a lump in her throat, "so he doesn't coddle me right into the insane asylum. You'd think anyone who rides bulls wouldn't blanch at the concept that he'll be busy changing diapers come Halloween."

"Hey, this having a baby is a sight more complicated than hanging on to a rope and keeping your balance," Walker objected.

While Jeff and Mary laughed at his mock indignation, Kalli gave him a warm, reassuring smile. He still had doubts about being a father and sometimes she wondered what on earth made her think she could be a mother, but they agreed that, together, they'd survive, maybe even thrive.

"Look, cowboy, you've got the easier end of this bargain. You're worrying about me coping with an eight-pound baby, but I'm wondering if you're going to escape an eighteen-hundred-pound bull."

"Maybe you've got the weight advantage, but how about time? I'm on the bull eight seconds. This pregnancy is a nine-month ride."

The dual laughter from Jeff and Mary brought their heads around.

"Nine months?" asked Mary, smiling lovingly and knowingly as she looked from one to the other of them. "Try a lifetime. A lifetime of fretting and loving and wondering and joy. That's the deal when kids enter your life."

Kalli felt Walker's hand move gently against her abdomen. When she looked up, she met the blue, blue eyes of the man she loved, and knew he was thinking the same thing.

A lifetime would do just fine.

*   *   *   *   *

Dark secrets, dangerous desire...

Three spine-tingling tales from the dark side of love.

This October, enter the world of shadowy romance as Silhouette presents the third in their annual tradition of thrilling love stories and chilling story lines. Written by three of Silhouette's top names:

LINDSAY McKENNA
LEE KARR
RACHEL LEE

Haunting a store near you this October.

Take 4 bestselling love stories FREE

Plus get a FREE surprise gift!

MONTANA
Mavericks

Stories that capture living and loving beneath the Big Sky, where legends live on...and the mystery is just beginning.

This September, look for

THE WIDOW AND THE RODEO MAN
by Jackie Merritt

And don't miss a minute of the loving as the mystery continues with:

SLEEPING WITH THE ENEMY
by Myrna Temte (October)
THE ONCE AND FUTURE WIFE
by Laurie Paige (November)
THE RANCHER TAKES A WIFE
by Jackie Merritt (December),
and many more!

Wait, there's more! Win a trip to a Montana mountain resort. For details, look for this month's MONTANA MAVERICKS title at your favorite retail outlet.

Only from ▼ *Silhouette*® where passion lives.

Is the future what it's cracked up to be?

This August, find out how C. J. Clarke copes with
being on her own in

GETTING IT TOGETHER: CJ
by Wendy Corsi Staub

Her diet was a flop. Her "beautiful" apartment was
cramped. Her "glamour" job consisted of fetching
coffee. And her love life was less than zero. But
what C.J. didn't know was that things were about
to get better....

The ups and downs of modern life continue with

GETTING IT RIGHT: JESSICA
by Carla Cassidy in September

GETTING REAL: CHRISTOPHER
by Kathryn Jensen in October

Get smart. Get into "The Loop!"

THE PARSON'S WAITING
Sherryl Woods

A life of harsh assignments had hardened correspondent Richard Walton. Yet his heart yearned for tenderness and warmth. He'd long ago given up the search for these precious qualities—until town parson Anna Louise Perkins entered his life. This courageous, loving woman's presence could be the cure Richard's soul so desperately sought....

Don't miss THE PARSON'S WAITING, by Sherryl Woods, available in September!

She's friend, wife, mother—she's you! And beside each Special Woman stands a wonderfully *special* man. It's a celebration of our heroines—and the men who become part of their lives.

Don't miss **THAT SPECIAL WOMAN!** each month—from some of your special authors! Only from Silhouette Special Edition!

TSW994

WHAT EVER HAPPENED TO...?

Have you been wondering when much-loved characters will finally get their own stories? Well, have we got a lineup for you! Silhouette Special Edition is proud to present a *Spin-off Spectacular!* Be sure to catch these exciting titles from some of your favorite authors:

HOMEWARD BOUND (July, SE #900) Mara Anvik is recalled to her old home for a dire mission—which reunites her with old flame Mark Toovak in *Sierra Rydell's* exciting spin-off to ON MIDDLE GROUND (SE #772).

BABY, COME BACK (August, SE #903) Erica Spindler returns with an emotional story about star-crossed lovers Hayes Bradford and Alice Dougherty, who are given a second chance for marriage in this follow-up to BABY MINE (SE #728).

THE WEDDING KNOT (August, SE #905) Pamela Toth's tie-in to WALK AWAY, JOE (SE #850) features a marriage of convenience that allows Daniel Sixkiller to finally adopt...and to find his perfect mate in determined Karen Whitworth!

A RIVER TO CROSS (September, SE #910) Shane Macklin and Tina Henderson shared a forbidden passion, which they can no longer deny in the latest tale from *Laurie Paige's* WILD RIVER series.

**Don't miss these wonderful titles, only for our readers—
only from Silhouette Special Edition!**

SPIN5

Silhouette

SPECIAL EDITION

WILD RIVER

Maddening men...winsome women...and the untamed land
they live in—all add up to love!

A RIVER TO CROSS (SE #910)
Laurie Paige

Sheriff Shane Macklin knew there was more to "town outsider"
Tina Henderson than met the eye. What he saw was a generous
and selfless woman whose true colors held the promise of love....

Don't miss the latest Rogue River tale, A RIVER TO CROSS, available
in September from Silhouette Special Edition!